I0550386

THAT'S THE WAY
THE COOKIE CRUMBLES

Book #4, The Mac 'n' Ivy Mysteries

By

Lorena McCourtney

Scripture used in this book, whether quoted or paraphrased by the characters, is taken from the Holy Bible, New International Version® (NIV®). Copyright© 1973, 1978, 1984, 2011 by Biblica, Inc.™ Used by permission of Zondervan. All rights reserved worldwide. www.zondervan.com. The "NIV" and "New International Version" are trademarks registered in the United States Patent and Trademark Office by Biblica, Inc.™

This book is a work of fiction. Certain actual locations and historical figures mentioned in the book are portrayed as accurately as possible but used in a fictional manner. All other names, places, and incidents are products of the author's imagination. All characters are fictional, and any similarity to people living or dead is purely coincidental.

Lorena McCourtney

CHAPTER 1

IVY

The honeymoon is over. Sigh.

And what a glorious honeymoon it was! At the last minute, rather than driving the motorhome into Baja as we'd planned, Mac and I left BoBandy and Koop with a friend and flew down to Cabo San Lucas at the tip of the Baja peninsula. Although problems bringing a dog and cat back into the States were unlikely, we didn't want to risk a worst-case scenario of not being able to bring one or both of them back without a long quarantine.

So we had two wonderful weeks with a room just a few feet from the beach. We went whale watching and walked barefoot on white sand under the stars. We took a glass-bottomed boat to see underwater sea life. We visited El Arco, the spectacular arch where crashing seas meet at Land's End. We found colorful shells on the beach and watched a flamenco dancer with flashing eyes and stomping feet. We ate shrimp tacos and spicy tamales and a creamy flan. We kissed in the rain when a tropical storm blew in. We celebrated Christmas Eve at a little church where everything was spoken in Spanish, so we understood only a few words, but the solemn holiness of Christmas came through in music and flickering candles, and the good will came through in shy, friendly smiles.

It was everything a honeymoon should be, nary a dead body anywhere, and we thanked the Lord for bringing us together in this gray-haired era of our lives. I optimistically thought the honeymoon might also be a dividing line between the past and a future where we'd never encounter a dead body or murder again. And perhaps we'd soon find the perfect place to end our transient life in the motorhome and settle down permanently.

Now, after retrieving BoBandy and Koop from our friend over in Arizona, we were on our way to a mid-California town that might eventually become our permanent home. A businessman we'd met in Cabo had described San Isolde as an older town, not too large and not too small, a little old-fashioned but lively, great weather, and friendly people. And, important to us, an impressively low crime rate.

He'd offered us a free spot to park the motorhome just for keeping an eye on his aunt, with the possibility of buying the property at a very reasonable price as soon as he could persuade her to move into a retirement home. He described his aunt Eleanor as a sweet little lady but a bit . . . and he'd paused, as if searching for the right word, before concluding with, "unpredictable." He'd also said, with a frown, that he wasn't too sure about that boyfriend of hers, and we might keep an eye, a very *sharp* eye, on him as well and let him know if we noted anything suspicious.

So here we were, just driving into San Isolde, on a sunny afternoon in January. Mac was in his old khaki shorts, me in my Baja T-shirt and fuzzy shark slippers. After being disappointed about not seeing sharks on one of our boat trips, Mac had bought the slippers for me at a souvenir shop. The slippers, with oversized, bloody teeth and a black fin sticking up on top, were a bit kitschy, maybe even garish, but they were so comfortable for traveling that I'd been wearing them all day. And they continually reminded me of what a wonderful honeymoon we'd had.

We'd never had GPS installed in the motorhome, but we did have a map Blake Houston had drawn for us that showed Eidenburg Road on the far side of town. We passed through an Old Town area with faded brick buildings mostly converted into antique and craft stores, but newer-looking homes sprawled over a nearby hill. I decided I should change out of my shark slippers and into something a bit more dignified before meeting Eleanor.

The house at 29427 Eidenburg was older, single-story, tan stucco with brown shutters and a red-tile roof. Probably three bedrooms but only a single bathroom, fine for us. A deep overhang of the front roof made a shady covering for a concrete patio underneath, and a windchime of silvery pipes hung from the edge of the roof. At least an acre of land encircled the house. Plenty of room for the motorhome out back for now, plenty of space for a big garden if we bought the place. I'm not the greatest gardener, and neither is Mac, but he assures me that together we can do anything. BoBandy and Koop would love the place. BoBandy was already peering out a window and wagging his tail.

An impressive palm tree shaded the grassy front yard, and a new-looking concrete sidewalk connected an open front door with the road. Winter-bare trees crowded the far side of the road, the nearest house several hundred yards away. All very serene and private, a place that indeed looked like a great possibility for settling down permanently.

Serenity interrupted when an older woman with bare feet and a tornado of short, blond curls streaked out the open door and down the sidewalk. Her wail blasted the last of the serenity as she zipped past the motorhome.

"Miranda! Oh, Miranda, where are you! Where did you go?"

I yanked the fastener on my seat belt, and an indignant Koop leaped out of my lap. The woman was already racing down the center of the road, a gauzy cover-up flying behind her. I stumbled out of the motorhome, still in my shark slippers, Mac right behind me.

This must be Aunt Eleanor. Who had she lost? A worker or caretaker? A friend? A *child*?

We raced down the road after her. No sidewalks in this edge-of-town area, so we took the center of the road too. She was surprisingly speedy for a woman whom the man in Cabo had said was about our age.

"Wait!" I yelled. "We'll help you!"

The woman ran another thirty feet before she stopped and leaned over, hands on her knees as she gasped for breath. A car rounded the sharp curve a little farther down the road. Mac caught up with the woman and edged her over to the weedy shoulder so the car could pass by.

"She was right there in the living room!" the woman gasped. "And now she's gone!"

"We'll help you look. Rest a minute," I said when I caught up with them. "How long has she been gone?"

"I don't know. I fell asleep while I was sunbathing, and when I woke up she was just *gone!*"

For the first time I realized what she was wearing under the gauzy cover-up. A bikini. A *ruffled red* bikini. Blake Houston had described his aunt as *unpredictable*, and I figured we might have an example of that right here. She wasn't Playboy material in the bikini, although she might be tough competition in a Ms. Golden Oldies contest.

"Can you describe Miranda for us?" Mac asked. "How old is she?"

"I don't know." She gave a distracted flip of her hand. "Maybe a couple months."

Which was a first clue that perhaps we weren't dealing with a human runaway here. Two-month-old youngsters do not take off down the road. A puppy, perhaps? Or a scared cat? Then a more chilling thought. Maybe it *was* a baby— "Could she have been kidnapped?"

The woman lifted her head and gave us a startled look. "I thought she ran away— But maybe she *was* kidnapped!"

Mac repeated his request for a description, but the woman just gave a frantic look around and wailed, "Oh, where is she?"

I fumbled for my cell phone to call 911. Oh, no, I'd left it in the motorhome again—

"There she is!" The woman took off down the road again, a plaintive "Miranda-a-a-a!" trailing behind her.

Mac ran after her and, after a moment's hesitation, I followed. An SUV and a pickup drove by, both slowing to watch this odd display of senior behavior.

The young guy in the pickup braked when he came to me. "Everything okay here?" He sounded wary.

I could ask him to call 911, but what could he say? *I'm out here on Eidenburg Road and there's these weird old people running down the road. An old lady in a red bikini, yelling her head off. An old guy with knobby knees chasing after her. Another old lady trying to run with something like grinning sharks on her feet.*

Practically an invitation for a whole herd of guys with big nets to come capture us.

I brushed hair off my face and assured the guy we were all okay, but his look was still wary, as if he suspected we could be escapees from some local institution for mentally unstable oldsters. Or maybe outer-space aliens masquerading as human seniors. Which was when I realized a rock in my left, shark-toothed slipper was cutting into my foot. I yanked off the slipper and shook it.

Pickup Guy's mouth fell open as if he feared imminent alien/senior attack. He pulled up a cell phone and snapped a photo, then gunned the engine and burned rubber into the asphalt. I saw myself as I'd just been captured for posterity. Little old lady with possum-gray hair falling across her face. Baja T-shirt scrunched up to expose little-old-lady midriff. Toothy shark slipper raised in elderly menace.

How soon would the photo show up on the internet? Like a California-road version of those strange "Walmart People" pictures that are always popping up on Facebook. Would I be displayed between a droopy-jeans man bent over to expose a crack the size of the San Andreas fault and an oversized woman bulging out of a thong as she licked a carton of strawberry ice cream?

While I stood there, a little black-and-white dog appeared out of nowhere and yapped ferociously. A larger creature following it gave a quieter but more ominous growl.

I was in no mood for threats. I growled back, and both dogs slunk away, apparently deciding my growl outranked theirs. Ahead of me, at the sharp bend in the road, the bikini-clad woman left the road and scrambled over an embankment. The floaty cover-up caught on a few weeds, but she plunged on.

"There she is! Miranda-a-a-a!" the woman repeated. Her head disappeared over the embankment. Mac's head followed.

A little late to the party, I finally dashed up and peered over the edge of the steep embankment.

What did I expect? Definitely not what I saw. Which was the woman picking up a round object, shiny black, a foot or so in diameter, that had crashed into a stump at the bottom of the embankment. She cradled the item in her arms.

We don't own one, but I recognized what the round object was, and, although I was relieved it wasn't a dead body, I felt a bit irate. We had risked life and limb racing down the road, braving traffic, hostile dogs, and a photo-snapping stranger, to chase after a runaway *robot vacuum cleaner*?

With an aid from Mac, the woman struggled back up the embankment, robot still clutched in her arms.

"Are you Eleanor?" I asked when they reached road level. I realized the question sounded a little grumpy, but at the moment I felt as if we had just been led on the goosiest of wild goose chases. "Eleanor Ridgeway?"

"Well, yes, I was Eleanor," she conceded. She was breathing a little hard but didn't seem in danger of collapse from her run down the road. "I'm Elena now."

She dismissed the name change as if it didn't require explanation and gave the robot a tap of rebuke. "Bad Miranda, running away like that."

Miranda, in spite of a tumble over the embankment and an encounter with a tree trunk, appeared to be none the worse for wear in her dash for freedom. I'm not sure I could say as much for myself. I'm not a total couch potato, but neither do I tend to make mad dashes down roadways in fuzzy shark slippers.

"Do you name all your appliances?" Mac, too, sounded a little disgruntled now.

"No, of course not." Eleanor-Elena looked us over with suspicion, as if we might be peculiar people who did name everything from microwave to body parts. "Do you?" she challenged.

"Of course not," Mac said. True, although long ago I did call my first car Trouble, but that was reasonable because trouble was what it was.

"The only reason I gave Miranda a name is because she . . . needed one." She shrugged as if that was explanation enough. "My nephew Blake got her for me. He's always buying me things." She sighed. "I appreciate that, especially the new sidewalk. I was always stumbling over the bumps in the old dirt path. But now he's bought me an air fryer. Can you imagine? Frying something with *air*?"

"Did you name her Miranda for some particular reason?" I asked, still feeling a little cantankerous. The connection I made with *Miranda* surely wasn't one that would occur to her. Maybe she was remembering that long-ago movie star, Carmen Miranda, who always had a pile of fruit on her head.

"It's because she always seems so *curious*, slipping under things or prowling around in corners. There's that law, you know, that people have to be told their rights, their Miranda rights, when they're arrested and questioned, and the name seemed to fit. As if she should be offering dust bunnies their rights before sucking them up."

It was a roundabout and unlikely connection to make, and Eleanor/Elena's knowledge of the basics of Miranda rights certainly surprised me. No connection with a fruit-topped movie star here. Hers was the same connection I'd made with the name.

"You're familiar with Miranda rights?" I asked.

"Of course." She gave me an *isn't everyone?* look, and I wondered if that meant she'd had personal experience with Miranda rights. Were there facts about his aunt that Blake Houston had neglected to tell us, something more ominous than *unpredictable*? My suspicions notched upward when she said, "Miles told me. He said if I was ever arrested that they had to read me my Miranda rights before questioning me. And that I should ask for a lawyer before I said anything."

"And Miles is—?"

"Miles Willoughby. My boyfriend. Although that's kind of a ridiculous term to use at our ages, isn't it?"

"Did he think you were in danger of being arrested?"

"Oh, no." She clutched Miranda a little tighter, and, despite her denial, a little twitch of her eyes gave me the unexpected thought that she might indeed be fearful of an arrest at some point. "But you never know."

This unlikely turn of conversation made me want to know more about this Miles who was apparently the man Blake had said we should keep a sharp eye on. Maybe boyfriend Miles had some personal experience with the law that made him familiar with Miranda rights? Mac jerked the conversation back to the original subject.

"How did Miranda happen to get away from you?" he asked.

"Usually she comes out by herself to clean later in the day, but I'd spilled some blueberry muffin crumbs in the living room when I was watching TV so I put her in there to clean up. Then I went in my bedroom to sunbathe under the window. That's why I'm wearing my new bikini, of course. I want a nice tan for the honeymoon."

Honeymoon? Mac and I exchanged glances. Nephew Blake hadn't said anything about a forthcoming honeymoon. Did he know about it?

"You're planning a honeymoon?" Mac asked.

"Oh, yes. As soon as Miles gets a business trip and a few other matters taken care of, we'll drive over to Reno and get married." She extended the fingers on her left hand, and I now saw a ring on her finger. Not a large diamond, but the small diamond was nicely set in a swirl of diamond chips.

"Well . . . congratulations." I felt a little hesitant saying this, considering her nephew's reservations about the man. Then I pointed out to myself that Mac and I had married rather late in life, and Elena was certainly entitled to do the same. Maybe nephew Blake was just an overprotective or worrywart type. We didn't know him all that well, and we didn't know boyfriend Miles at all.

"Miranda has always been so well-behaved, so industrious and efficient. Who'd have thought she'd run away? Though she has gotten lost a time or two. Once I had to look all over before I found her stuck in a closet and another time she got tangled in a sock under the bed."

I had no idea how robot vacuum cleaners were supposed to behave, so I didn't know if what this one had done today was aberrant robot conduct or not.

"But it never occurred to me that just because I left the front door open to let in some fresh air that she might run off." Elena broke off and her nicely penciled eyebrows scrunched, as if this were a hurtful display of disloyalty. Then she brightened. "But maybe she didn't actually run away. Maybe she just went walkabout! Yes, I think that's what she did. She just got tired of going back and forth on the same old carpet and went walkabout. That's the word Miles would use. Several of his cruises took him down to Australia."

I used my own handy-dandy word suitable for all occasions. "Umm." It seemed appropriate for a conversation about a robot vacuum cleaner's motive for a runaway/walkabout excursion and a boyfriend who knew about Miranda rights. "And then once she was outside," Elena went on, "I don't know how she got turned to go down the road. Usually she just goes in a straight line until she runs into something."

Which was apparently how she'd escaped out the open door. The patio was on a level with the concrete floor of the house, so she hadn't run into anything to make her turn and she'd just kept going. Then, instead of turning with the sharp curve in the road, she'd kept going straight ahead and plunged over the embankment.

"Maybe she hit something on the far side of the road to make her turn," I suggested. I gave myself a mental whack for referring to the robot vacuum cleaner as *she*. Mirada was machinery, perhaps an eccentric piece of machinery, but not a "she."

"I suppose." Elena gave the robot another reproving tap, as if she was still a bit annoyed with it.

"By the way, we're Mac and Ivy MacPherson," Mac said. "Perhaps your nephew Blake mentioned us?"

"Oh, yes. You're the people with the motorhome that he met on one of his trips. He said you'd be coming." She looked us over, with a momentary pause on my shark slippers. Her tone went a little cooler when she added, "You're welcome to park out back, of course, but I'll tell you right off that I do not need a caretaker or

Lorena McCourtney

babysitter or whatever Blake wants you to be. I know he means well, and I know he'd like me to go live in a retirement home. But I'm fine right where I am, and I won't be alone after Miles and I are married." She hesitated, then added, with what I thought was a hint of defiance, "Miles is a few years younger than I am."

Yes, there was definitely a wanna-make-something-of-it? challenge in the way she mentioned the age difference.

I said, "Umm," and then added another congratulation. "I hope you'll be very happy together."

Elena might have a peculiarity or two, but it didn't appear that she and Miles needed, as she put it, a babysitter. Although I had to admit to a smidgen of suspicion. How much younger was this boyfriend/fiancé? Did he see Elena as a ticket to free room and board, with a generous nephew as a bonus? Or perhaps Elena had hidden financial assets, and he had nefarious plans to glom onto them?

Or maybe it was nephew Blake of whom we should be suspicious. Were we just players in some underhanded scheme to railroad his aunt into a retirement home so he could grab her property?

Okay, so I'm a suspicious little old lady. Maybe running into a murder here and there does that to you. But, as I reminded myself again, we knew nothing about boyfriend Miles and very little about nephew Blake. We didn't even know much about Elena, except that her nephew considered her unpredictable and she had a rather flamboyant taste in bikinis.

"Perhaps we should just be running along," Mac said.

"Oh, don't go until you meet Miles," Elena said. "He's coming over for dinner, and then we're going to make pretzels. Have you ever made pretzels?"

"No, I don't believe I ever have," I admitted.

"Neither have I! But Miles is a marvelous cook, and he says we can add some collagen to the pretzel dough to make it more nutritious. And he tells the funniest knock-knock jokes."

My suspicions of Miles stumbled. Somehow nefarious plans don't seem to go with pretzels and collagen and knock-knock jokes.

14

"And you're welcome to park out back too. At least until Miles and I get married. We haven't decided yet if we'll live in my place or his townhouse. I just don't want any misunderstandings about my needing to be looked after."

"How soon will you be going to Reno to get married?" I asked.

"As I said, Miles has some matters to take care of, so we haven't set an actual date. Maybe we'll get a motorhome, too, and do some traveling. Yours looks very nice."

She peered down the road to where our motorhome stood in front of her house. It isn't a newer model—we definitely couldn't afford the price of a new one—but it is quite nice. And comfortable. A slide-out to enlarge the living room space. A queen-sized bed, a generous-sized refrigerator/freezer, and an oven that worked as both microwave and convection.

I could see an orange lump behind the big windshield that meant Koop was curled up in a favorite spot.

"We live in it full-time now. But we're looking for a place to settle down and live permanently." I decided not to mention that it was *her* place we were eyeing.

Elena winced as she started back toward the house on the rough asphalt, and we both looked down at her bare feet. The feet were blackened and dirty, with painted toenails like little pink headlights peeking out of the dirty toes. A raw spot marked where she'd stubbed her big toe, and a torn strip of the gauzy cover-up drooped down her leg. Where her ankle sported a tiny butterfly tattoo.

"Right now, I think we should get you and Miranda back to the house," Mac said.

"I may have overexerted myself a bit," Elena admitted.

"I'll carry Miranda for you," I offered.

I reached for the robot, but Elena set it on the road and pushed a button. It cheerfully started off on another journey, apparently unfazed by the unhappy end to its earlier jaunt. We all followed it, but after only a few feet a red light came on and it slowed to a stop.

"I think that means her battery is run down. Or something is jammed in the cleaning brushes. At the house, when she's done working or the battery gets low, she goes back to her docking station and recharges."

An enviable ability. There are times I'd like to retreat to a docking station and do a quick recharge. Elena, too, looked as if she could use a recharge. She winced again as she took a few more steps on the asphalt.

"Look," Mac said, "you two wait here, and I'll go get the motorhome so you won't have to walk back to the house."

Elena hesitated only momentarily before nodding, and Mac headed down the road toward the motorhome. I looked around for someplace Elena and I could sit down, and that was when I spotted something back in the trees beyond the stump where Miranda had crashed. Something red.

Given past experience, an ugly possibility instantly occurred to me. I scoffed at it. Surely the red thing was just some discarded old rag. The mat of fallen leaves under the trees probably concealed all kinds of trash.

But that old bugaboo of mine, what a police officer friend had once called my mutant curiosity gene, made me step closer to the edge of the embankment for a better look. I could immediately see that the red thing was a T-shirt. And it had a disturbing *fullness*. As if it were something other than a discarded piece of clothing . . .

But it couldn't be what it looked like. No, no, surely not. No way. The honeymoon was a dividing line between past and future experiences with such discoveries.

Elena was looking now too. "What is that?"

I didn't want to investigate more thoroughly. But if the thing beneath the trees was what it appeared to be, I couldn't *not* investigate.

I slid down the embankment and into the trees, and a moment later I could tell that what made the T-shirt look *full* was exactly what I didn't want it to be.

The admirably low crime rate of San Isolde may have just taken a jump upward.

CHAPTER 2

MAC

I pulled the motorhome to the far edge of the shoulder at the wide spot where the road curved sharply. From the height of the motorhome window I could see Ivy and Elena leaning over something back in the trees.

BoBandy wanted to come with me when I opened the door, but I pushed him back inside. There was something odd about the way Ivy had her hands linked behind her back while she studied something on the ground. I'm not given to astute intuitions, but I had a knot-in-the-belly feeling about this.

"What's going on?" I called as I rounded the front of the motorhome.

"We've found . . . something," Ivy called back. Elena moved closer to the thing on the ground, and Ivy reached out to grab her. "No, don't touch—"

Too late. Her warning went unheeded as Elena did more than touch the red thing on the ground. She turned it over, and there was no mistaking what it was from the flopping head and arms. I skidded down the embankment and put an arm around Ivy's shoulders. Then, when Elena spoke, I realized, unpleasant as finding an anonymous dead body was, something worse was going on here.

"It's Miles," Elena whispered as she stared down at the face. "It's Miles and he's *dead*."

Elena's boyfriend dead? It seemed an incomprehensible statement, totally out of context. We've chased an errant robot vacuum cleaner down the road and now there's a dead boyfriend?

Elena didn't start screaming or sobbing. She was apparently too stunned to do anything more than simply stare in disbelief. The dead man was silver-haired, with a short, neatly trimmed beard and mustache and a wiry body.

"But how could he be *dead*?" Elena protested.

Taking a closer look, I suspected the bullet hole in his chest had a lot to do with it.

"He was there at the house just last night! We barbecued burgers and watched an old John Wayne movie . . . *Rio Bravo.* Miles loves that old movie! Tonight we're going to watch *Four Weddings and a Funeral* and make pretzels." She said all this as if the movies and planned pretzels meant Miles surely couldn't be dead.

But he was. Miles would not be making pretzels or telling knock-knock jokes tonight. And our awesome honeymoon had not ended our involvement with dead bodies and murder as I know Ivy had optimistically hoped.

Of course, it was possible this wasn't murder . . .

Yeah, right. It was possible that hole in the man's chest was just a strange decoration printed on his T-shirt, something even more tasteless than those shark slippers I bought for Ivy. But not likely.

Ivy stepped away from me and wordlessly put her arms around Elena.

I said, "I'll get my phone and call nine-one-one."

With surprising presence of mind, considering how stunned she looked, Elena reached under the gauzy thing she was wearing and unclipped a cell phone case from her bikini. She, unlike Ivy, was apparently never without her connection to the world. She handed the phone to me, and I tapped in the numbers. I gave the woman who responded at 911 the information, and said no, we weren't in in any danger. She asked a few more questions about identity and location, and I gave Elena's address and said we'd wait at the scene for someone to arrive. I think the woman wanted me to stay on the phone, but I tapped the Off button. Unpredictable Elena had a skittery look that made me think I needed to be ready for whatever she might do next.

Ivy touched Elena's arm. "Let's go sit in the motorhome," she coaxed.

Elena suddenly came to life. She jerked away. "No, no we can't leave him just lying here! We can move him up to the road—" She bent over and grabbed his arm as if she fully intended to do a one-woman fireman's carry up the embankment.

I jumped forward, ready to physically restrain her from destroying evidence by moving the body again, but Ivy had better technique.

"We'll all stay right here with him," she soothed. "You can hold his hand if you want."

I had many questions, and I knew Ivy did too, but this wasn't the time to ask them. Elena still wasn't crying, but she looked more than stunned now as she let dead Miles fall back to the ground. Her blue eyes had a scary-movie glaze, as if she might go into head-spinning mode any moment. And then, without warning, before she could take the dead man's hand, she simply collapsed.

She hit the ground like a boxer on the receiving end of a knockout blow. I didn't think we should let her just lie there on the moldering leaves, so I scooped her up and struggled up the embankment with her. She wasn't heavy, but I was glad I didn't have to carry her a mile or two. Ivy opened the motorhome door and I managed to twist Elena sideways to get up the steps and through the door. I thought we'd have to call 911 again, this time to ask for an ambulance, but she'd halfway returned to consciousness even as I set her on the sofa.

"Did I *faint*?" She sounded appalled with herself. She struggled to sit up.

Ivy patted her arm, and BoBandy sniffed her bare feet. "Just for a minute or two."

"I didn't imagine it, did I? Miles is *dead*."

"I'm afraid so," Ivy said.

"He has a bullet hole in his chest." She clutched her arms around herself and rocked back and forth on the sofa. "Somebody killed him! My sweet, sweet Miles. Somebody *killed* him."

She didn't ask the questions it seemed to me most people would ask at this point: *Why would anyone want to kill him? Who did it?*

Some of us may know people who might not grieve if we accidently ingested a plate of poisoned lasagna, but not many of us know people who actively want to shoot us.

"He should have gone to see Nicole. I was always trying to get him to, but he never would. Maybe she could have told him he was in danger. Maybe she'd have warned him!"

"Who's Nicole?" Ivy asked.

"She's Miles's niece. The Cookie Lady. She sees things. She knows things. He liked her, but he always laughed at her readings. He said only silly old ladies would ever believe any of her cookie-crumbling nonsense."

I knew this statement would not endear Miles to Ivy, even if he was now dead. She tends to take umbrage with anyone who couples a word such as "silly" with "old ladies." However, before either of us could ask for details about "cookie-crumbling nonsense," a police car rolled up and we had to get out of the motorhome and start answering questions.

Names. Addresses. A bit of confusion when we couldn't provide an address where we actually lived. Our relationship with the dead man. What we'd seen. How we'd found him. Finally, tears did trickle from Elena's eyes as she talked about "sweet Miles" and showed them her ring. Ivy kept a supporting grip on Elena's arm. A police photographer started documenting everything in the area, and yellow crime scene tape went up.

More police cars arrived. Police radios squawked. A few curious onlookers appeared. Elena looked as if she might crumple again at any moment, and her bikini bottoms had taken an unfortunate scrunch-up on one side. For modesty reasons, they needed yanking back into place, but the idea of discussing bikini adjustment with an almost-stranger woman tends to give a man of my age and old-fashioned nature definite heebie-jeebies.

We stood around watching a little longer, Elena growing more agitated every minute. She suddenly tried to rush back down to Miles, and an officer had to hold her back. Ivy finally asked permission to take her back to the house, and, after the officers did a quick search of the motorhome because it was part of the general crime scene, they let us go. With the warning, of course, that we all stay at the house until someone came to question us further.

I helped Elena back into the motorhome, and Ivy retrieved Miranda from between the front wheels of a police car, only a few inches away from being squashed. By the time we got back to the house, the ruffled bikini bottoms had, thankfully, slid back into a more modest position. Elena insisted on immediately returning the robot to its docking station.

"After all," she said, "she risked getting run over to lead us to Miles. She's really a *heroine*. Who knows how long before he'd have been found if she hadn't done that?"

It was indeed possible that the body might not have been found for some time, but I didn't give the vacuum cleaner credit for some multi-tasking ability that enabled it to track down dead bodies as well as pick up dirt and debris. She . . . no, *it* . . . had just happened to smash itself into a stump down below the road by accident. The fact that the boyfriend's body was nearby *was* an odd coincidence, but it was strictly coincidence.

Elena got the vacuum cleaner properly docked at the station, giving it several nice strokes of appreciation, and it started blinking a pink-and-blue light. If I wanted to grant "she" status to the robot, I might think the blinking did look a bit smug, as if the robot was pleased with a task well done. But it was just a machine.

Ivy talked Elena into changing into a flowered robe rather more substantial than the flimsy thing she was wearing and then persuaded her to lie down in the bedroom. Elena protested, saying she had to call Miles's niece, Nicole the Cookie Lady. Ivy said she'd do it, that Elena needed to rest now. Ivy closed the drapes to darken the room.

Back in the kitchen, Ivy found a pitcher of iced tea in the refrigerator and poured a glass for herself and me. We plopped down in a little breakfast nook tucked into a corner of the kitchen. Elena's cell phone was still in my pocket, and I set it on the table.

"I wonder how long it will take them to come here to question us," Ivy said.

"Hard to tell. Probably not until after someone from the coroner or medical examiner's office, whatever they have in this county, comes."

Ivy drew damp circles on the blue-topped table with her glass. "They're going to be suspicious of Elena."

I nodded. With Elena's fiancé connection to Miles, and her finding the body, they would certainly look at her as a possible suspect. Strangers commit murders, of course, lots of them, but more homicides are committed by someone with a personal connection with the dead person. Fact gleaned from one of the many articles on crime in Ivy's files. "They're not going to credit a robot vacuum cleaner with leading the way to the body. They'll suspect Elena already knew it was there."

We silently pondered that. I could almost read Ivy's mind: Elena seemed an unlikely suspect in a murder and her shocked reaction to her fiancé's dead body seemed genuine, but *everybody's a suspect.*

"Is there any reason to think it *isn't* a murder?" Ivy sounded hopeful.

I suppose there is some way a man could have a fatal gunshot wound in the chest without it being murder. A poorly planned suicide. Some bizarre mishap involving a loaded gun and a deadly game of Russian roulette. It could be a tragic accident. Maybe that old standby, he didn't know the gun was loaded and it went off accidently while he was cleaning it.

But it was doubtful Miles had been playing Russian roulette or cleaning a gun down there among the trees alongside the road. I shook my head, unable to supply a helpful answer to Ivy's question.

"He was apparently killed sometime after he left here last night," Ivy said. "Did he just walk out the door and *bang!* someone shot him and then dumped the body where we found him? Or was he killed right where we found the body?"

"He must have come here in a car. Where is it?"

"Yes, a *car.* Maybe somebody killed him to get the car."

Even disturbing as that thought was, that someone would take a man's life just to grab his car, it wasn't an uncommon crime. I knew Ivy had been wondering, as I was, if Elena had some motive to kill

Miles. The idea that he'd been killed in a car hijacking was somehow more acceptable than Elena as a murderer. Even if she was unpredictable.

"I suppose I'd better call this niece and tell her what's happened," Ivy said.

She didn't sound eager to do it, but she picked up the cell phone from where I'd set it on the table. I headed to the motorhome to let BoBandy out for a few minutes while she made the call.

CHAPTER 3

IVY

"San Isolde Bakery," a cheerful voice said. I'd found a number for a Nicole on the contact list on Elena's phone. Two numbers, actually. The one I'd chosen was apparently where she worked. "Blueberry muffins are just coming out of the oven. Want some?"

"Well, umm . . ." Actually, at the moment—inappropriate as it seemed—I suddenly did want a blueberry muffin. But what I said was, "May I talk to Nicole?" Elena's contact list hadn't given a last name.

"This is Nicole."

"Cookie Lady Nicole?"

"Well, yes, but I don't do cookie readings here at the bakery. I can make an appointment at my home for you, if you'd like."

"Actually, this is about something else. I'm calling from Elena . . . Eleanor . . . Ridgeway's home. I think you know both her and her friend Miles?"

"Yes, of course."

"I believe Elena said Miles was your uncle?"

"In a way."

"I'm afraid something has happened to Miles. I hate to have to tell you so bluntly, but we just found his body—"

"His *body!*"

"Yes. The police are at the scene now. It's just down the road from Elena's home."

"Miles is *dead?* I can't believe it— What happened to him?"

Tell Nicole that he had a bullet hole in his chest? I hesitated. I had no firm reason for hesitation, but that "in a way" reference to the uncle-niece relationship seemed a little odd. *Everybody's a suspect.* Maybe I'd just see what she had to say.

"I think the police will be coming here to the house shortly. They may have more information." It wasn't an untruth, although it was certainly a non sequitur and dodged around the few facts we knew.

"Where's Elena?"

"She's resting now."

"Is she okay?"

"I think so. This has been a terrible shock for her."

"How did you find his body?"

"It's rather strange, but Elena's robot vacuum cleaner got out on the road and—"

"*Miranda* found him?"

"It was a coincidence, of course. She . . . *it* . . . just happened to crash near his body."

Brief silence as she absorbed the oddity of that. "How did Miles die?"

I couldn't squirm out from under the direct question, but I didn't have to be specific. Maybe she already knew more than I did. "It appears to have been a homicide."

"Homicide! You mean someone killed him?"

I repeated my earlier line. "The police will probably have more information later."

"I'm coming right over."

**

Mac came back inside after taking BoBandy out for a potty break. We watched cars, some with police insignia, some unmarked, come and go. Mac went out again to check around in back and came in to say there were electrical, water, and sewer hookups behind the garage, apparently set up for an RV at some earlier time. Getting the motorhome away from all the coming-and-going traffic on the road seemed like a good idea, so Mac unhooked our little pickup and moved the motorhome around back.

I looked in on Elena a couple of times. I'd slipped out of my shark slippers and was also barefoot now. She was sleeping, but restlessly, her head of blond curls tossing back and forth on the pillow. I now noted a photo in a leather frame on the nightstand, Elena and a man who must be Miles together on a beach. They both looked happy; he, with a black cap set at a rakish angle and a rather mischievous grin, quite dashing; she almost girlish in white shorts and sleeveless blouse tied at the waist.

A sharp contrast with the road dirt and scratches now on her bare feet. I wondered if I could wash her feet and put salve on the cuts without waking her. I was just coming out of the bedroom, planning to return with a washcloth and pan of soapy water, when the doorbell tinkled. I heard the door open without the visitor waiting for a response to the doorbell.

The woman and I practically collided in the hallway. She was thirty-ish, attractive, nice figure, especially for someone who apparently had blueberry muffins available on demand. Her dark hair was pulled into a prim bun at the back of her head, not the most flattering of styles but perhaps suitable for work in a bakery where a stray hair in the muffins might be a major disaster. She wasn't tall, but taller than I am. As almost everyone is.

"You're the person who called me about Miles?" she demanded.

"Yes. Ivy MacPherson. We're friends of Elena's nephew, Blake Houston."

She frowned, as if that wasn't necessarily a five-star recommendation. But all she said was, "I'm Nicole Keller. I need to know more about this. Don't go away. But first I have to see Elena."

She apparently knew her way around the house and rushed on by me to Elena's bedroom. When I peered through the open doorway she was just standing there looking down at Elena. Her hand rested lightly on Elena's shoulder and worry lines cut her forehead, but she seemed reluctant to wake the sleeping woman.

"Let's let her sleep," I said. "Come on back to the kitchen. There's iced tea."

"Why are her feet so dirty?"

"She ran down the road barefoot trying to catch up with Miranda."

Nicole nodded as if that was a perfectly normal thing for Elena to do. I guessed the fact that she'd been wearing a bikini for the chase wouldn't surprise Nicole either. It occurred to me that perhaps it was a good thing Elena hadn't wanted an all-over tan, or she might have been running down the road in even less than a ruffled bikini.

Nicole hesitated a moment more and then gave Elena's shoulder a gentle pat. "Yes, let's let her rest. She must be devastated about Miles."

We went to the kitchen, and I poured the iced tea. Mac was still outside getting the motorhome set up. Nicole slipped into the padded bench seat of the little breakfast nook and shook her head. I sat down across from her.

"I can't believe this. You're *sure* it was Miles, and you're *sure* he was dead?"

"Elena identified him. And I'm sure he was dead."

"You found him down there by where all the police cars are parked?"

"Yes. We'd just arrived in our motorhome and Elena ran out of the house yelling that Miranda was missing. At the moment, we didn't know who . . . what . . . Miranda was, of course. But we followed Elena down the road, and then Miranda tumbled off an embankment. And that's where we found Miles's body."

"A strange coincidence, that Miles would be right where Miranda went off the road."

"Elena gives Miranda credit for finding him."

Nicole almost smiled. "She would. Twice she's lost earrings and Miranda found them for her both times." She cut the almost smile and appraised me across the table. "You say you're friends of Elena's nephew Blake?"

I explained how we'd met Blake down in Baja, and how he'd offered us this space to park our motorhome in exchange for keeping an eye on Elena and helping out when she needed it. I didn't mention the possibility of our buying the property or that nephew Blake thought Miles also needed watching. Considering Miles's unfortunate demise, I was more curious than ever now why Blake thought that.

"You met Blake while you were in Cabo on vacation?" Nicole asked.

"We were there on our honeymoon, but Blake was there on business. He's some kind of salesman/consultant for a big company that designs and builds specialized heavy equipment for big construction projects, mostly overseas. He does a lot of traveling. But I suppose you know all that."

"You'd just met him, and out of the blue he suggested you live here and watch over Elena?" She sounded skeptical.

"I guess we struck him as trustworthy people."

She made no comment. I suspected she wasn't putting us in a trustworthy category yet. Perhaps because she also didn't consider Blake trustworthy? I didn't see any reason to be suspicious of her, but neither did I see any reason to put her in a trustworthy category. There was way too much we didn't know about this entire situation. As Miles's niece, did she stand to inherit something from his death? Was there some conflict between her and Miles? She was at work when I called, of course, and sounded shocked at the news. But I was almost certain Miles had been dead for hours . . . his body had seemed limp when Elena turned him over, so rigor mortis had already started to leave his body . . . so being at work was no alibi for her.

"And the police are calling this a homicide because—?"

"He had a gunshot wound in his chest."

That seemed to hit her hard. She tilted her head down and put a hand on her forehead and seemed almost overcome with emotion. Genuine, or a competent act? I still didn't understand what that Cookie Lady identity was about.

"I understand Elena and Miles were about to be married," I offered tentatively.

"Yes, that's right." Nicole hesitated, as if she were about to say something more, but she instead just swallowed hard and managed another sip of iced tea.

She didn't seem inclined to offer any further information, so I tried again. "Miles is your uncle?" I asked.

"Yes. Well, no, not really. He's actually my ex-husband's uncle, not mine. Miles and I stayed friends after the divorce, but it was a rather awkward situation. I think he could see that Stan had, as the

28

old saying goes, done me wrong, but Stan was the only family Miles had left. I think he also had investments or an IRA or something set up with Stan."

"I can see how Miles might feel uncomfortable, if he felt he was caught between you and your ex-husband. And then you're also good friends with Elena, and she was his fiancée."

"Miles is . . . *was*," she corrected with another swallow of emotion, "good looking and charming and fun to be around."

I could agree with the physical part of her description of Miles. Even in death, I could see he'd been a good-looking man, although the tan that had no doubt added to those good looks in life had looked strangely artificial in death, almost painted on.

"I could see why Elena fell in love with him," Nicole went on in that same choked voice. "I hoped everything would work out great for them."

She didn't add a *But* to that statement, but I thought it was there. I was also reminded that Blake had said to keep an eye on Miles. I suspected there might be various interesting side trails to follow in this information, but at the moment I took a stab in the dark. "You introduced Miles and Elena?"

"No, no. They did meet at the bakery, but I didn't actually *introduce* them." She didn't say it in so many words, but from her emphasis, I suspected she hadn't wanted them to meet. That seemed odd. "We had a plate of blueberry-muffin samples set out—they're the bakery's specialty and both Miles and Elena loved them—and they happened to reach for a sample at the same time. Elena said it was love at first bite for both of them."

Love at first bite. That was kind of sweet. I guess love at first sight . . . or bite . . . can happen. Although it wasn't what happened to Mac and me, and I have to admit to a certain suspicion of love that arrives at falling-off-a-cliff speed. Yes, Mac and I had felt an attraction from the beginning, but we detoured around the idea of committing to marriage for quite some time. Through several dead bodies and murders, actually.

"I was concerned for Elena. She's in no way *dumb*. She can work those sudoku puzzles faster than I can. She always knows the answers to quiz show questions. But she may be a bit . . . naïve," Nicole said. "I've always liked Miles, but I warned her that I didn't think he was marriage material, and she should be careful."

"What did she say to that?"

"She said that was fine because she wasn't looking for a husband."

"And yet they were planning to get married."

"Yes. That love at first bite thing, I guess."

Something about the lines that crossed her forehead made me ask, "But you weren't happy about that?"

"Again, I was . . . concerned. I hoped it would work out. But I was afraid Miles would—" She broke off. "I just didn't want Elena to be hurt."

"You were afraid Miles would do something to hurt her?"

"It doesn't matter now. He's dead." She spoke as if that closed the subject, but I wasn't about to let that happen.

"I can see you don't want to say anything negative about Miles, and I can certainly understand that. But you may be asked by the police what you know about him and his relationship with Elena. The police may be suspicious that she has some connection with his death."

She looked up. "Elena? Oh, no. No, never!" She sounded aghast. "She's all starry-eyed and crazy in love with him. They were planning to go to Reno and be married in some chapel there, just the two of them. She'd *never* do anything to hurt Miles. Actually, she's such a sweetheart she'd never hurt *anyone*, human or otherwise. She was heartbroken when her cranky old cat Ricardo died a few months ago. She'll throw a tissue over a daddy longlegs and carry it outside rather than squash it."

"Her nephew Blake described her as unpredictable."

"Unpredictable? Well, that's true, I suppose. She surprises me every once in a while. Like the short blond hair and curls. She always had gray hair in a long braid and hardly ever wore makeup. Now she reads a makeup magazine and knows all about eyeliner and blush."

I've tried eyeliner. It makes me look like a racoon with a hangover. Maybe I should have read a makeup magazine first.

"But a murderer? No way. Besides, what does Blake know?" Nicole scoffed. "He buys her stuff, sure. He bought this house for her to live in, and furnished it too. But he's so busy chasing around the world making money that Elena could be dating an ax murderer and he wouldn't know. He lives right down in San Diego, but he's hardly ever there."

"You've met him?"

"I met him at Elena's once. Later he called and suggested we have dinner together. I was impressed with him. He's an . . . attractive guy, and Elena always had such good things to say about him." She waved a dismissive hand. "And then he never showed up. Dumb me, I sat there waiting for something like three hours, but he never called, nothing. All I got was a message three days later from a secretary saying he'd had to make an 'emergency trip to Hong Kong,' and I never heard from him again. But I never told Elena he'd bailed on me."

The discussion about Miles had gotten sidetracked into a critique of Elena's nephew, and I understood now why our coming here because we knew Blake was not a gold-star endorsement. But none of that had anything to do with murder. I jumped back to Miles. What if he'd changed his mind about marrying Elena? What if last night, over burgers and *Rio Bravo*, Miles had told her the wedding was off, maybe said something especially hurtful about her being too old for him? Would she have had a woman-scorned reaction at a murderous level? I wondered if the police had found a gun there with the body. Or if there was one hidden here in the house. I gave an uneasy glance toward the hallway to Elena's bedroom.

Nicole took several long sips of iced tea. "But if I have to provide unfavorable information about Miles to help Elena, I'll do it." She sounded determined.

"Would this unfavorable information have anything to do with who killed him?"

"It might."

I waited until she apparently made a decision. She planted her elbows on the table and started talking.

"Okay, this is it. Miles's first wife died before I ever met him, so I don't know much about her or that marriage. They lived back East somewhere. But I know that not long after her death, he was downsized from a longtime job with an insurance company, and the timing cut him out of most of the retirement pension he expected."

"Sometimes companies do really awful things like that."

"Right. He didn't exactly go off the deep end, but he did make a rather drastic change in his life."

"In what way?"

"From what Stan said . . . did I mention that Stan is my ex, Stan Moore, otherwise known as The Villain? I took back my maiden name, Keller, after we divorced. Anyway, Stan said Miles had always lived a quiet, very conservative life working for the insurance company. He and his wife didn't have children, and she was kind of a recluse with a lot of health complaints. Stan called her a hypochondriac but maybe that was unfair, because she did die. But after her death and the demise of the insurance company job, Miles dumped his whole past life and started work with a cruise line as a 'cruise ship host.' I don't think a lot of money was involved, but he got free travel and a place to live and meals too, of course. So it was an interesting way for someone with limited finances to live."

"What does a cruise ship host do?" I've never been on a cruise.

"He greeted passengers and helped them with any small problems that came up. He introduced people and helped less socially-adept ones from becoming isolated." She smiled wryly. "But basically, he was a dancing partner and social companion for unattached older women passengers. He made the cruise more fun for them."

"You mean he romanced these older women as a *job*? Is that legal?"

"I doubt *romance* was part of the job description, but I'd guess some of the women thought his attention was more than just a job for him and took it seriously."

"I suppose that could happen."

"Like I said, he was a good-looking guy. In great shape too. Fun. He could talk to anyone. And also a great dancer. Elena said he was teaching her. The guy knew everything from jitterbugging to salsa."

"That seems at odds with the quiet life you said he'd always lived."

"Yes, it does, doesn't it? Maybe he'd always felt his life was boring or restrictive, and just . . . cut loose after his wife died. Took dancing lessons or something. Or maybe he had a secret double life even before she died. Who knows?" She paused as if that thought troubled her, but then she smiled again. "The thing was, however, he never got over getting seasick on every cruise. And it's difficult to be an effective host when you have to rush off and barf every few minutes. Or take a seasick pill that has you falling asleep in the middle of a conversation."

"So he gave up being a cruise ship host and found some other job or source of income?"

"Maybe he was getting by on the reduced retirement he got from the insurance company. Maybe his investments with The Villain were paying off. I don't know. He never had any actual job that I know of, but he never seemed short of money. He and Elena didn't go out to expensive restaurants or shows, but he drove a recent-model SUV and had a nice townhouse in Sunshine Valley. Mostly they liked driving over to the beach or hiking or just staying home and cooking or watching DVDs together. But they did go dancing occasionally, and he bought that ring for her."

"So?" I didn't see anything here that would put Miles on a marriage-market blacklist and make Nicole reluctant to introduce him to Elena. The cruise ship 'work' was a little questionable, but he'd given that up, and he was apparently financially stable. "What would any of this have to do with someone murdering him?"

"I think, after he quit the cruise ship work, that he maintained relationships with some of the women he'd met." She paused and rattled the ice in her glass. "Actually, I've wondered if he started the cruise ship work with the specific idea of meeting women with money. Afterward, I think he may have been getting money . . . from them."

33

I was startled. "You mean some kind of con thing? Preying on wealthy older women?"

She smiled uneasily. "Well, that's putting it a little bluntly, but something like that. And I think that may have been his actual source of income. He went off on trips occasionally."

I remembered Elena saying Miles had a 'business trip' to make before they got married. "He took trips to exotic places?"

"I don't know. All he ever let slip was one time he said something about getting out of Kansas just before a big snowstorm hit there. But when I asked him about it he wiggled out with some fuzzy story about it being a snowstorm years ago that he was talking about."

"So you're saying he took these trips to see women? Or maybe go on trips with them?"

"He didn't share his itinerary with me. Or who he was with. But he'd be gone several days or a week or more at a time."

Unidentified trips sounded rather suspicious, of course, but Kansas seemed an odd place for a romantic getaway. But maybe it made sense for a man who got seasick on cruises.

"These trips were before or after he met Elena?"

"I only knew about the trips after he and Elena got together. Before that, Stan and I saw him occasionally, but not regularly enough to know if he'd been away. And, at the time, my mind was more on what sneaky things Stan was up to, not what Miles was doing. Anyway, now that Miles is dead, I'm wondering if one of those women turned vengeful when she realized he was playing her for money. Murderously vengeful. It happens, you know."

This certainly put a different perspective on Elena's "sweet, sweet Miles." A Lothario with a side-hustle going with one or more cruise women? Yes, indeed, murder was possible. Although this didn't necessarily absolve Elena. He could have told her he was breaking off with her so he could marry one of those women. Or maybe he wanted to continue the con games with other women even after he and Elena married, and he openly suggested that to her. And Elena's murderous reaction had been a bullet hole in his chest?

Or perhaps a murderous reaction from her came from a different possibility. "Do you think he was conning Elena for money?"

"Elena hasn't much in the way of assets, as far as I know. Her husband's huge medical bills pretty well wiped them out before he died. She lost the home they had, and Blake bought this place for her to live in."

Which rather sank my side suspicions that Blake might be recruiting us to stay here while he hustled Elena off to a retirement home so he could grab her house.

"But Miles may have been living beyond his means. Who knows?" Nicole added. "Maybe he figured Elena had a ready supply of funds from Blake and was willing to marry her to get in on that."

Was that why Blake was suspicious of Miles and wanted us to keep an eye on him? "When did she change from Eleanor to Elena?"

"About the time she met Miles. Which was also about the time she went blond and started wearing makeup and got that butterfly tattoo on her ankle. I think she felt a little insecure about being older than Miles and wanted to, you know, update herself for him."

"Elena is my middle name, actually. It isn't as if I just grabbed it out of thin air."

Nicole and I both jumped. I had to grab her glass of iced tea to keep it from crashing to the floor.

"Elena!" Nicole exclaimed. She slid out of the breakfast nook. "We thought you were asleep."

"Obviously," Elena snapped.

How long had she been standing there listening to us? Long enough, obviously. She scrunched the belt of the robe tighter and looked as if she might like to strangle both of us with it. "Sitting out here talking about me—and Miles!—as if he were some sleazy con artist and I'm a gullible old fool with delusions of glamour."

"Oh, Elena, sweetie, I'm sorry!" Nicole gasped. "You know I've never thought of either of you that way. It's just that—"

Elena sagged against the wall. "Well, it doesn't matter now. He's dead."

"Yes. Ivy told me. It's such a shock. That he's dead. And an even worse shock that someone killed him."

A ring of the doorbell ended any further discussion on that subject. "The police officers are probably here to interview us," I said uneasily as I stood up.

"They think I did it," Elena said. She straightened and crossed her arms over her chest. "They'll probably be even more suspicious when they find out about my gun."

CHAPTER 4

MAC

I walked in the back way just in time to hear Elena say, "They think I did it."

I was surprised. I'd thought Elena was too shocked, too stunned . . . or maybe too naïve . . . to realize that her connection with Miles plus finding the body had no doubt landed her on a suspect list. Maybe she wasn't nearly as shocked and stunned about Miles's death as she'd let on? Or, to be fair, more likely this realization of the police suspicions had come to her later, while she was lying there in the bedroom.

I also didn't believe the officers had come to as definite a conclusion as she made it sound. At this point, she was surely just a "person of interest." I wasn't totally unsuspicious of Elena myself. But then, at this point, we were probably all under a certain amount of suspicion from the police. Maybe they were even thinking a three-way conspiracy, Elena and us together. Or maybe they'd include Miranda and make it a four-way.

Elena went to the door and let two officers inside. One was older, a beefy build, an air of experienced authority; the other was younger, tall, muscular. He exuded a certain brash eagerness. A rookie on his first murder investigation? I wasn't sure if these officers had been at the scene of Miles's body, but they weren't ones we'd talked to earlier. It looked as if the local police department didn't have a separate division of plainclothes detectives.

The uniformed officers came into the living room, and I could see the older cop expertly taking in everything from the vase of flowers on the coffee table to Elena's dirty bare feet. Ivy's feet were also bare, her shark slippers parked by the kitchen door. He asked a few questions about names and connections with the dead man, the same questions we'd been asked before. We were all still standing. He jotted everything in a small notebook, giving us each an appraisal much more penetrating than the innocuous questions. I felt as if I'd been scrutinized from eyebrows to toenails, with maybe a pit stop at my midsection. I self-consciously sucked it in. I'm not into pot-belly stage yet, and Ivy calls me a silver fox, but neither do I have an impressive six-pack of muscle these days.

Since there were four of us now, I figured he was taking his time deciding whether to separate us for full questioning here or have us come to the police station. The younger officer kept rising up on his toes, apparently impatient for action.

Then, while Nicole was telling the officers about her semi-niece connection with Miles, I noticed something else. Miranda, apparently recharged now and working on her regular schedule, had left her docking station and was working the living room, deftly dodging furniture. She was behind the officers, barely making a sound as she covered the room in diagonal strips. They seemed haphazard strips at first, but then I could see she was managing to cover the carpet quite thoroughly.

Then I noticed something else. It was surely just part of her programming, but she almost seemed to be stalking the officers. She'd probe their feet delicately from behind, dart away without actually touching them, then sneak back. The officers didn't seem aware of her presence. They were concentrating on the four of us.

"As the victim's nephew, we'll need your ex-husband's name and address too," the older officer was saying to Nicole, his pen poised over the notebook.

The younger officer studied a framed sketch hanging on the wall. It was a drawing of a woman, perhaps a much younger Elena. The officer took a step forward, apparently to take a closer look at the drawing.

Which was when Miranda, in some robot change of mind about avoiding direct contact, struck. She slammed directly into Younger Officer's heel. I might even think it was a gleeful slam.

He yelped in surprise, jumped, and banged into the other officer. The older officer took a startled step backward and tripped over the coffee table behind him. Notebook and pen arced across the room. The coffee table flipped, like some would-be gymnast, and skidded across the carpet. Water from the vase flying off the coffee table targeted Older Officer as he went down.

Older Officer hit the floor, his feet tangling with Younger Officer's leg. Younger Officer went down too. The vase smashed under him. Older Officer said something very un-officer-ish and not to be repeated. He bounced to his feet and came up with a gun in his hand. He instantly crouched, his head swiveling to keep us all in view, ready to take on all comers.

Miranda got him on the side of the foot. He didn't react as forcefully as Younger Officer had, but he looked down and kicked. Miranda took a quick zig to the side, nimbly avoiding him. No doubt a coincidental rather than deliberate zig, of course. Unless robot vacuum cleaners are programmed to dodge hostile police officers.

Younger Officer, still on the floor, scrambled for his gun and tangled his hand in a wet jungle of tiger lilies and carnations and baby's breath from the broken vase.

Miranda prudently scurried away. The four of us just stood there like characters in a video game unexpectedly frozen on screen as we faced two officers, one standing, one sitting. One with a big wet blotch, one dripping with flowers. Both with drawn guns.

"Nobody move," Older Officer growled. A growl somewhat diluted by the fact that the water from the vase had hit him well below the belt, and the result was the look of a rather indelicate personal accident. None of us moved anyway.

Miranda disappeared behind a potted lemon tree. Younger Officer got to his feet, his back side plastered with flowers like some long-ago flower child about to start singing *Kumbaya.* Loose, there seemed to be a lot more flowers than there were when in the vase. More water too. He brushed the flowers away with his free hand, but a spray of baby's breath clung to the hair behind his ear.

Elena rushed over and rescued a few of the fallen flowers. She clutched them to her chest and looked at the officers accusingly. "Miles gave me these flowers!" she wailed.

Older Officer, as if aware they'd put on something of a Keystone Kops display, finally holstered his gun with dignity. Younger officer did the same and then picked up pieces of broken vase. He didn't seem to know what to do with them and finally handed them to me. Also with dignity. I took them to the trash can in the kitchen and came back with paper towels to soak up the waterlogged carpet. Older Officer retrieved his pen and notebook. I wondered if water had affected what he'd written in it.

"You'll all have to come down to the station for interviews," Older Officer stated. He managed to sound stern and authoritative in spite of the wet blotch on his pants, although I suspected the choice of venue might be because he didn't care to conduct interviews sitting in damp underwear.

"Now?" Elena objected. "You want us to come to the station *now*?"

I also had a mild objection. "We already told the officers out at the crime scene everything we know." I always try to be cooperative and helpful dealing with authorities, but we really didn't have any more information to give and Ivy looked as droopy as the fallen flowers. She certainly didn't need any more stress today. "We arrived here only a few hours ago and we'd never even met Miles when he was alive."

Neither Ivy nor I often play the age card, but now Ivy said, "It's been a hard day for people our age. Finding a dead body and all." She drooped the back of her hand against her forehead.

I noted she didn't mention this wasn't exactly a unique event for us. We've been involved with a few dead bodies and murders before. But I didn't mention that either.

"I have appointments I really need to keep," Nicole said.

Older Officer frowned but relented slightly. "Okay, the three of you can come in tomorrow. But you—" He stabbed a finger at Elena. "You come to the station with us now."

I figured what he was doing was separating their most important witness, the one with the closest connection to Miles, from the rest of us so we wouldn't discuss the situation. Discussion can alter the perspective of witnesses and may even implant mistaken ideas of what they've seen. Especially if one person is *trying* to implant false ideas.

"Come in for an interview or an *interrogation?*" Elena demanded.

"You may call it whatever you like, Mrs. Ridgeway," Older Officer said, his statement rigidly polite. "But we need your statement."

"I want my Miranda rights," Elena snapped.

"We aren't arresting you." Older Officer's patience was beginning to fray. Younger Officer rose up on his toes and put a hand on the handcuffs that dangled from his belt. "It shouldn't take more than an hour or so. We'll bring you home afterward."

"I think I want a lawyer," Elena said.

If they were already suspicious of Elena, which I was fairly certain they were, I doubted she was doing her case any good. Although she certainly had the right to a lawyer, of course. Maybe she needed one.

Ivy tried to help. "I don't think Elena is feeling well. She had a blackout spell earlier. Perhaps she could wait and come in with us tomorrow?" To Elena she added, "I'm sure you can have a lawyer if you want one."

"I want my Miranda rights," Elena repeated.

Although I didn't think it was required without an arrest, Older Officer gave her the standard Miranda rights spiel. He spread his feet in a belligerent stance to emphasize his authority, then apparently realized the spread feet only made the wet blotch more obvious. He scooted his feet back together and did an aggressive squaring of shoulders instead. I wondered if I should hand him a pillow from the sofa for concealing purposes.

Elena nodded when he was finished with the Miranda rights. She had a self-satisfied look. "Thank you."

"And you'll have to come to the station with us now."

"I *have* to come?"

"No, you don't *have* to—"

"Then I don't believe I will."

Older Officer gritted his teeth. "We'd appreciate it if you'd come to the station with us now for an interview."

"I'll come along if you'd like," Nicole offered to Elena. "I can call and postpone my appointments."

Elena lifted her chin. "I can do it on my own." She tightened the already tight belt on her robe. "I'll need a few minutes to dress."

Older Officer waved her off, and she marched toward the hallway to her bedroom. But she hadn't gone a half dozen steps down the hallway before she thunked to the floor, again dropping as if she'd been nailed by a heavyweight. I dropped the paper towels and ran to her. The small mob of Ivy, Nicole, and two officers filled the hallway behind me.

I had to wonder, was this something Elena could do on demand? Just lose consciousness and keel over like those fainting goats I've seen on TV? I picked her up and her head dangled limply over my arm. Older Officer stepped up beside me and looked down at her. I suspected he was trying to decide if she was faking.

"Do you want me to carry her out to your car so you can take her in for questioning?" A facetious question, of course. Who could be so heartless as to demand an interrogation of an elderly woman in her condition? Elena's eyes were closed, not even a flutter of eyelids, and her mouth sagged. If she was faking, it was a great fake. If she wasn't faking, maybe we should get her to the hospital as soon as possible.

"We'll postpone the interview until tomorrow," Older Officer muttered.

Ivy had stepped up beside me. "We'll bring her in when we come. Unless her physical condition precludes that, of course." *Precludes* isn't a word Ivy uses in everyday conversation, but as a librarian for many years before she retired, she is familiar with such words and can drag out some impressive ones when needed.

"Okay. So all of you, *all* of you," the officer emphasized with a hard glare at each of us, "be at the station tomorrow morning." He had his growl back, but it seemed a little forced.

He turned and headed down the hallway. Unfortunately, the wet splotch had seeped around to his backside. His gait was a little stiff legged. Perhaps walking in wet underwear does that to you.

I felt a certain sympathy for him. I think he felt he'd been outmaneuvered. Maybe he was right.

"Thanks for coming," Ivy called politely after him. "We'll see you tomorrow."

At the end of the hallway I heard Older Officer growl something to the younger officer. I think he told him to take those stupid flowers out from behind his ear.

Police officer training, thorough as it is, perhaps doesn't cover situations such as stray flowers and wet blotches. I was glad I hadn't also been in the pathway of the tumbling vase or I might be walking stiff legged too.

CHAPTER 5

IVY

Mac deposited a limp Elena in the bedroom, and we went back out to the living room. I'd call an ambulance if she didn't regain consciousness soon, but I had the feeling she might recover rather quickly. Mac straightened the overturned coffee table, but the legs stuck out at odd angles and it couldn't stand upright. Nicole used more paper towels to soak up water from the wet carpet. I found a jar in the kitchen, filled it with water, and gathered up flowers that weren't too badly mangled. I wasn't really surprised when Elena charged down the hallway only a few minutes later, apparently fully recovered.

"Where's Miranda?" she demanded. "I'll sue the police department and the city and every one of those officers if they hurt her!"

I didn't think Miranda had been damaged, but I didn't know where she'd gone. I got down on the floor to help Elena look for her. Several items of furniture we crawled around were newer and expensive, probably pieces Blake had bought for her: the blue sofa, two burgundy recliners, a big, flat-screen TV. A computer and printer were set up on a sleek, modern desk. But a dark, corner hutch filled with knickknacks was definitely older, probably a leftover from the house Elena had lost, as were an old-fashioned, cane-bottomed rocking chair and a heavy old rolltop desk. The coffee table, now lopsided with the off-kilter legs, was an older style too.

Some purists might roll their eyes and call the mixture of styles a mishmash, but I liked the mixing of old and new. Maybe because it's a little like me: some parts jump to what's new and modern, some parts cling to what's old and familiar.

We found Miranda wedged into a narrow space between the rolltop desk and a potted cactus. She apparently turns herself off when stuck. Elena cooed endearments to the robot and took her to the docking station. Then she turned on Nicole, who was still on her knees swabbing at the carpet.

"I suppose when you're interviewed you'll spout all that nonsense about Miles being some sort of con man," she snapped.

"I think I have to tell them," Nicole said. "It may be important. It's quite possible some woman Miles conned was angry enough to kill him. Don't you think it would be good for the police to have some suspect other than *you*?" she added pointedly.

"But *con man* makes him sound so *sleazy*. And he wasn't! He was a wonderful man. Though he may have—" Elena broke off sharply.

Nicole leaned back against her heels. "May have what?"

"Nothing. He may have been . . . too nice for his own good. He was not some con man preying on gullible women," she finally stated with a firmness that gave me an uneasy thought: *Methinks she doth protest too much.*

"Do you know where he went on those trips he took?" Nicole challenged. "If he wasn't running off to see other women, where did he go and why? Why didn't he invite you to go along?"

"I did go with him once, remember? We drove to some little town up north of Sacramento. And he wasn't visiting some woman *there*."

"But that wasn't like his other trips," Nicole insisted. "You weren't gone overnight. And he didn't drive on his other trips. He flew then, didn't he? And was gone several days at a time?"

Elena didn't respond, but her uneasy look said she didn't know where or by what means Miles had gone on those other trips or why she hadn't been invited. Finally she muttered, "He said they were business trips."

Nicole's unladylike snort gave her opinion of what kind of "business" Miles had been involved in, and I made a mental note to dig into the subject of Miles's mysterious trips. A little later Nicole

45

got up off her knees, dumped her wadded paper towels in a trash can, and said she should get on home for her appointments. By that time it was almost dark.

She paused at the door. "I wonder if they'll call Stan and tell him about Miles."

"You gave the officer Stan's name and address, didn't you?' Elena said.

"It may take them a while to notify him. It will probably be on the news, but Stan never pays attention to anything but national news and the stock market. But I can't call and tell him. I don't even have a phone number for him. And I'm certainly not going to rush over and pound on his fancy door."

"I may have a phone number for him," Elena said. "Miles used my phone to call him one time when his cell phone battery was dead, and I saved the number in case I ever needed it. This was back before he and Stan had their falling out, but the number is probably still in my contacts list." But she, too, sounded as if calling Stan was right up there with playing toesies with a carrier of foot fungus.

Not a popular guy, this Stan The Villain. I had to wonder, of course, did he have any murderous reason to get his uncle out of the way? "How about if I do it?" I offered.

Nicole and Elena both looked as if I'd just rescued them making personal contact with Godzilla, and Nicole said, "Yes, please!"

Mac's glance was more skeptical, and I could guess what he was thinking. Was I really being helpful or was my mutant curiosity gene kicking into gear again?

Actually, I did want to be helpful. This was something neither Nicole nor Elena wanted to do, and I could do it. No problem. Although I had to admit to a fair amount of curiosity about Stan The Villain too.

"Is it an office number or his home?" Nicole asked.

"I have no idea. I never had any reason to call him." Elena was already scrolling through her contact list. She scribbled a number on a scrap of paper and handed it to me.

"Okay, I'll leave you two to notify Stan. But don't bother to do it if you don't want to. Some official will probably notify him eventually. By the way," Nicole added to me, "if you talk to him, when Stan wants to appear dignified and important, he uses his full name, Stanton. When he wants to be a good ol' boy he's Stan. Or it might be Spider Woman who answers."

"Spider Woman?"

"The new and improved Mrs. Moore. Saun-dra." Nicole stretched the single word into two long, snide syllables. "And be sure to get that 'u' in there. *Saundra*, not Sandra. And she must be at least part spider, considering the clever web she spun to trap Stan." She smiled wryly. "Not that I hold a grudge or anything."

"You could stay and have dinner," Elena offered, her annoyance with Nicole over the con-man allegation apparently softening.

"Thanks, but I do have those appointments tonight." Nicole glanced at her watch. Her tight bun had come undone while she was swabbing the carpet, and strands of dark hair hung around her face. It was actually a softer, more attractive look for her.

"Cookie Lady readings?" I guessed, and Nicole nodded. "The cookie business must be flourishing," I added.

"I'm not getting rich but it helps. And I certainly need the money. Thanks to The Villain."

"Is reading cookies like reading tea leaves or cards?"

"Something like that," Nicole said.

"I've done a few tea leaf readings, and had my palm read too, but Nicole's cookie readings are much better," Elena said. "A few weeks ago she told my friend Marjie that she should take better control of her temper or it was going to get her in trouble. And sure enough, Marjie mouthed off when an officer stopped her for speeding and got a big ticket."

"Do you really believe in tea leaves . . . and crumbling cookies?" I asked Nicole.

"I believe in the cookie crumbles!" Elena put in, with enthusiasm.

"Well, I never did," Nicole said, her tone more reserved than Elena's enthusiasm. "I always thought all that stuff was only for the gullible. But lately it's begun to look as if there really is something to what the cookies reveal." She tilted her head thoughtfully, then smiled and shrugged, apparently not ready to argue the point. But I suspected she could put on a very convincing show for her clients, however one does a cookie-reading show. "Come on over sometime, and I'll do a reading for you. Most of my clients think it's fun. And then we'll have tea and cookies afterward."

I didn't feel it was the time to offer my views on tea leaves or any other form of fortune telling, but Biblical references are quite plain that the Lord doesn't approve of such activities even if they are just for "fun" and you get to eat cookies too. So all I said was, "Umm."

After Nicole left, we were going out to the motorhome to fix dinner, but Elena suggested we stay and eat with her. "I have pork chops I was going to fix when Miles came over for dinner this evening." A choked silence as we all thought about the fact that Miles would never be coming for dinner again. Finally she managed to add, "Too much food for just me."

"Our cat and dog are probably getting tired of being alone in the motorhome for so long," Mac said. "So we really should—"

"Bring 'em over," Elena said. "I miss not having a kitty around."

I guessed she didn't want to be alone after what had happened today, so Mac brought Koop and BoBandy inside and we stayed for dinner. BoBandy made quick friends with Elena, then explored the house with enough speed to suggest a time limit on getting it done. Bo is mid-sized, brown, droopy-eared, a pedigreed Mutt, friendly with almost everyone.

Koop is more reserved, making me suspect something about Elena, but he found Miranda at her docking station, batted at her blinking light as she recharged again, and inexplicably curled up on top of her shiny surface. Koop is orange colored, one-eyed, stubby-tailed, and totally lovable, but he does have one quirk that made me ask Elena a question.

"Are you a smoker?"

"I used to be, but Miles hated it, so I quit." She gave her fingers a guilty sniff. "But I had a cigarette earlier. I'd hidden a few away. For an emergency, I guess. And all this . . . felt like an emergency. But I had just *one*."

I nodded, but I suspected Koop wouldn't warm up to her anytime soon. I've never known why . . . something before we joined pathways in life . . . but he has an almost fanatic aversion to smokers and usually stalks away from them with stubby tail jerking in displeasure. One cigarette was enough to earn Koop's ire.

There was a formal dining room, but it was rather unused looking, and we ate at the cozier breakfast nook. Mac offered the blessing, and we had a nice dinner of pork chops and gravy, Elena's homemade biscuits, and coleslaw. Good, down-home type food, although Elena nibbled more than ate. She teared up every once in a while, but she managed to keep from breaking down. Afterward, she brought out brownies for dessert.

"They're fortified with wheat germ and whey," she said. "So they should be healthy. At least as healthy as brownies can be."

"I'll have to try that. I've been hearing about some grain called quinoa. Have you tried it?"

Elena wrinkled her nose. "I have some up in the cupboard. I'm trying to like it. But it's kind of *blah.*"

So we sat there and ate brownies and talked health food and supplements. Mac and I had just started taking probiotic capsules, and Elena was quite knowledgeable about that. We drank decaf coffee with the brownies. Unhappily, at our ages, real coffee keeps us awake and staring glassy-eyed at late-night infomercials on TV.

We hadn't talked much during dinner, determinedly avoiding the topic of Miles's death and murder, so I was surprised when after our health foods discussion, Elena now came out with, "I know both of you thought I was faking when I passed out there in the hallway when the cops were here."

I used my handy-dandy "Umm."

"But I really did pass out," she insisted. "I don't think it was for any *medical* reason. I mean, I'm *fine* physically. I think it was because I really didn't want to go in for more questioning, and my brain just told my body to do a swoon thing."

"They are going to question you sooner or later," Mac pointed out. "You can't avoid it."

"I know. But I needed more time to decide what to tell them."

I took a guess based on what she'd said earlier. "About your gun?"

She nodded.

"What about it?" I asked.

"Should I tell them about it? Maybe even take it along and show it to them?"

"That might be a good thing to do," Mac said. "They can test it and compare it with the bullet that killed Miles."

"Then they'll know you're innocent," I added. And surely she *was* innocent.

"You're assuming the bullet that killed Miles was still in his body, or that they found it somewhere under his body, so they'll have something to run tests on for comparison. But if the bullet *wasn't* there, because he was killed somewhere else and brought there, they won't have anything to compare my gun with." It was a rather convoluted statement, but she apparently knew something about guns and how they can be connected with bullets fired from them. "So maybe taking the gun in would only make me look even more guilty. I mean, if they don't have the bullet, who's to say the fatal shot *didn't* come from my gun?"

Interesting point.

"I could just tell them I don't have a gun." She glanced hopefully between us. "Or maybe they won't even ask. I mean, who'd think an old lady like me would have a gun? Do *you* have a gun?"

Mac and I keep thinking we should have a gun for protection when we're on the road . . . we do seem to run into situations where a gun would be handy . . . but so far we've never gotten one. "No, but if we did, we'd tell them," I assured her. "It's usually less complicated just to tell the truth to begin with."

Elena gave me back an "Umm" and a frown.

"Even if you tell them you don't have a gun, they may decide to get a search warrant anyway. If they find the gun then, it might look even worse for you," I added. "As if you'd been trying to hide it."

"I suppose so."

"I'm wondering, did you hear a shot after Miles left here?" Mac asked. "Or something that you didn't identify as a shot at the time but may have been?"

Elena shook her head without hesitation. "No. All I heard was Miles's car start up and leave. There's an old guy who drives by occasionally in a pickup that's always backfiring, but I didn't hear anything last night." She sighed and stood up. "Well, I'd better go find the gun and take it in tomorrow. Because it *isn't* the gun that killed him."

She marched down the hallway and we heard her rummaging around in the bedroom. Then she went on down the hall to another room and rummaged there. Finally she came back to the breakfast nook looking flustered and frustrated.

"I can't find it. I sure I just stuck it back in my nightstand after the last time Miles and I went target shooting. That's where I always keep it." She paused. "Although sometimes I forget and put things in strange places."

Me too. The last time my glasses went missing, I found them in the refrigerator. But right now I was more surprised with what Elena said about shooting.

"You and Miles practiced target shooting?" She'd probably surprised a few other people there at the shooting range. She looked as if she should be home baking brownies instead of banging away at a target. I wondered if the targets were man-shaped. I think I'd find that a little disconcerting.

"Of course we practiced. As Miles said, there's not much use having a gun if you don't know how to use it. He taught me how to take it apart and clean it too. And one time he mentioned identifying how they could tell if a bullet came from a certain gun."

"Are you a good shot?" I asked.

She gave me a sharp look. "Not *great*. But good enough to shoot someone in the chest at close range, if that's what you're asking," she added, her tone tart.

"Did Miles have a gun too?" Mac asked.

"His is a Glock, much bigger than my Swiss and Wesson. He said the S and W is more suitable for a woman's hand."

"He bought it for you?"

Elena nodded. Well, that was something to think about. Had he bought the gun for her simply because he thought a woman needed a gun for general self-protection? Or did he have a more specific reason? Such as thinking some vengeful cruise woman might come after Elena for stealing a man she thought was hers, so Elena should have a weapon and know how to use it?

We decided the gun should be found, and we all looked for it. High and low, here and there and everywhere. Under the beds in both bedrooms, in the closets and kitchen cabinets and rolltop desk. In dresser drawers, dirty-clothes hamper, and the pots-and-pans drawer under the oven. Behind the Tide and dryer sheets in the laundry room and inside a cat food sack left from when the cranky cat Ricardo was alive. I had to admire Elena's housekeeping. Doing such a search in our motorhome would surely turn up traveling dust bunnies, but her house hadn't so much as a baby bunny.

BoBandy followed the search, conscientiously splitting his time between Mac and me. Koop snoozed and Miranda blinked. I wondered if perhaps we should get her going on a search for it. If she could find earrings and a dead body, maybe she could find a gun. I realized I'd succumbed to "she" and "her" in regard to pronouns for the robot. Apparently I'd also succumbed to the idea that she'd found Miles's body.

Finally we regrouped at the breakfast nook. No gun.

"I can't imagine where I could have put it that three of us together can't find it," Elena fretted.

"Could someone have taken it?" I asked.

"Why would anyone take it?" Elena asked. Then she touched her lower lip as she realized what my question suggested. "You mean someone might have taken it and shot Miles with it? *My* gun may have *killed* him?"

She didn't carry the thought further, but I did. Had someone stolen the gun, killed Miles with it, and now planned to frame her for the murder?

"Who knew you had a gun?" Mac asked.

"Well, let's see. It isn't something I broadcast, but Nicole knew, of course. My friend Marjie too. She may have told some other friends. They've all talked about how they should have a gun for self-protection. And occasionally we ran into someone Miles knew at the gun range."

"How long has it been since you and Miles were at the gun range?" Mac asked.

"Maybe three weeks or a month."

"Who's been in the house since then?"

"Oh, my. That's a long time to remember. Let me think." She tilted her head back and squeezed her eyes shut. "Miles himself has been here many times, of course. But *he* certainly didn't take the gun. Nicole comes over fairly often. She brings me blueberry muffins or cookies and tells me funny stories about people who come in the bakery. But *she* certainly didn't kill Miles."

She took a break to take a sip of coffee. "Marjie comes over every few days. Which reminds me, I need to call and tell her about Miles. Helen and Sharla come with her sometimes, when we're playing pinochle. A young man from down the street stops in once in a while to see if I need anything done. My house insurance lady came once. A carpet cleaner man came to make an estimate on what it would cost to do the whole house. He did some measuring in the rooms. And probably some other people I can't remember now."

Elena was not, it appeared, an isolated woman who sat home alone all day.

"Did you contact the carpet cleaner or was he just in the neighborhood and offered to make an estimate?" Mac asked.

The thought occurred to me that this was good information for future use, in case *we* ever needed to get into someone's home. We could carry a tape measure for authenticity. *Free estimate! Fifteen percent discount if you order through us today!* Then I chastised myself for the thought. We do not go around making up stories to get into people's homes, no matter how suspicious . . . or curious . . . we may be.

"I called him," Elena said, dousing my suspicion of someone using subterfuge to get into her home. "And I was with him in every room while he was measuring. He didn't have any chance to take the gun."

"It could have been taken by someone not making a normal visit," Mac pointed out.

"You mean like a burglary? But I've never had a burglary."

"Maybe someone came inside while you were gone and you didn't even know it. Do you always lock your doors when you go out?"

"Well, I didn't today when I ran out looking for Miranda. But I don't usually go dashing out of the house and running down the road in my bikini. Today was an emergency."

"Do you always lock *all* your doors, not just the front one?" I asked. "On your non-emergency trips, I mean."

"Well . . ." She looked mildly guilty. "I guess I don't always check the back door that comes in through the laundry room. But it's a hard door to get to from outside. Someone would have to go all the way around the house to find it."

"I came in that way after I parked the motorhome," Mac said. "It wasn't locked then."

"I'll be more careful after this," Elena promised, and I was reminded of that old adage about the futility of locking the barn door after the horse was out. I suspected she'd been warned before. She affirmed that thought.

"I know I should be more careful. Miles told me I should always lock all my doors. And when Blake was here, he said the same thing," she said. "So are you saying someone could have stolen the gun with the deliberate idea of killing Miles with it?"

"Possibly. But it could have been a random burglary," Mac said. "Someone just looking for something to steal. Nothing connected with Miles. But then—"

Elena grabbed onto the random burglary possibility. "That's probably what happened. Just an everyday burglary." She dismissed the subject with an airy flip of hand. "Weren't you going to call Nicole's ex-husband?" she added to me.

CHAPTER 6

IVY

Mac went out to the motorhome and brought my phone in. He used the back door, still unlocked. I tapped in the number Elena had found in her contact list. It took seven rings but someone finally picked up.

"Hello."

A simple, non-informative greeting but spoken in an oddly wary tone. I was tempted to ask if this was Stan The Villain but I didn't, of course. Remembering Nicole's comment about Stan using his full name when he wanted to sound important, I went for flattery instead. "Is this Stanton Moore?"

An odd silence, as if he might simply be going to hang up. So much for flattery. Then, "If you're a member of the Secure Your Future Investment Club, a phone number is not currently available. You should write to the mailing address listed on your certificates."

His still-wary tone made me also feel wary, and before he could hang up I hastily said, "Mr. Moore, I'm calling about your uncle, Miles Willoughby." I didn't intend to tell him this was an official call, but neither did I intend to announce that this was something other than official notification.

There was a brief silence, and I thought he was either going to deny being Mr. Moore or simply continue with the hang-up, but he finally said, "What about Miles?"

"I'm afraid I have some bad news. Mr. Willoughby's body was found earlier today on Eidenburg Road."

"His *body*!" He sounded shocked, but I know from experience that killers can be quite adept at sounding shocked. I hadn't any definite reason to be suspicious of Stan The Villain, although it was likely he stood to inherit from Miles's death. "What happened?"

"Details are not being released at this point. We just wanted to inform you of his death and ask if you've been in the Eidenburg Road area within the last forty-eight hours or so. If perhaps you'd seen or heard anything that might be helpful?"

"No, of course not. I'm not even sure where Eidenburg Road is." He paused and then went with the shocked voice again. "Are you telling me Miles's death was something other than a natural heart attack or stroke or something like that?"

"Indications are that Mr. Willoughby's death was a homicide."

"Homicide! You mean someone *killed* Miles?"

"Yes, I'm afraid that's what happened."

"Oh, wait. Elena, that woman he was planning to marry, lives on Eidenburg Road, doesn't she? Elena . . . what? Ridgeway. Elena Ridgeway, that's it." He paused as if evaluating the connection between his uncle and Elena from a new perspective.

"You know Mrs. Ridgeway?"

"We've met her a few times when Miles brought her here. But I can't say we really *know* her. We've never been to her home." He paused. "Is Elena okay?"

Asking about Elena's well-being sounded like something of an afterthought, but perhaps that was an unfair conclusion. His first concern would naturally be for his uncle.

"She's doing okay. In shock, of course. But she wasn't involved in the . . . incident."

I left the statement hanging, hoping Stan would fill the silence with comments or information about Elena or someone else.

He didn't. All he said was, "Do they know yet who did this to Uncle Miles?"

"No information is being released at this point." I segued into a question. "Has Mr. Willoughby recently confided to you any concerns about his safety? Or perhaps you have some personal knowledge of enemies or threats?"

"No, Miles was a great old guy. Everybody loved him. I can't imagine him having any enemies."

"We understand Mr. Willoughby occasionally went out of town on business trips. Do you know where he went or what kind of business he was involved in?"

"Wait, I don't get this. Are you from the police or the hospital or morgue? Who are you?"

I didn't want him to know I'd found the body or that I was in any way connected to Elena or Nicole. *Everybody's a suspect,* and I had a sudden, mental-gong reminder about killers who take a murderous view of someone they think knows too much. Or is too nosy. It's happened to me before. "I'm very sorry for your loss, Mr. Moore. Please accept my sympathies."

"Thank you, but—" I disconnected while he was still talking.

Which didn't hide my identity, of course. My number would show on his phone. It wouldn't mean anything to him, but would he be curious enough to use a reverse cell phone search to find a name that went with the number?

**

We took BoBandy and Koop out for a do-their-business walk and then I got on the computer, still wondering if that photo of me might show up on Facebook. I couldn't find it, which was a relief. Although I did find another Walmart person, a woman in a chicken outfit wearing shoes with foot-high platform soles. She appeared to be shopping for beer.

It was some consolation that even if my photo did show up on some internet site, next to her I wouldn't appear quite so weird.

Afterward, Mac and I shared a Bible reading in Luke and went to bed fairly early. Elena didn't, however. The light was still on in her bedroom when I made a trip to the bathroom about 1:30. Not unusual, of course, when you've just lost the man you loved and planned to marry. I remember the first terrible weeks after my husband Harley passed away long ago. Maybe Elena was looking through old photos or mementos, reminiscing and crying. I'd done that. Or maybe she was still looking for the gun.

Or hiding it in some new place . . .

The thought occurred to me that if she had killed Miles, perhaps the whole revelation about owning a gun, and the search for it, was a big charade. That she actually knew exactly where the gun was and was not about to let it be found.

Oh, Ivy. What a suspicious little old lady you are. And perhaps I was overthinking the whole gun situation.

Next morning, Mac, Elena and I all went together to the police station to be interviewed and give our statements; Nicole was taking off work to go in by herself later. We went in Elena's older Ford Fiesta so we wouldn't all be scrunched into our Toyota pickup's small cab. Mac drove. Fortunately, he's accustomed to stick shift. . . not many people these days are . . . because our old pickup is also stick shift. She said Blake had wanted to buy her a new car with an automatic transmission, but she'd told him no; she liked her old Missy. So she'd told us a bit of a fib earlier; she had named more than one piece of equipment. We could see down the road that a couple of police cars and a van were still at the crime scene, but not the crowd from the day before.

Elena wore blue slacks and a demure white blouse with a bow at the throat, along with pearl earrings and sensible blue sandals. Her blond curls were nicely tamed. If she was purposely trying to project a non-murderly image, she succeeded. She looked sweet and unsophisticated, a "wouldn't harm a flea" innocent. She said she'd decided to tell them she did own a gun and it was missing.

They interviewed us individually, of course. Even married couples aren't questioned together. I don't know who questioned Elena, but Older Officer from yesterday did both Mac and me, Mac first.

When my turn for questioning came, I noted that the officer's trousers were nicely un-blotched today, sharply creased, and his name tag read A. Hutchinson. I didn't think it necessary to volunteer the information that I'd talked to Stan Moore yesterday. Officer Hutchinson didn't try to intimidate us into staying in the area for further questioning, but he did ask for a cell phone number where we could be reached if we moved on.

Actually, it was a very brief interview before he led me back to the waiting room, shook my hand, and thanked me. I didn't feel totally invisible, as I sometimes do, but I certainly didn't feel he'd taken much notice of me. Good! It's much easier to slip around poking into things when you're in an LOL-invisible state. That's how I tend to think of myself as a little old lady, an LOL.

I reminded myself I'd felt distinctly uneasy "poking into things" when I talked to Stan The Villain. But I also sighed. A little thing such as that wasn't likely to deter that mutant curiosity gene. It's as persistent as a mosquito on a hot night.

Then we sat and waited for Elena. They questioned her for considerably longer than they had either of us. We watched people come and go. For an area with a reportedly "low crime rate," the police station was quite busy.

Finally, Elena came out. She didn't look completely frazzled, but her eyes were red and swollen, as if she'd spent some of the time crying. Her innocent look apparently hadn't kept them from digging deep with their questions. In the car, however, she was more grumbly than tearful. She said the only questions they *hadn't* asked were if her hair was natural blond or what she'd had for breakfast.

I didn't delve into hair color, but I did say, "Speaking of breakfast, did you eat any?"

She admitted she hadn't. "My stomach felt a little queasy," she admitted. "But it's much better now."

Some people think that if you're innocent, a questioning by police is no big deal. All you have to do is relax and tell the truth. But I'd argue with that. Sometimes just being in the presence of police officers can make me jittery enough to feel guilty about *something*. I certainly didn't consider Elena's earlier queasiness about being questioned of any significance. I did ask her what the questioner's reaction had been to her information about owning a gun.

"Actually . . . at the last minute I didn't tell them."

"Did they ask?"

"Yes, they asked," she admitted. "But I got this gut feeling that it would be better not to mention it. And you know what they always say, *when in doubt, go with your gut feelings.* So I did."

"They" apparently being people with gut feelings more reliable than mine usually are. Mine have all the reliability of a late-night infomercial. I made no comment.

"Actually, it wasn't really a lie," she added. "I mean, we all *looked* and couldn't find the gun anywhere. So what I told them is true. I don't have a gun."

"Did they ask if you'd *ever* had a gun?"

"No, they didn't ask that."

We were getting into that squiggly line between truth and untruth here, one that I seem to encounter all too often.

She suggested a coffee shop near the Old Town area and directed Mac how to get there. We'd eaten in the motorhome, of course—we aren't go-without-breakfast people—so we just had coffee and split a bagel. Elena downed French toast and bacon, with an extra egg and a fruit cup on the side.

Afterward she guided us on a mini-tour of the town: the city park, a shopping mall, a good Mexican restaurant, a statue of an old prospector and his donkey outside a small museum. The tour ended with an excursion through the winding streets of the hillside subdivision of new homes, referred to in general as The Hill. She said Stan lived in there somewhere, but we didn't go by his place.

From a viewpoint at the top of the hill, which passed as a hill only because the surrounding area was so flat, we could see the town and vineyards spread out below. Far to the east, snow sparkled on rugged mountains. Also visible was an impressive church down on Hillside Boulevard, all stone and glass and spires, with a parking lot large enough for a UFO landing site.

When we're in a new area, we always search out a church to attend until we move on. We usually find one rather less elaborate than this edifice, but Elena was eyeing it with interest.

"Miles said we should start going to church," Elena said. "He said he'd started reading the Bible, right from the beginning. He planned to read it all the way through."

Hey, good for him! Although the cynical thought also occurred to me that sometimes people get "churchy" when they're feeling guilty, thinking maybe they'd better do something to get in good

60

with God before he decides to zap 'em. Did Miles have something to feel guilty about, perhaps something involving cruise ship women?

Mac said, "A fine idea. Perhaps you'd like to go with us this Sunday?"

"This one looks a little . . . intimidating," Elena said.

My thoughts exactly. Although a grand and impressive structure doesn't mean a church is preaching a worship-God-and-get-rich message rather than offering the true message of salvation, of course. "We could look for a smaller church closer to Eidenburg Road," I offered.

Elena didn't commit herself. "I'll think about it," she said finally. "But I don't know. Without Miles . . .." Her voice trailed off uncertainly.

"We'll check with you again later," I said, and she nodded.

**

We ate a late lunch when we got home, then took the animals out for a walk while Elena napped in her bedroom. After we got back, Mac inspected the coffee table. He thought he could fix the off-kilter legs, but he didn't have the drill he'd need to put in some new screws. When Elena came out, he asked if she had one. She didn't, but she said Miles had some tools at his place.

"We could go over to the townhouse and see if there's a drill. He wouldn't mind. I have a key."

She didn't sound reluctant to do that; in fact, she sounded unexpectedly eager.

"The police may be there," Mac said. "They'll surely do a complete search of where he lived."

"Will they close it up so nobody can get in?"

"That's usually what they do."

"Does that mean they think he was killed there at the townhouse?" The thought seemed to chill Elena; she drew her sweater closer around her.

"Not necessarily, but they'll investigate all angles. They'll look for evidence of a crime committed there, of course. But even if he wasn't killed there, they'll look into his computer and phone or

61

anything else that might offer information about possible suspects. He does have a computer, doesn't he?"

"Oh yes. He's very competent on it. Much better than I am. You wouldn't believe what I saw on a site I thought was about waffle recipes."

I could believe it. I've accidentally stumbled into a few sites that made me blush with both embarrassment and outrage that such sites existed.

"How long will they have the townhouse closed up?" Elena asked. Then as if it were suddenly urgent, she said, "Let's drive over there right now. Maybe we can get inside before the police search it. If I don't get in now, I'll probably never have a chance to. Stan will have the locks changed."

"Stan?"

"He's Miles's only living relative, so he'll inherit it."

I'd suspected that before, but now it loomed as a definite motive for murder-by-Stan. Were there other assets that enlarged that motive?

Checking out the townhouse right now sounded good to me. Was Miles's car there? What about his Glock? Maybe we could get a peek into his computer and find information that gave even more credence to Stan as a killer. Or perhaps, to be fair to Stan, we'd find incriminating information about cruise ship women and the mysterious trips Miles had taken.

We went in Elena's car again. San Isolde is located several miles off the freeway, and Miles's townhouse was in a condo/apartment/townhouse area called Sunshine Valley closer to that main north-south interstate. Elena said it was more of a bedroom-type community than an actual town, that most residents, if not retired, worked in bigger towns nearby, some going all the way up to Modesto or down to Fresno. Although the area was flat, the streets were winding, not easy to negotiate, probably designed to slow down the speed of traffic.

But it was a pleasant and quiet area, lots of trees and grass, a huge flag flying atop the tallest condo building, blooming flowerbeds of hardy pansies, a swimming pool full of water but unoccupied at the moment. A landscape worker was industriously planting a new tree in a freshly worked-up oblong of earth, more trees with balled-up roots lying nearby. A couple of the condo buildings were seven or eight stories, tall by my standards, but Miles's townhouse, the end space in a long row of townhouses, was just two stories, with a garage under one side of each unit.

The first thing we saw was that we definitely hadn't arrived before the police. A car with a county sheriff's department logo and a white van were already parked in front of yellow crime scene tape marking off a corner unit. Apparently the San Isolde city police and the county sheriff were investigating the crime together.

We sat and watched for a while. Once an officer came out and talked on the car radio. Another time two men in white jumpsuits carried a two-drawer file cabinet to the van. Elena said that the file had been in the extra bedroom Miles used as an office, but she had no idea what he kept in it. I wondered if he had a file on every cruise ship woman he'd met. And conned. I suspected Elena wondered that too.

She didn't share her thoughts, but she obviously found the scene upsetting. She moved restlessly in the back seat, rolled the window down, then hastily rolled it back up as if she didn't want to be caught watching.

Finally she muttered, "I want to go home," and Mac started the engine.

She looked back as we drove away, and I had the unexpected feeling that she'd wanted to get into the townhouse before the police—or Stan—for some reason other than finding a drill Mac could use.

CHAPTER 7

IVY

Mac efficiently drove us directly back to Elena's house, no wrong turns. Just because I can get to someplace doesn't mean I can immediately find my way back, but Mac seems to have a reverse trip map automatically installed in his head. He said he'd try to fix the coffee table without a drill. Elena didn't have anything to say on the trip.

I was surprised to see a car parked in the driveway when we got back to the house, winter daylight already fading. The car was small, but it was an expensive-small, not economy-small. Metallic burgundy color, one of those that looks as if it's breaking the speed limit even standing still.

"Someone you know?" Mac asked Elena.

"I don't recognize the car," she said. She lifted her head cautiously to peer out the window. "But I think it's—oh, yes, it *is* him. They probably got another new car." She scrunched back down in the seat. "Can you get rid of him? I really don't feel like talking to him now."

Mac and I slid out, leaving Elena in the back seat. A man walked toward us, tall, blond, tanned. In a dark gray business suit and light blue shirt, he moved with a confident stride. A man who looked as if he'd be equally comfortable giving a speech to thousands, riding a surfboard, or playing a mean game of golf or tennis. It didn't take a name tag for me to guess this was Stan The Villain.

I felt a nervous squiggle of electric worms up my spine. Had he already discovered the identity of who called him and had now come calling himself?

No, I assured myself. A premature worry. Logically, even if he'd somehow managed to connect my name with the phone number showing on his screen, he couldn't know where I was located at this moment.

"Hi. I'm looking for Elena Ridgeway. Or perhaps it's Eleanor. This is her address, isn't it? I'm not familiar with the area, and we had a hard time finding it."

"Yes, this is Elena's home, but she's feeling indisposed at the moment," Mac said. He didn't make a giveaway glance in the direction of the car where she was sitting. "I'm afraid she isn't up to seeing visitors right now."

"I'm so sorry. We should have called. But we wanted to offer her our deepest condolences and ask if there is anything we can do." He held out a hand to Mac. "I'm Stanton Moore, Miles Willoughby's nephew. I'm assuming you also know about his tragedy?"

I noted he'd used *Stanton*. Apparently he felt Mac was worth impressing, so he was in dignified-and-important mode

"Yes. I'm Mac MacPherson, and this is my wife, Ivy. We're friends of Elena's nephew Blake and just happened to be here at this sad time."

He also shook hands with me. It was a good handshake, firm but not crushing. He was wearing an evergreen-y aftershave lotion, brisk and masculine. Although it didn't cover another scent. Stan Moore was definitely a smoker.

"From what the police tell me, the person who killed Miles has not yet been identified, and it may be several days before his body is released. I thought we and Elena should discuss final arrangements for Miles. Perhaps she has some preferences, or perhaps Miles discussed preferences with her?"

I thought including Elena in the decisions was rather gracious of him. He could have ignored her completely, given the fact that she and Miles weren't married yet. Although the fact that he wasn't sure if she was Elena or Eleanor seemed odd.

"Perhaps Elena will feel up to talking to you in another day or two," Mac said.

"She can contact me, or we'll come back another time. I really do need to talk to her."

I glanced back at the car. Elena hadn't gotten out, but I could see she was rather furtively peering out the window again. I quickly looked away, not wanting to draw Stan's attention in that direction. So I now also saw that a woman was sitting in Stan's car. Spider Woman? I restrained myself from dashing over to get a good look at her, instead just offered a little wave in her direction. She didn't respond, but I decided that was because her gaze was targeted on Stan and she just didn't see me; she wasn't deliberately ignoring me. Or perhaps it was LOL invisibility at work. I was trying to decide if I should go over to the little sports car and speak to her when another car pulled in behind Elena's.

Nicole jumped out. She charged across the yard in full attack mode. "What are you doing here?" she demanded of Stan.

"Saundra and I came to offer our condolences." If his voice was any colder, we'd have been dodging ice projectiles.

I didn't even hear the car door open, but the woman suddenly appeared at Stan's side, fast as a car salesman cornering a hot prospect. "Nicole. How nice to see you again." She gripped Stan's arm tight enough to cut off circulation.

I caught the real meaning of the words. *Nice as seeing a tarantula in my soup.*

Nicole's response was a stiff nod. The hostility between them sizzled like a downed electric wire.

Saundra was a surprise. From what Nicole had said, I expected a woman young and gorgeous, a trophy-wife type, someone capable of spinning a spiderweb of seduction. Saundra wasn't that. She certainly wasn't *un*attractive, but she was at least a dozen years older than Stan's thirty-five-ish, a tall, husky woman, her curves sturdy rather than stunning. She was wearing what I think is called a power suit, and the fuchsia color complemented her dark hair, but the general impression was more efficient office manager than web-spinning temptress.

"We'll tell Elena you were here," Nicole said.

"I don't think that will be necessary." Stan nodded over Nicole's shoulder.

I turned to look and saw Elena hurrying toward us with unexpected speed.

"Stan . . . Saundra," Elena said. "It's been quite a while since we've . . . since *I've* seen you."

Stan stepped out to meet her. "We came as soon as we heard." He gave her a hug that looked genuine enough, although her response was on the limp side. "This is such a shock about Uncle Miles."

"Thank you for coming. You know Nicole, don't you? Oh yes, of course you do." Elena was obviously flustered, apparently to the point of momentarily forgetting that Stan and Nicole were unfriendly exes. "I'm sorry. I'm just not . . . myself, I guess. I can't believe it really happened, someone shooting Miles."

"The police notified you?" Nicole asked Stan. Even though she knew I'd intended to call him, she sounded suspicious of why Stan was here.

"Yes. Actually, a couple of agencies contacted us."

His identifying both calls as from "agencies" suggested he hadn't looked up a name to go with the cell phone number that came with the call from me. Good!

"I'm going to the police station tomorrow for an interview," he added. "I want to help any way I can, but I don't think I have any useful information to offer them."

"We've already been questioned," Nicole said. Not subtly, she added, "The innocent have nothing to fear from their questions."

"Speak for yourself," Elena snapped with sudden spirit and even a small hint of humor. "They don't do waterboarding, but they're pretty handy with the good-cop, bad-cop technique."

"Surely they don't suspect *you*," Stan said.

I expected a sharp retort from Elena, but she suddenly wilted. "I have no idea what they think," she said. "I just know it's been *awful*. Seeing Miles lying there dead under the trees, and then answering all those questions . . ."

Nicole put a protective arm around Elena's shoulders. "C'mon. I'll take you inside."

"We'll help," Stan said. He put a hand on Elena's arm, and the exes glared at each other over the small woman between them.

Neither of them was willing to let go, and they marched toward the door like some hybrid species trying to figure out how to manage six legs. Stan's head banged into the windchime, setting it into a musical tinkle at odds with the frigid atmosphere. He swatted at the windchime, and it tinkled more energetically. I hoped he and Nicole wouldn't get into a tugging match, with Elena as the prize. She might have to do another of her swoons.

Mac was close behind them, and I maneuvered closer to Spider Woman to follow them. She didn't seem to have even noticed me yet. LOL invisibility still at work? Her gaze was locked on her husband. She wore a light, flowery perfume, quite attractive.

"I suppose you and your husband were close to Miles?" I asked.

She jerked, as if a post holding up the patio roof had unexpectedly spoken to her. She turned her head to look at me, finally noticing me for the first time. "Oh, yes! Miles was a wonderful man. So intelligent and fun."

"I understand he was also an excellent dancer."

"Really?" She looked at me as if baffled that I'd make such an irrelevant remark.

"Something to do with his former work with a cruise line."

"Perhaps so."

I wanted to ask if she knew anything about Miles's "business trips," but I'd asked that of Stan on the phone, and I didn't want a similarity of questions to give away my identity as that earlier caller. So what I said was, "It's good of you to include Elena in a discussion about Miles's final arrangements."

"We were looking forward to welcoming her into the family, and I welcome the opportunity now to get to know her better."

I considered that statement. If they were so friendly and welcoming, how come they'd never been to her home here on Eidenburg Road?

Saundra's gaze shifted to her husband's ex. "I suppose Nicole is still doing her bizarre little cookie readings?" She asked the question with a kind of amused tolerance, the way you might ask if a dear aunt was still shoplifting on the sly.

"I think so. Although we arrived only a short time ago and don't really know her. Have you had one of her readings?"

"Me?" Saundra shuddered lightly. She leaned closer, pulling me into a small conspiracy with her next words. "Given how Nicole feels about me, I imagine she'd come up with quite a grim future for me. Maybe washed out to sea by a sneaker wave or crushed by a falling safe." She smiled. "And not averse to pushing that safe out of a building to make it come true."

"Umm."

She unexpectedly put a hand on my arm and squeezed. "My apologies for the snarky remark. You probably don't know it, but my husband was formerly married to Nicole. She can definitely be a trial. But it was an uncalled-for remark, and I do apologize. I know Miles liked her. But then, Miles liked everyone."

Up close, I caught a whiff of smoker's scent on her too, not as prominent as her husband's, but definitely there. "I'm sorry I never had a chance to know him."

"I'm afraid I didn't catch your connection with Miles and Elena. Are you relatives of Elena's?"

"No. We're friends of her nephew Blake's. We met him down in Baja." I considered our status for a moment. "We're just passing through."

"How fortunate for Elena that you're here to help, then, when this terrible tragedy struck."

Inside, we settled into a rather odd group in the living room. Something less than a social gathering, not quite a battleground confrontation. Stan and Nicole sat at far ends of the sofa, Elena between them. They exchanged polite words about Miles, Elena occasionally giving a reluctant answer to a question about him, Saundra adding a few complimentary comments about what a great person he was. I wiggled my toes and counted the knickknacks in the corner hutch. I'd thought a purpose of this visit was to discuss final arrangements for Miles, but no one even mentioned that subject, and I couldn't see that this sitting around playing nice was accomplishing anything. Although it was probably better than an all-out brawl on the carpet.

After the conversation deteriorated into a discussion of the weather, I finally figured out what was going on. Neither Stan nor Nicole was willing to leave first; somehow this had become a non-physical tug of war. Regardless of why either of them had come, whoever stayed longest was the winner, whoever left first the loser. Ridiculous, but there it was.

By now I knew there were thirty-seven items in the hutch, including nine little skunk figurines. Miranda came out, and everyone watched as if her trips across the room were fascinating. I finally asked if anyone would like something to drink. It wasn't until I'd made coffee in the kitchen and returned with a tray of cups and saucers, sugar and cream, and saw the surprised looks on Saundra's and Stan's faces that I realized they'd thought I was offering liquor-type drinks.

But they all drank coffee graciously, Saundra even commenting on how good it was, until Elena herself finally broke the stalemate.

She jumped up and said, "Thank you all for coming. I appreciate the support. Stan, I hope your interview with the police goes well and you will be able to provide some helpful information for them. Saundra, so good of you to come. Nicole, I'll come by the bakery in a day or two to pick up some blueberry muffins."

Elena herded the three of them toward the door. Nicole went out first, with Stan and Saundra following. I thought Elena had handled that rather well, although the thought occurred to me that perhaps we should leave too. Then Nicole made an unexpected end run to victory. She scooted around her ex and his wife and darted back inside. She stood there with her arm around Elena's shoulders, victorious smile on her face.

"So good of you to come," she called sweetly after Stan and Saundra. She closed the door on them and peered through a window to be sure they did go. "There are two people who really deserve each other," she declared. "Bottom-feeding partners in both marriage and business."

I wasn't sure what she meant by "bottom-feeding," but I doubted it was a compliment. "Are you suggesting they may have had something to do with Miles's death?" I asked.

She touched her chest and raised her eyebrows as if shocked I'd suggest such a thing. "Stan and Saundra? Not necessarily. But who knows?" She smiled. "Although I'm probably not the most impartial person to ask."

I didn't know whether to applaud her success or denounce her sneakiness in winning the claiming-Elena contest. Stan and Saundra had, actually, been quite civil during the visit.

"I wonder why they came," Elena fussed.

I reminded her that they'd said they wanted to offer their condolences and discuss final arrangements for Miles.

"But they didn't do that, did they?" Nicole pointed out. "They had something else in mind. Something they didn't want to talk about after I showed up."

"Have you ever been to their home?" I asked Elena.

"A few times. With Miles, of course. It's one of those newer places on the Hill. Very nice. But that was quite some time ago."

"How did Miles feel about them?"

"I'm not sure. They were on friendly terms when I first met him," Elena said, "and Miles never actually said anything *against* them, but he and Stan had some kind of falling out. And I think they came today for some reason other than what they said."

71

CHAPTER 8

MAC

I got up before Ivy the next morning. Koop was still curled by her side. I didn't want to wake either of them, so I clipped a leash to BoBandy's collar and tiptoed outside. The police cars and crime scene tape were gone from the curve down the road, so we strolled in that direction. It was a fine, dewy January morning, a feeling of early spring in the air.

Evidence of something happening at the curve remained. A maze of vehicle tracks crisscrossed the wide shoulder of the road. Crushed weeds littered the embankment. The old leaves beneath the trees beyond looked as if a heavy-footed giant had caroused through them.

BoBandy sniffed everything, a talent I've envied before. What was he smelling? Hidden clues? A killer? Or maybe just an old sardine can? BoBandy is a great but definitely non-discriminating sniffer. All I could get was a musty scent of old leaves and the reek of fumes when a battered pickup rattled by spouting a series of earsplitting backfires.

On the way back to the motorhome, I met another man out walking his dog. His black retriever and BoBandy exchanged doggy greetings, and the guy and I discussed what had happened here. He said the police had questioned everyone up and down Eidenburg Road.

"I don't suppose you saw or heard anything?" I asked.

"I might have." He straightened his shoulders in a self-important way. "I was looking out the window before I went to bed the night that guy got killed. I saw a car go by and shortly afterwards another one. Usually not much traffic here at night so it was probably the guy who got killed and somebody following him."

"Which way were they going?"

"Back toward town."

"You could identify the cars?"

"Well, no. I just saw headlights and taillights."

I didn't want to belittle his information, but unidentifiable vehicle lights passing by in close succession didn't strike me as a cutting-edge clue. They were also going the wrong direction, away from the embankment where we'd found Miles's body.

As if he suspected I wasn't overly impressed with his observations, he added, "The taillight on the vehicle doing the following was dim and flickering. I told the police about it, of course. I think they thought it could be an important observation."

"I'm sure the police appreciate any information they can get."

"Well, it's more important than the rumors that're going around, that's for sure."

"Rumors?"

"I heard someone say that guy who got killed was really hiding out from the Mafia and they killed him with a machine gun with a silencer on it. Someone else said Mrs. Ridgeway was running down the road naked before the cops got here. And some other older woman wearing bloody shoes was chasing her."

I had to admit his information about a flickering taillight was probably more important than a rumor about a machine gun with a silencer, something that didn't exist. Although the rumor about an older woman in bloody shoes made semi-sense. I'm not sure what I was thinking when I bought those ridiculous shark-toothed slippers for Ivy, even though she seems to like them.

The old pickup went by again, going the other direction this time and still backfiring. It sounded like gunshots, a shoot-out at high noon. The driver, an old guy probably even older than I am, seemed oblivious to the ruckus he was causing.

"Is that one of the vehicles you saw the other night?" I asked.

"Nah. That's old man Donaldson. Lives over on Rightly Road. He takes that old rig out for a drive about once a month. Sounds like a traveling gunfight tearing through the neighborhood. When it really gets bad is when he decides to do it at night. But he's kind of a harmless old guy, and I guess everyone is entitled to a joyride once in a while." He surprised me by laughing and dismissing the noisy, one-vehicle parade with an indulgent smile before returning to gloom and doom. "The really bad thing about all this murder stuff is what it'll do to the neighborhood. Property values are sinking even as we speak." He looked down at our feet as if the very earth might be dissolving beneath us.

I didn't hear any sympathy for the dead man or Elena, just that concern for property values. "You're planning to sell?"

"No. But I don't like to see property values going down. And they are. Mark my words."

On that gloomy prediction, we parted company.

Maybe I'll toss those slippers in the trash when Ivy isn't looking. Before rumors have a naked, bloody-footed older woman running down the road with a machine gun.

**

IVY

Koop and I were up by the time Mac and BoBandy got back from their walk, sitting out in the grassy area between the motorhome and the garage, where daffodils looked almost ready to bloom. He was telling me about meeting a man spouting rumors about everything from the Mafia to machine guns, saying he'd seen two vehicles out on the road the night of the murder, one with the prime clue of a blinking taillight, when Elena came out and suggested we have scrambled eggs and pancakes with her. She said she'd add flaxseed meal to the pancakes for extra nutrition.

"I have some real maple syrup to go with them too. Miles got it on one of his business trips back East. It's really good."

We finished breakfast—the flaxseed meal really wasn't noticeable—and Mac took the coffee table out to the garage to see what he could do to repair it without a drill. I was still in the kitchen with Elena when Stan showed up again, this time minus Saundra.

"I knew he'd be back," Elena muttered as she peered out the window. "I don't trust that man any farther than I could throw an elephant. After the way he treated Nicole . . ."

I looked out too. Stan was more casually dressed on this Saturday morning, jeans and a country club sweatshirt. He was also driving a different vehicle, a big blue SUV. Was this his version of slumming?

Then, as if she were talking to herself more than to me, Elena added, "But I shouldn't be complaining about him, should I? He's Miles's *nephew*. He's probably just trying to be nice."

She went to the door and apparently managed to quell her unwelcoming feelings enough to invite him into the kitchen for coffee.

He accepted the offer and mentioned he'd heard on the news that the police were following several promising leads on the case. "They'll have it all figured out before long." He offered his own views on what had happened: a robbery gone bad or perhaps a case of mistaken identity. Someone killed Miles thinking he was someone else.

"Oh, by the way, Saundra and I got to wondering about Uncle Miles's will," Stan said oh-so-casually.

My immediate epiphany: so that was the reason they came yesterday and then didn't mention it because Nicole was here, and why he was back again today. He's wondering how soon he can glom onto Miles's assets.

"Would you happen to know where he kept it or who his lawyer was?" he asked Elena.

"No. He never mentioned anything about a will to me," Elena said. "But I don't think you need to worry. You're his only heir."

"We were hoping a will would say something about his preferences for a funeral and burial," Stan said, his dignified tone suggesting the reason for his interest in a will was only a noble caring for his uncle.

Then I felt a bit guilty for my suspicions. Maybe I was being unfair thinking he was an impatient heir-in-waiting. Maybe he really did want the will for unselfish reasons only.

"The will might be there in the townhouse," Elena said. "Do you have a key?"

"No, no I don't."

I noted Elena didn't helpfully announce that she did have a key and he was welcome to use it.

"I wonder if the police will search the townhouse?" Stan added.

As if she didn't want to admit we'd been there and seen for ourselves that they were doing exactly that, Elena turned to me. "Didn't Mac say they'd probably do that?"

I nodded. "I think it's standard procedure."

"I hope they don't trash the place while they're searching it. I've heard they sometimes do that," Stan said.

"Didn't Miles have some kind of investment with you?" Elena asked. "An IRA or something?"

"He did. Not an IRA, but a great investment that paid excellent dividends. But he sold everything a while back. He never mentioned anything about that to you?"

"No, he didn't. But maybe he sold it in anticipation of our getting married," Elena said.

"I thought it was an unwise move at the time, but that was probably it," Stan agreed.

An unpleasant thought occurred to me. Had Miles sold the investment because he needed money to pay off some cruise woman to keep her from making known the fact that he'd conned her?

"Perhaps I'll contact a lawyer and see what should be done if we can't locate a will," Stan said.

"We'll discuss final arrangements for Miles another time?"

"Yes, of course. I'm so upset about all this that the matter of arrangements slipped my mind for a moment." Stan lifted his wrist to look at his watch. I'm not familiar with high-priced brands, but this one looked as if it had enough dials to track satellites and perhaps double as a time-travel machine. "I have an appointment today, but yes, we'll do it another time."

**

The next day was Sunday. We hadn't yet spotted a church we wanted to attend, so we decided we'd just drive around until we found one that looked appealing. I went over to the house to ask Elena if she'd like to come along. I found her in the kitchen sipping tea and looking downhearted and sad.

"I'm really not feeling up to it yet," she said.

If I'm feeling down, singing and worshipping with other believers in the Lord's house lifts my spirits, and I regretted that Elena didn't also have this spiritual comfort. "Perhaps next Sunday, then."

"I'm thinking maybe I'll start reading Miles's Bible before I go."

"I can give you a Bible to start with right now—"

"No, I want *Miles's* Bible." She sounded stubbornly determined, as if his personal Bible held information other Bibles didn't, but she suddenly brightened. "Maybe they've finished searching his place by now. We could go back over there this afternoon. And Mac still needs a drill to fix the coffee table."

I was pleased with her eagerness to get hold of Miles's Bible. But I was also reluctantly suspicious that she still wanted inside the townhouse for some other reason.

"Maybe I'll just drive over myself while you're at church, then," she said.

I was a little concerned about unpredictable Elena. She seemed determined to get into Miles's townhouse. "If the yellow crime scene tape is up, you can't go inside, you know. Even if you do have a key and no one's there."

"I know. And technically everything belongs to Stan now anyway."

"He'll probably be happy to let you have the Bible."

She gave a humorless snort. "Sure. After he goes through every page to make sure Miles didn't leave a dollar bill or two tucked inside."

After breakfast, Mac and I drove around until we found a little stucco church with the door open and went inside. It was a good choice. A friendly young woman said she hadn't seen us there before and welcomed us. The sermon was good, a message about the comforting assurances and basic truths of Jesus's words in John 14. *Do not let your hearts be troubled. You believe in God; believe also in me.* Afterward, several people made a point of asking us to come back.

I was afraid when we got home we'd find Elena was off sneaking into Miles's townhouse, so I was relieved to find she was just watching Miranda briskly vacuuming around the sofa where Stan had been sitting last night. After lunch I asked Elena if she'd like to drive over to the townhouse again. She immediately jumped on the idea.

"Maybe that police tape will be gone and we can go inside."

**

The yellow tape was not gone. It twisted gently in a slight breeze. We'd come in Elena's car again, Mac driving, and she sat there looking out the rear-seat window with frustration. I had the uneasy feeling she was thinking about just ducking under the tape and going inside or maybe even tearing it down.

A woman suddenly came around the corner of the townhouse. Youngish, dark hair in a short, spiky cut. Not overweight but large, big-boned and athletic looking. Dangly silver earrings in a large and rather alarming butcher-knife shape hung from her ears. Jeans, black sweatshirt, something in her hand. What was it? Oh, a cell phone, of course. She lifted it above the yellow tape and took a quick photo, then spotted us watching her and dashed to a car parked at the curb. She didn't burn rubber leaving, but her departure was definitely on the getaway side.

I turned to look at Elena, wondering if she recognized the woman. "Someone you know?"

"Maybe she's a reporter."

Could be. There hadn't been much on the local news lately about the murder, but, since I hadn't seen any video equipment, maybe she was from the local newspaper snooping for a follow-up story?

"Although . . ."

"Although what?" I prodded.

"I think maybe I've seen her before."

"Since Miles died? Or before?"

"Before. Something kind of odd happened." Elena's forehead wrinkled in thought. "Miles was cooking dinner for us here that

78

night, and just as I walked up to the door, a woman ran out. She was angry about something, so angry she practically ran into me. She'd have flattened me if we'd collided. Then she yelled back at Miles, 'I'll believe that when we get the money! You aren't going to get away with this! I'll see to it.' She ran on by me and got into a car and roared away. Just like this woman did just now."

"The same car that this woman was driving?"

Elena shrugged. "Maybe. I'm not sure."

Elena's ability to identify vehicles apparently matched mine. That the car was white was the limit of my observation of it.

But, if this was the same woman Elena had seen here before, who was she? A cruise lady Miles had conned? She seemed young for that. Or maybe Miles's repertoire of conned cruise ladies covered a wider age group than I'd assumed?

"What did Miles have to say about this?"

"He just laughed. He said she was a saleslady selling time-share condos in Tahiti and someone had given her his name, and he was kind of interested for a while, thinking it was something he and I might enjoy. But then he asked for nitty-gritty details and figured out what a risky deal it really was. He said he'd pointed that out to the woman, and she got mad that he had her figured out and wasn't buying."

I said a noncommittal "Umm." Elena apparently accepted the explanation Miles had given her, and I had to give him credit for a good spur-of-the-moment story. He'd couched it in terms of his and Elena's relationship. But I wasn't buying it. The woman's parting shot at Miles about "the money" just didn't fit with his supposed rejection of a time-share. It sounded more like a threat.

And if this was the same woman, what was she doing snooping around here today?

We were still sitting there looking at the townhouse when another vehicle cruised by. A big blue SUV. I couldn't see the driver's face because he was looking at the townhouse and the yellow tape. But it looked a lot like the SUV Stan had been driving earlier.

The townhouse was a popular place. The police were looking for evidence in it. A reporter—or some angry young woman Miles knew—was snooping around it. Stan wanted in to look for Miles's will. And Elena wanted in for . . . some reason.

**

Back at the motorhome, Mac and I talked about Elena and the townhouse, the unidentified woman, and Stan. If there was some connection, we couldn't fit the pieces together. I unenthusiastically decided it was time to do a stove cleaning I'd been putting off. But while I was gathering supplies for the cleaning, Elena knocked on the motorhome door.

"Blake just called! He's in one of those foreign places he's always going to for business, but when I told him about Miles he said he'd get back to the States as soon as he can and come right up here. It will be so good to see him again!" Her enthusiasm abruptly fizzled. "He probably thinks he can get me to move into a retirement home now that Miles is gone."

"Will you?" I asked.

"I don't think so." She hesitated. "But . . . maybe."

Which meant this place might be available after all. Mac and I looked at each other. Were we interested? One of our standards for a place on which to settle down was that it be a murder-free zone, which Eidenburg Road was not. Did we want to relax that standard? Or maybe we should just stay out of this, let the police take care of it, and be on our way. Our friends Magnolia and Geoff were down around Padre Island in Texas now; maybe that's where we should be too.

A mutant curiosity gene surely can't jump up and down in protest . . . *you can't just run off and leave without finding out what happened here!* . . . but it certainly felt as if mine was doing exactly that.

Then Elena came up with an idea much more appealing than cleaning the stove. Although I have to admit it doesn't take much of an idea to dissuade me from stove cleaning.

CHAPTER 9

IVY

"Blake loves my apple pies, and I want to make one for him when he gets here," Elena said. "I'm going to run over to the farmers market and pick up some apples. It's only open on weekends. Want to come along?"

"Go," Mac urged. "It'll do both of you good to get out and do something. I'll go to the hardware store while you're gone and pick up some glue and try fixing the coffee table with that."

"We could use some fresh tomatoes and lettuce," I said.

So we got in Elena's little car and drove to a farmers market set up on a parking lot at the north end of town. It was a great place, with all kinds of fresh vegetables and fruits, plus various stands selling everything from tacos to taffy. A live trio played cheerful old tunes, going from "Johnny B. Goode" to an old favorite of mine, "Blueberry Hill." We were eating almonds while we listened, but the song gave me an unexpected craving for blueberries.

I couldn't find any fresh berries, too far out of season, but I did find bags of another favorite, satsuma mandarins, and added them to my tomatoes and green leaf lettuce and little green onions. Elena grabbed a bag of the mandarins too.

"Oh, Nicole loves these! Okay if we go by her place and take some to her?"

Fine with me. If I got back to the motorhome too soon I might feel obligated to clean that stove.

Nicole's apartment was in a modest, U-shaped, pink stucco building, her #17 at a corner of the U. Nicole came to the door in an ankle-length, flowered dress with a lacy white apron tied around her waist, her hair in a puffed-up pompadour like you see in old-fashioned photos.

"Are we interrupting something?" I asked as Elena handed her the mesh bag of mandarins.

"Oh, satsuma mandarins! You know how much I love those, don't you? C'mon in." She took the bag and waved us inside. "No, you're not interrupting anything. I have a Cookie Lady reading scheduled for later, and I'm just getting things ready."

The interior of the apartment smelled deliciously of vanilla and cinnamon. A blue loveseat, a recliner rocker and a couple of bookcases, a catty-corner desk, and a wall-mounted TV had been arranged to make the most of the small apartment space. A stuffed giraffe in one corner lent a touch of whimsy, and pots of African violets, which I suspected I could kill just by touching the pots with what friend Magnolia calls my Thumb of Death, flourished on a kitchen windowsill.

"Your cookies smell so good!" I said.

"Sometimes I bake my own, but today's are leftovers from the bakery. Cookies that aren't too fresh crumble better. The scent comes from a pan of vanilla and cinnamon simmering on the stove. A little deceptive, I have to admit. But the scent gives a nice ambience, don't you think? The dress too. I mean, who could doubt pronouncements of a sweet lady in a granny gown?" She gave a graceful little curtsy.

"Maybe you could do a cookie reading for Ivy before your clients get here," Elena suggested.

"Oh, I'd love to—"

"Thank you, no," I said hastily.

"Then do a new one for me," Elena said.

Nicole glanced at the clock on the wall. "We won't have time for tea and cookies afterward because of my client, but sure, I can do a quick reading. Let me get these mandarins put away first."

"Tell me more about your cookie readings," I said as she put the fruit in the bottom of the refrigerator and got a tray of cookies covered with plastic wrap from the top of the refrigerator.

"I always have a variety of cookies for clients to choose from because what a client chooses is a part of who they are." Nicole made the statement sound learned, as if it were a scientific undertaking. I could identify oatmeal raisin cookies, chocolate chip, sugar cookies, and various other frosted and unfrosted varieties on the tray.

What would I pick if I were actually doing this? A plain sugar cookie, I decided. Because they're my least favorite, and I didn't see any point in ruining a favorite such as the chocolate chip by crumbling it. I'd rather eat it. Did that say something about me?

Nicole lifted a hand with a dainty strand of lace tied around her wrist and motioned to an open door. "Come with me, ladies, to the inner sanctum of the Cookie Lady."

Nicole was too young to remember the creepy, squeaking door of that old *Inner Sanctum* radio program, and there was certainly nothing creepy about the small, second bedroom of the apartment that she'd turned into a special room for her cookie readings. The furnishings were simple: a high, round table with a skirt of blue-flowered fabric that turned into a ruffle at the floor, curtains of the same delicate pattern, and two tall chairs with padded backs and seats. A small table by the door held flyers. I picked up one.

There was a photo of Nicole in a dress similar to the one she was wearing now. In the photo she was studying cookie crumbs, a client's back to the camera. The wording said:

Puzzled about your life? Confused? Let the Cookie Lady help!
Insights
Understanding Yourself
Discernment
The Future

"Help yourself, if you'd like to have one," Nicole said. "Or take several. Give them to everyone you know!"

Umm, no.

She turned on a floor lamp that gave a soft, pinkish glow and set the tray of cookies on the table. The table already held a square of wood, like a kitchen cutting board, and a bowl with an assortment of tools: a knife, a spoon, a small pair of pliers, tongs, a hammer-shaped metal meat tenderizer, and a plastic glove. A pile of napkins stood beside the bowl.

The tools struck me as a little odd for dealing with cookies. That meat tenderizer thing looked mean enough to take out a burglar, and the pliers looked more suitable for overhauling a car than crumbling a cookie. But other than that, she'd set up the perfect ambiance for intimacy and trust, no distractions.

"Have a seat, Mrs. Ridgeway," Nicole said as if Elena were an actual client. She motioned to one of the tall chairs at the table and sat in the other one herself.

"Oh, I will, but may I use your bathroom first? I ate some nuts at the farmers market and there's a chunk stuck in this tooth that's been bothering me." She wiggled her jaw. "I really need to use some dental floss on it."

Nicole waved her off.

"What are all the tools in the bowl for?" I asked.

"The first thing I do is have a client pick a cookie. What kind she chooses is meaningful, and also whether she uses her fingers or tongs or a napkin to pick it out of the pile. Oatmeal-cookie-crumblers tend to be on the old-fashioned side; sugar-cookie-crumblers like things simple. It gives me a starting point."

I suppose that could be true, although it also seemed to me that someone might choose a cookie simply because it was the top cookie on the pile. But maybe doing that had some significance too.

"Then I ask her to crumble it, and I note whether she uses a tool or if she does it with her fingers or her fist."

"Fist?"

"Oh, yes, some clients are very dainty crumblers, but some do a real smash job with a fist. Other smashers pick that meat-tenderizer tool."

"And you really do think the way she does it and the way the cookie crumbs fall say something about that person's future?"

"I read some books on reading tea leaves and fortune-telling, so I figure if it works for tea leaves, why not cookie crumbs too? Such as seeing a cow in the tea leaves is a sign of coming prosperity. So is seeing triangles, trees, or a bridge. Or angels. Seeing a ring means marriage. But seeing a coffin or a snake or a monkey is bad." She wagged a disapproving finger. "Very bad. But what I do is really more of a character analysis than a prediction of the future. Our character affects our future, of course, as I always tell people."

"But don't people usually want a fortune-telling prediction for the future?"

"Yes, but I try to make the answer rather generic. Not, yes, you should divorce that louse of a husband, but that you should look to your inner self. Talk to that inner self about the relationship. Think about consequences. Release your potential. Beware of false positives or self-denial." She smiled. "And whatever other psychobabble I can think of at the moment."

"You don't take this too seriously, then."

"I didn't when I started doing it, although I'm kind of changing my mind. The thing is, the pattern in which the crumbs fall so often does seem accurate. Sometimes almost eerily accurate. I've done readings for myself, of course."

"And what do the cookies say about you?"

"The first couple of times I did it, they didn't say anything. The crumbs were just a big, disorganized mess. But then one time they showed birds flying. They really did . . . flying birds! That's a symbol of something good coming your way. And along with it was a car shape. I'd been thinking about buying a friend's car, so I did buy it, and it's the car I still have. A great car! And I probably wouldn't have bought it if the cookie crumbs hadn't told me it was the right thing to do."

"But what if someone does what you say and it goes terribly wrong? What if someone is thinking about quitting her job and starting her own business, and she interprets what you say as encouragement to start a new business . . . maybe a combination tattoo parlor and ice cream shop . . . and it goes down like a leaky canoe."

Nicole smiled at my unlikely business venture. "Point well taken." She made a small dip of her head. "But if the crumbs say even an unlikely business venture will work, maybe it will."

"What if you tell her a ring you see in her crumbs means marriage, and she takes that to mean the next guy she meets is the one she's supposed to marry? And he turns out to be an axe murderer or serial killer?"

Nicole looked momentarily startled, but then she laughed. "Or maybe a cheating philanderer, like I married?"

"How did you get started doing this?"

Nicole went out of cookie-reading mode and leaned her elbows on the table. She had a pensive look.

"I was working in Stan's office. At the time, it was the only place I'd ever worked. Stan is several years older than I am. He'd graduated college before I met him and was working in his father's investment business. I was about halfway through my second year of college, and we met when he came to talk to one of my classes. And the fact that this successful businessman turned out to be interested in little ol' *me* just bowled me over. I dropped out of college within a few months to marry him. His father died not long afterward, and Stan took over the business. I was never involved with actual investments, just a receptionist and general gofer, but even I could see that the company started going downhill almost immediately. Stan was great at public-relations and drumming up new clients, but he wasn't anywhere near the businessman his father was. The business was sinking like your tattoo parlor and ice cream shop."

I couldn't see that this had anything to do with cookie-crumbling and a granny dress, so all I said was, "Umm."

"Eventually I began to suspect that Stan had something going on the side. Some other woman. But I wasn't prepared for what happened."

Elena returned from her freshening up and perched on the other tall chair. Nicole didn't seem to notice. She was momentarily caught in the past.

"I came home from the office at the regular time that evening, but Stan stayed to work late. Yeah, I was gullible enough to swallow the working-late myth. I was baking cookies for him—" She paused and laughed. "Can you believe that? I actually used to bake cookies for the man, and that evening I was making the crinkly chocolate kind he especially liked."

I glanced over at the cookie tray. No crinkly chocolate cookies. Perhaps they were banned.

"Anyway, he came in and grabbed a cookie, and then, as casually as if he were telling me he'd stopped to fill the gas tank on the way home, he said—and I remember this word for word—he said, 'You know, babe, I've been thinking. This just isn't working, is it? I saw a lawyer this afternoon. I'm filing for divorce.'"

"He may be Miles's nephew, but he's a jerk," Elena muttered.

"I was flabbergasted," Nicole said. "Dumbfounded. I had my suspicions about him, yes, but I hadn't realized we were at this point. I asked him if there was someone else. He denied it, said I was imagining things because of my 'immaturity.'"

"A total jerk," Elena emphasized.

"And I said, 'But you can't end a marriage without even *talking* about it.' And he said, 'Oh, yes, I can.' I guess I still looked astonished or unbelieving or something, and he said 'That's just the way the cookie crumbles, babe.' And he picked up another cookie and squashed it in his hand and let crumbs fall all over the floor. Then he walked out, except he stopped at the door and said, 'By the way, you don't need to come into the office tomorrow.' And I, still dazed, asked him why. And he said, 'Because you don't work there anymore.'"

"That was it?" I said.

"That was it. Except that I was too stunned even to cry and I just sat there for I don't know how long. Then I got mad. And madder. And then I said out loud, even though I was there all alone, I said, 'I'll show you how the cookie crumbles!' And I started smashing cookies. Every cookie I'd baked. Smash, smash, smash!" She pounded her fist on the table. "The kitchen looked as if there'd been a cookie-crumb tornado."

"And then you started doing cookie-crumb readings?" I asked doubtfully.

Nicole laughed. "No, not right away. We got the divorce, and I got the house in the property settlement. Which was a big laugh because the payments were way over my head and I lost it within a few months. I couldn't find a decent-paying job, which puzzled me at first. Then I found out that when I gave Moore Investments as a job reference, which was the only work experience reference I had to give, they were saying all this critical stuff about me. About my questionable work ethic, inability to follow orders, and on and on. Maybe that I had bad breath and smelly feet, for all I know."

"Stan was doing this?"

"I don't know if it was him or Saundra, but someone did it. Did I mention that by then Stan and Saundra were married and living happily ever after? Because there definitely was someone else all along. Saundra. She was working at the office too. And, from what I heard from a friend who still worked there, things picked up considerably at the office after Saundra got into it. Maybe she's a better businessperson than Stan."

"Why would they want to keep you from getting a good job by giving you a bad reference?"

"I think it was their do-it-yourself, get-rid-of-the-ex-wife plan. They figured if I couldn't get a good job I'd just pick up and leave the area. Maybe go to Georgia where my father and his wife live. Or maybe it was just general maliciousness."

"Isn't giving an unwarranted bad reference unethical, maybe even illegal?"

"I don't know." She shrugged as if it no longer mattered. "I worked in a taco stand for a while and then found this job with the bakery. It's kind of a dead end, I suppose, but it pays the bills . . . and I get all these leftover cookies. And I'm doing Cookie Lady readings of course. I started them as just kind of a getting-even-with-Stan thing, making fun of him, actually. Then friends told friends, and pretty soon I had an actual money-making business going." She smiled. "So that's the way the cookie crumbles."

"Stan is worse than a jerk," Elena said. "He's a—"

Nicole shushed Elena before she came out with a word or two I suspected were considerably more derogatory than *jerk*.

"So, to get on with your reading, Elena, pick a cookie."

Elena selected a peanut butter cookie, the top one on the pile, and crumbled it with her fingertips, holding the cookie up high and giving a little flourish at the end so crumbs scattered all over the wooden board. Nicole studied them carefully. Elena licked crumbs off her fingers.

"You're a remarkable woman, Mrs. Ridgeway. Precise at times, but with a touch of playfulness. Or perhaps it's adventure . . . yes, a definite touch of adventurousness, maybe even recklessness! You're willing to take chances. Unpredictable! You've had a recent disappointment in life—" Nicole pointed to a dense swirl of crumbs.

"Yes," Elena agreed. "Miles."

"But the most identifiable portion of the crumbs shows a . . . let's see . . ." Nicole moved the wooden board a fraction of an inch. "A cat. Yes, it's a cat!"

I leaned over to peer at the scattered crumbs. A cat? I couldn't see anything that remotely resembled a cat. Unless those three long strands and a larger blob of crumbs above them were a three-legged cat wearing a sombrero.

Elena studied the crumbs too. I had the feeling she couldn't see a cat any more than I could.

"But you're the one who can *see* what's in the crumbs," she said confidently. "And if you see a cat— Maybe Ricardo is trying to get in touch with me!" She paused and addressed the scattered crumbs on the wooden board. "Ricardo, sweetie, is that you? Do you have something to tell me?"

I was startled. Was Nicole really going to let Elena think her cat was trying to contact her from some dead-cat world?

I was relieved when Nicole shook her head. "No, the cat in the crumbs isn't Ricardo. The crumbs are telling you there's *another* cat in your future."

"Another cat?" Elena sounded doubtful.

"Ricardo would want you to have one, don't you think? He wouldn't want you to be lonely. Yes, another cat is definitely in the crumbs. And this square-ish shape over here? That's the county animal shelter. You're going to the county animal shelter, where another cat is waiting for you! You'll have a wonderful new cat friend and the cat will have a wonderful new home. And that's the way the cookie crumbles."

Elena hesitated only momentarily before saying enthusiastically, "I'll do it!"

Nicole looked at me over Elena's shoulder and gave me a quick wink. She swept her hand across the wooden board, brushing away what I was pretty sure was just a cookie-crumb mess. The landline phone rang and Nicole went to answer it.

"See?" Elena said triumphantly. "Nicole's cookie crumbs told my future. A new cat."

We waited until Nicole finished with her phone call, and then Elena opened her purse.

"I want to pay your regular rate."

Nicole gave her a hug. "The mandarins are plenty of payment. Enjoy your new kitty."

I hung behind while Elena headed for the door. When she opened it, I could see a light rain had started falling.

"I couldn't see any cat in those crumbs," I said to Nicole and added bluntly, "I don't think you could either."

Nicole tilted her head and smiled. "Okay, so sometimes you have to use a little imagination to see anything in the crumbs. Elena should have another cat. So I just helped steer her in that direction."

I had to concede it was probably a good direction. Koop had eventually forgiven Elena for the cigarette scent on her hands that first day he met her, and they were good buddies now, but she needed a cat of her own. Nicole had even thrown in instructions for how Elena should acquire that new cat. A new cat for Elena; a new home for a homeless kitty. A win-win situation.

Though I still wasn't comfortable with prophecy-by-cookie-crumbs.

Nicole sighed. "Although I have to admit it would probably have been more helpful if I could have come up with information on who killed Miles, wouldn't it? But at the moment, I think that's something only the killer himself knows."

I said what I knew to be true, no cookie crumbs needed. "The Lord knows. There are no secrets from him."

Nicole lifted her eyebrows but didn't comment. "I've been thinking about something else. It's kind of about Miles." She hesitated, then backpedaled on the statement. "Or maybe not."

I made a noncommittal murmur. The cookie-crumbs thing seemed harmless enough, yes, and Nicole had worked it around to something good for Elena. But still . . .

"The thing is, quite some time ago, this old man came into the bakery. He had a wrinkled old face and a mole on his chin. I couldn't see his hair because he was wearing an old tweed cap. He shuffled around, kind of bent over, and he asked for muffins in a croaky old voice. I certainly didn't know him, but somehow he seemed kind of familiar."

I didn't say anything, just nodded for her to keep going.

"Then, just as he turned to leave, I saw he was wearing a ring, a heavy, gold ring with a ruby stone in it. Miles always wore a ruby ring just like that because his birthday was in July, and ruby is the birthstone for July."

"Umm."

"I wondered at the time if Miles was wearing a mask and playing some kind of joke on me. Although it certainly didn't *look* like a mask, just like leathery old skin, but I asked him about it later. I mentioned the old guy wearing a ring that looked like his. He just laughed and said sometimes he felt all wrinkled and bent over, like I described the old guy, but he hoped he wasn't in that bad shape yet. He said he did have a ruby ring but he hadn't been wearing it lately because it had gotten too loose on his finger."

"Did the old man ever come back to the bakery?"

"No, at least I never saw him again. And I never saw Miles wear his ruby ring again. But I don't know why I'm mentioning any of this now. It surely doesn't have anything to do with Miles's death. It was probably just one of those odd coincidences."

A coincidence? Maybe. Maybe not.

Odd? Yes.

Nicole suddenly changed the subject. "Are you guys doing anything this evening? That phone call was from my clients cancelling their appointment. At the last minute, no less. I should send them a bill and a message from the cookies that says they're both going to get fat and bald and have ingrown toenails."

"That'll fix 'em," I said.

Nicole laughed. "But I wouldn't really do that, of course. But now I have a long empty evening alone ahead of me. Unless . . ." She gave me a speculative glance. "Maybe all three of us could go out to dinner and a movie. I haven't been to an actual movie theater in ages. How about it? Girls' night out."

"I'll check with Elena and Mac and give you a call."

CHAPTER 10

MAC

Repairing the coffee table with glue did not go well. Ivy tells me I'm a great fixer, and ordinarily, I can indeed be fairly competent at repairing things. But on this project I seemed to have all the fixing talent of a toadstool.

First, I assumed . . . mistakenly as it turned out . . . that with four table legs and four holes to fasten them into, that it didn't matter which table leg went in which hole. For some unknown reason, at least unknown to me, I found after a lengthy time trying to put uncooperative table legs into uncooperative holes that each leg had to be fit into a particular hole.

Okay, got that figured out. Then I got a sliver in a finger on my right hand. After considerable time, and a considerably bloodied finger trying to dig the sliver out left-handed with a pocket knife, I gave up. Maybe Ivy could manage it when she got home. I went over to the motorhome, covered the injured area with a Band-Aid, and determinedly returned to give the coffee-table project another try.

Sometimes determination and persistence make as much sense as trying to make coffee with a tea bag.

It was dark by the time Ivy and Elena got home, and I'd just managed to glue my finger to the underside of the coffee table. With this glue that guarantees you can fasten two items together and nothing will separate them, proven by an advertisement showing a lawn mower hanging from items glued together.

I'd never quite believed the glue could be that powerful, but certainly nothing seemed inclined to separate me and the coffee table, and it appeared I could be destined to spend the rest of my life lugging around a coffee table attached to my hand. An awkward situation that might change Ivy's mind about my competence as a fixer.

Anyway, by the time she came into the garage to find me with a finger affixed to the coffee table, apparently for life, I did not have a cheerful attitude toward girls' night out.

**

IVY

After gouging the underside of the coffee table with a screwdriver in order to detach it from Mac's finger, and removing a sliver from another finger—which looked as if it had been worked on by a doctor-wannabe who'd never managed to get into medical school—I went back to the house.

"Mac isn't feeling well, so I think I'll stay home with him this evening," I said to Elena without explaining details of why I was backing out on the girls' night out we'd talked about on the way home. Mac is usually so even-tempered and such a good fixer, but tonight's encounter with the coffee table had turned him into Grump with an Attitude. I didn't want to complain about that to Elena, however; I figure a good husband is entitled to an occasional Sour Husband Day. Perfection could be intimidating to live with, since I fall rather short of it myself.

"Oh, that's too bad." She sounded disappointed. "I hope it isn't anything serious."

"I think he'll be fine. No reason you can't go ahead and go."

Elena sighed. "Oh, I couldn't. I probably shouldn't even have considered it to begin with. With Miles gone . . ."

"I think Miles would heartily approve. And it will do you good."

She hesitated another moment and finally nodded. "I'll give it a try."

Elena called Nicole, who wanted to come pick her up, but Elena insisted on driving over to Nicole's apartment and they could go from there. I could see Elena was determined not to become a person who always needs things done for her. It's an attitude I had to admire, although I didn't necessarily approve in this situation.

Mac and I spent a quiet evening watching TV and went to bed early, only a little past nine. Elena wasn't home yet.

I woke sometime later. I thought it was the middle of the night, but the clock showed only a few minutes after ten. I got up and then, wondering if Elena was home yet, pushed aside the curtains across the broad front windshield of the motorhome so I could see out. The house lights weren't on, but faint flickers of light showed from Elena's bedroom window on the back side of the house.

I was just thinking how odd that was when Mac voiced the same thought from right beside me.

"That's odd, isn't it?"

"It might be a flashlight. What could she be doing?"

"I believe we've already decided her nephew was right when he said Elena is unpredictable."

Right. Elena could be over there doing anything from dancing in the dark to making pretzels. Or she might be ill. "I think I'll just run over and make sure everything's okay."

I slipped on a robe and slippers and headed for the motorhome door. I didn't get it closed before Mac came out behind me. He was carrying something.

"You have a *baseball bat*? When did you get that?"

"When I was buying glue to fix the coffee table."

"You're planning to take up baseball?"

"I'm planning to have something available for protection in case we need it. We've talked about getting a gun, but we've never done it. I'm keeping the bat alongside the bed now."

Damp grass brushed my feet as we crossed the yard to the back door. There was no yard light back here, but some light spilled from the yard light out front. I unexpectedly shivered. There was something almost eerie about the light and shadows. I was glad Mac had come along. And had the bat.

I knocked. No response. I tried the door. Unlocked, as it usually was.

95

We slipped inside. No sounds, no flickering light. Why hadn't we brought a flashlight of our own?

"Elena?" I called softly. "Are you home?"

No answer. We moved down the hallway.

And then something barreled out of Elena's bedroom. A shadow . . . a person! In the hallway, here reached only by a faint seep of light from the outdoor yard light, I couldn't see much, but I had the impression of a bulky person all in black. Did unpredictable Elena wear black pajamas? Maybe—

The shadow crashed into me and I sprawled backwards, stumbling over Mac's feet as I went down. Shadow Person hurtled on by me. Mac whacked with his baseball bat and collided with something. Shadow Person *oofed*, stumbled and hit the wall but managed to bounce off and head for the door we'd come through. I held my head and sat up, groggy.

An oblong of faint light showed as the back door opened, momentarily silhouetting the bulky figure of someone lurching through the opening. I struggled to my feet to give chase, stumbled again. Mac grabbed me, half to support me, half to stop me from carrying out my lame-brained idea of chasing this person.

"You okay?" Mac said.

"Someone was in here. They got away!"

"I'm new at this. I should have hit harder."

I heard the front door open. Burglar returning? No. Burglars do not race out a back door only to instantly return by a front door. A light snapped on in the kitchen, and we staggered down the hallway.

Elena stared at us. We stared at her. She looked quite nice after her evening out, all dressed up in a skirt and boots, a lively shine in her eyes.

"What are you doing?" she finally asked.

"We saw a flickering light over here, so we came to investigate," Mac said. "Someone ran out of your bedroom and knocked Ivy down. Then the person ran out the back door."

Elena rushed to Ivy. "Are you okay?"

I jiggled my shoulders and stomped my feet lightly. "Everything seems to be working okay."

She patted me down as if checking to be sure all the parts were intact before saying, "I wonder if they took anything."

We followed Elena back to the bedroom. She flicked the light switch. The bedroom looked undisturbed, bed unrumpled, closet door closed. She checked the nightstand drawers and opened a couple of dresser drawers.

"I don't see anything missing."

"I think we should call the police anyway," Mac said. "Maybe they just didn't have time to grab anything before we interrupted."

Elena tapped her fingers on the dresser top. Finally she said, "I'd rather not."

"Why?" I asked.

"Well, the person didn't actually take anything, and you didn't actually get hurt, and they were probably wearing gloves so there wouldn't be any fingerprints. And the police . . . I don't know, make me kind of nervous, I guess. They already look at me as if I'm Suspect Number One, with Guilty stamped on my forehead. They'll also think I'm stupid or senile or something for leaving the back door unlocked. Anyway, I don't want to call them."

"Well, okay," Mac said reluctantly.

We asked how the girls' night out had gone. Elena said they'd had a great dinner at a Mexican restaurant she'd never been to before and saw a strange but rather interesting older movie set on some other planet where all the people were blue.

**

Next morning, even though Elena was eager to jump into her foretold future and acquire a new cat, we didn't get started until after lunch because Elena wanted to have a new bed and dishes all ready for a new cat. She didn't have a cat carrier to bring a cat home, so Mac loaded Koop's carrier in her car and we were off.

And soon discovered the shelter wasn't open on Mondays. A couple of vehicles were parked inside the fence, and several dogs barked back there somewhere, but a metal gate barred our way. A sign said they'd be open on Tuesday 9:00 a.m.

I said the obvious. "We'll just have to come back tomorrow."

"I suppose so."

But she didn't start the car, and for a moment I had the awful feeling we were going to try a cat-snatching burglary. Then she turned the car around, but we didn't head for home. I asked where we were going. She said she just wanted to run by Miles's townhouse and see if anything was going on there. I didn't think there could have been any change since the last time she was over there, but I supposed there wouldn't be any harm in taking another look.

Famous last words.

The townhouse looked exactly the same as before, except there was no police car or white van parked out front. Yellow tape blocked the front door and circled around back of the unit, which was possible only because it was the end unit. Elena parked the car across the street. From here, the garage for the townhouse was on the left side, the bedrooms over it on the second floor. I couldn't tell if there was a car inside the garage.

After a while Elena said, "I'm going to go around back and make sure nobody's broken in or disturbed anything."

I intended to just sit and wait for her, but sitting and waiting is not my strong point. After tapping my feet restlessly for a couple of minutes, I got out of the car and followed the yellow tape around back.

An alleyway separated the row of townhouses Miles's place was in from the row behind it. Each townhouse had its own little just-above-ground-level balcony tucked into the back side, with a sliding glass door opening to the interior. The small balconies didn't offer any view, but most had potted plants, barbecues, and lawn chairs set up on them, as did Miles's place. A few bushes covered the space between his balcony and the ground. Drapes on the sliding glass door gapped open about ten inches, but it was impossible to see inside because the barbecue blocked the way. The yellow tape didn't cover the back side of the townhouse; it was just spread out loose on the ground.

Like an elderly jack-in-the-box, Elena bounced up and down as she tried to see through the gap in the drapes. "They took the yellow tape down back here so they must be through searching. If I could get up a little higher, I could see over the chairs and into the kitchen."

"What's there to see?"

"I don't know because I can't *see* it." Elena sounded exasperated with my question. "I need something to stand on."

I thought the tape had most likely blown loose, not been removed, and the police would be returning to continue their search any minute. And they might not take kindly to two LOLs wandering . . . sneaking? . . . around the place.

But it was also possible Elena was right. Maybe they had taken the yellow tape down back here and just hadn't finished removing it out front.

I reached through the balusters on the railing and jiggled a chair, but we had no way to lift it over the railing so she could stand on it. I didn't feel any great enthusiasm for an idea that occurred to me, but maybe it would be the quickest way to get us out of here before the police returned to continue a search.

"I could get down on my hands and knees and you could step up on my back," I offered reluctantly. "Just to take a quick glance."

"Stand on your back? Oh, I couldn't do that—" She gave me a speculative appraisal and apparently changed her mind; yes, she *could* do that. "It'll just take a second. I'll take off my shoes."

So there I was, down on my hands and knees, scrunched up next to the bushes growing under the little balcony, barefoot Elena clambering up on my back. I *oofed* as her bare toes dug in. She was heavier than she looked. They say muscle weighs more than fat, and if that was true, little Elena must have the muscle/weight ratio of a pit bull.

"Can you see anything?" I called up to her.

"Not really—"

I *oofed* again as she kind of bounced on my back, and then the weight was suddenly gone. Had Elena fallen? I floundered to my feet.

Which was when I realized what she was doing. Oh, no— "Elena, I don't think you should—"

Too late. She was already doing it. She'd used my back as a stepping stone to climb over the railing, and she was right now pulling a key out of her pocket and putting it into the lock on the door. A moment later she was inside.

"Elena!"

She stuck her head out the door. "Shh! Someone will hear you!"

She motioned me inside with a vigorous wave of arm and disappeared through the sliding glass door. I stood there a moment. This surely wasn't a good idea, was it? Was there a penalty for breaking into an area the police had cordoned off?

But, I reasoned, we weren't actually breaking in. Elena had a key. And maybe the police really had started to remove the tape. Squeezing through the bushes to get closer to the railing, and stretching my short legs to their utmost, I managed to get one foot up to the balcony floor, toes jammed between two balustrades. I bounced a few times and got a knee between two other balustrades. I rested a few moments and then, like an activated sandbag, floundered up and over the railing. I landed like a sandbag too.

Inside, breathing hard, I hastily closed the door and pulled the curtains shut tight.

The kitchen was shadowy in the gray light of late winter afternoon, but I could see that everything was clean and tidy. Miles had not been one of those bachelors whose living quarters look as if Godzilla and a couple of buddies camped there. Stainless steel, double-door refrigerator, kitchen range, microwave, dishwasher, all sparkling clean. A fancy coffee maker stood on the counter, plus a small toaster-oven. I opened the refrigerator . . . why? Who knows? I just did it, and a glare of light shone out. The refrigerator was still stocked with everyday essentials . . .milk, eggs, lettuce, ketchup . . . plus an unopened carton of brie and a bottle of red wine. Had Miles intended to contribute these to that evening of pretzel-making with Elena?

Sad, all their happy plans cut short—

But Elena wasn't in here bemoaning what was not to be. I couldn't hear her on the ground floor so she must be upstairs rummaging through a bedroom. I'd mostly discounted the

100

possibility she'd had anything to do with Miles's death, but at the moment that possibility rumbled back. Was she looking for something that could incriminate her in the murder?

Surely not. I didn't know what she was looking for, but what we needed to do since we were here was find something that pointed to a killer other than her, something the search people hadn't recognized as relevant and important.

Something to do with cruise ladies and a con scheme.

I opened a door that led out to the garage. One question answered. Miles's SUV was there, clean and shiny. Clean garage also. I peeked in the living room with a dining area at one end. A small but elegant teakwood table and chairs, gas fireplace, leather sofa and recliner. I didn't see any good place to hide con-scheme information.

I crept up the stairs and peeked into the bedroom where Elena was searching. She was down on her knees looking under the bed. I moved on to the other bedroom that Miles had used as an office. There was a desk and chair, a computer monitor and printer, but the computer itself was gone, of course, as was the file cabinet we'd seen the guys in white jumpsuits remove. I yanked the top desk drawer open, but it held only miscellaneous office supplies. A second drawer held bills and bank and credit card statements, neatly divided into sections. Oh, but there was a little red book . . . names and telephone numbers and addresses! How come they hadn't taken that?

I hadn't time to study the statements or the red book, but, doing a quick rationalization that if the officials had wanted the little book, they'd have taken it by now, I stuck it in the back pocket of my jeans. A diary or journal would have been better, but Miles apparently wasn't into journal-keeping. Or else they'd already taken that.

The closet. Maybe they'd missed something in there. I slid the mirrored door open.

Just regular closet stuff. Too shadowy to see much, but this looked like where Miles had kept the dressier part of his wardrobe. Suits, dress shirts, dressy slacks. His more regularly used everyday clothing must be in the bedroom where Elena was rummaging. I looked on the shelf above the clothes rod. A portable radio, a couple of tennis rackets, a stack of caps with visors, several shoeboxes up front, more boxes in back. I pulled down the shoeboxes. Maybe he'd hidden something there—

No. Only shoes spilled out and tumbled to the floor around me. Dressy loafers, unused slippers, a pair of old-fashioned, high-topped tennies.

The stack of caps collapsed too. Maybe caps he'd collected on his cruise trips? One had Tahiti embroidered on the visor, another said Hong Kong. But there was one that was different—

I picked it up off the floor. Nothing written on this one. It was just a plain, rather old-fashioned looking cloth cap.

A *tweed* cap.

Elena stuck her head in the door. "Let's get out of here."

I hesitated. There were other boxes farther back on the shelf—

She grabbed my arm to hurry me along. "I think a car stopped outside."

"Did you find anything?"

She held up a photo in a metal frame. "This picture of Miles and me when we went to Disneyland one time. Let's go!"

We'd run the risk of sneaking in here just so she could grab a sentimental memento?

"What about his Bible? Didn't you say you wanted that?"

"Yes, yes. I saw it on his nightstand."

She ran back to the bedroom and returned with a Bible tucked under her elbow. She grabbed my arm and hurried me down the stairs and out the way we'd come, through the sliding glass door. She locked the door behind us and was first over the railing, hitting the ground with a nimble plop. I was just crawling over the railing when someone came around the end of the townhouse. He stopped short when he saw Elena.

I stopped short too, one leg thrown over the railing.

"Well, Elena," Stan said. He didn't seem to notice me on the railing. "What are you doing here?"

Elena was not slow on the uptake. "What are *you* doing here?" she shot back.

I floundered over the railing and tumbled into the bushes below.

"I saw your car parked across the street. I came around to see what you're doing here. You're trespassing, you know."

"The door was unlocked."

I have a definite aversion to telling untruths, but I didn't feel obligated to point out that Elena was telling one here. I also thought she was saying too much; he wouldn't know we'd actually been inside, except that she'd just told him.

"But I locked it when we came out, so *you* can't get in," she added, sounding victorious.

I also realized that Stan hadn't really explained why he was here. I wanted to ask, but I prudently realized I was apparently invisible at the moment and I'd better stay that way. I scrunched deeper in the bushes. But I peeked out, of course.

"I see you took something," Stan said. He nodded to the picture frame Elena had managed to hold onto even as she climbed over the railing. I saw now that she'd dropped the Bible. I suspected that grabbing it was something of an afterthought anyway.

"Yes, I did. A memento that's very precious to me. But it belongs to you, of course. So if you want it—" She held the framed photo out to him as if daring him to take it.

Stan disdainfully waved the picture away. "I just want you off my property. And don't come back."

Good enough for me. I scrambled out of the bushes. All I had to show for this little excursion was a damp rump and grass stains on my knees. Oh, there was Miles's little phone book in my pocket, but Stan didn't ask if *I'd* taken anything, so I didn't feel obliged to tell him.

That brought me up short for a moment. Was I drawing a rather fine line between truths and untruths, something I'd perhaps better sort out with the Lord?

But at the moment, I just wished I'd grabbed that tweed cap from the closet and stuffed it under my shirt. Nicole had mentioned a tweed cap when she was telling me about the old man in the bakery. She might recognize this one.

Stan took a menacing step toward us. "You're not only trespassing on my property, you crossed a police line to do it. I can call and tell them—"

It seemed a good time to scurry out to the car and skedaddle, though I did swoop down and grab the dropped Bible on my way.

CHAPTER 11

MAC

Ivy and Elena were gone much longer than I expected, and I was getting concerned by the time the car pulled into the driveway. I'd stubbornly gone back to working on the coffee table, and it was back in the living room now. The glue job wasn't as solid as I'd like, but it should hold up as long as a herd of police officers didn't crash down on it.

I went out to meet Ivy and Elena just outside the side door to the garage. I thought they both looked a bit disheveled—Ivy had a piece of weed or brush or something caught in her hair—and Elena was barefoot. A trip to the animal shelter required a jaunt through the brush and a forfeiture of shoes?

"Did you get a cat?" I asked.

"The animal shelter is closed on Mondays," Ivy said. "So no cats were available today."

"What happened to your shoes?" I asked Elena.

"I took them off," she said.

That was obvious, and she seemed to think it was explanation enough. I looked to Ivy for something more.

"She took them off so she could stand on my back," Ivy said.

Did that make everything clear? Like LA on a high-smog day. But I decided it might be just as well, for the moment at least, not to inquire too deeply into what these two had been doing. Although it must not have been anything too bad, because Ivy had a Bible under her arm.

"Do you want to make apple pies yet today?" Ivy asked Elena.

"Not today," Elena said. "Maybe tomorrow. After we get back from the animal shelter."

Inside the motorhome, I got more information on both the Bible and Elena's lack of shoes. Hearing that Ivy and Elena had crossed the police barrier to go into Miles's townhouse, or at least dodged around the barrier, was a bit disturbing, but it was a little late to advise against their course of action now. The deed was done.

"How's your back where Elena walked on it?" I asked.

"A little sore, but it's okay," Ivy assured me. "I should take this Bible back over to her. She dropped it when she jumped over the railing at the townhouse."

Ivy's explanation hadn't included anything about jumping over railings, but all I said was, "Let it go until morning."

She didn't argue. I was glad I had soup and salad already started for supper, and she took a quick shower while I finished up. After supper we sat together on the sofa and leafed through Miles's Bible. It was a rather new-looking Bible, but he had underlined various verses that apparently meant something special to him. I know how it sometimes happens that one verse you've barely noticed before suddenly jumps out at you. Here he'd underlined one of the basic instructions from the Lord, the eighth of the Ten Commandments in Exodus. *You shall not steal.*

"Does it strike you that there may be a lot we don't know about Miles?" I asked as we paused on that verse.

"Oh, yes." She thought about that for a moment. "Elena too. I don't think she was so anxious to get into the townhouse just to get that picture of her and Miles or the Bible. I think she was after something else."

"Did she find it?"

"I don't know. She didn't carry out anything the size of a breadbox, but I'm not sure what she may have hidden in a pocket." She paused. "I hope Stan doesn't use Elena's sandals to get us in trouble for going in the townhouse. They're certainly proof we were there."

I pointed out a technicality. "Not proof that *you* were inside. And since you didn't take anything—"

"Actually, I did," she admitted. She went to the bedroom to retrieve her jeans and came back with a small red notebook. We browsed through it.

Miles apparently didn't keep familiar phone numbers in the little book. Elena's name wasn't there; neither was Stan's. This had only a minimal number of scattered names. But they were all women's names, along with addresses from all over the country.

"Cruise ship ladies?" Ivy asked uneasily.

"I wonder."

"I suppose we could call each of them and ask if Miles had been conning them out of money," she said.

Which might make for some awkward conversations, but I supposed we might have to do it.

For our Bible reading that night, we studied all the Ten Commandment verses there in Exodus. I kept coming back to the one Miles had underlined: *You shall not steal.*

Did he have a guilty conscience about shoplifting a toy car from the dime store back when he was a boy?

Or was he thinking about something larger and more recent, such as stealing from cruise ladies?

**

IVY

The next morning we strolled past rows of cages at the animal shelter and then the attendant took us into a room with an opening to an outdoor area. A number of cats were sleeping or playing together in the room. Cats, short- and long-haired, blacks and whites and calicos, oranges and one Siamese, males and females, shy introverts and active extroverts.

"They've all had their shots," the attendant said. "Males have been neutered, females spayed. We try to give them each some individual attention, but there isn't enough time and they're all hungry for more affection," she added as several wound around our feet.

"Oh, dear," Elena said. "I want them all."

She couldn't do that, but she did wind up with two calicos, older sisters that had come in together and the shelter was hoping to place in the same home. I, too, wanted them all, and it was so hard just to walk on by. A sweet, all-white, older kitty . . . a fluffy male with a cropped ear . . . a skinny black with gorgeous yellow eyes. I had to keep telling myself, *The motorhome can't hold any more animals,* or we'd have wound up with a traveling zoo of furry creatures.

Elena took care of the adoption paperwork, and then we settled the two cats together in Koop's cat carrier. There were some uneasy meows, but they didn't actually resist. Back at the house, where Mac had stayed to do some yard work, he brought the cat carrier inside. We made sure all the doors and windows were shut tight in case the cats—Fancy and Felicity by name—were frightened in a new place and tried to escape.

They came out of the cat carrier warily, looked around cautiously, and immediately scurried to find hiding places. Elena started to chase them down, but I suggested they needed time to adjust and feel safe; they'd come out when they were ready. She'd set out food and water this morning, plus a nice box padded with a blanket that she'd set out yesterday. Her cell phone rang from her purse as I was heading for the back door that went out through the laundry room.

It's rude to listen in on someone else's phone call, although I couldn't help but overhear when Elena answered the phone and then said, "Yes, this is Eleanor Ridgeway. Eleanor Elena Ridgeway." Her tone and the wary way she gave her name told me she was talking to someone she didn't know.

That mutant curiosity gene instantly surfaced, but I managed to overcome curiosity with propriety and kept going toward the door rather than stopping to listen. Then Elena stepped into the hallway and motioned me back as vigorously as she'd motioned me into Miles's townhouse, and who was little ol' curious me to argue with that? There wasn't even a railing to climb over.

She went to sit on the sofa, and I planted myself on the little cane-bottomed rocker. The phone conversation went on for some time, and I finally gathered it had some connection with Miles's will.

Interesting, but even more interesting for a moment was that one of the cats, Felicity, I think, cautiously crept into the living room. She accepted my stroke along her back before darting away again, but the small overture, even though minimal, was encouraging. The last thing Elena said on the phone was that ten o'clock the following morning would be fine.

It's also rude to ask what a phone call is about, but I didn't have to. Elena instantly volunteered the information.

"That was a lawyer, Bradley Effenshire. He said he wrote a new will for Miles a few weeks ago, and he's the executor. Miles had left instructions that if anything happened to him, the lawyer should contact me immediately. He said he hadn't called earlier because he's been out of town and didn't know about Miles's death until he got home and saw it on the news."

I considered the implications of that. "Does that mean Miles wrote a new will because he thought something might happen to him?"

"I don't know." She swallowed. "It almost sounds that way, doesn't it?"

"Did Miles leave you something in the will?"

"He left me everything." She sounded stunned and repeated the word. "*Everything*."

That was obviously a surprise to Elena. And would no doubt be just as big a surprise to the nephew who had chased us away from the townhouse because he assumed it was his. "What about Stan?"

"I asked the lawyer about Stan. The will mentions him. But only to state that he is to take nothing from the estate."

Wow. Miles hadn't minced words. They must have had a humdinger of a falling out. But Stan must have thought a blood relationship would trump a falling out and he'd still inherit everything.

"Stan apparently doesn't know anything about this, but it means he was way out of line telling you to get off his property," I said. "It's *your* property."

"It is, isn't it?" She sounded amazed and a little apprehensive. "Stan is not going to be a happy camper."

"Don't worry about it," I said. I'd guess, between the lawyer and Miles, the will had foolproof wording to keep Stan's greedy hands out of it. "Are you going to call and tell him about the will?"

"Do I have to?"

"Perhaps you could ask the lawyer to do it."

Elena brightened. "Yes! That's what I'll do. I have an appointment with him tomorrow to go over details and get the probate started. Actually, I feel a little . . . guilty about this. I know Miles and Stan had a problem or disagreement or something, but Stan is Miles's only living relative, and they'd probably have patched things up if Miles had lived longer."

"Miles must have given it a lot of thought, or he wouldn't have gone to the trouble of making out the new will. Perhaps he figured that since you'd be getting married soon, he'd just do the will a little ahead of time."

"But Stan may think I persuaded Miles to do this. That I—what do they call it?—that I unduly influenced him." She paused. "Maybe he even thinks I *killed* him, so I could inherit whatever Miles had. But I didn't! I didn't know anything about Miles having a will written, and I didn't kill him! I loved him. I still love him."

I had another uneasy thought. Would this new information influence the murder investigation? Learning Elena inherited everything certainly wouldn't *reduce* police suspicion about her, and her claim that she knew nothing about the provisions of the will before Miles's death probably couldn't be substantiated.

Ever curious, I also had to wonder, how much of an estate was there? Enough to inspire murder? Of course, whatever the size of the estate, that didn't mean Elena had done the murder. If Stan thought he was going to inherit everything, and he might know more about Miles's assets than Elena did, there was still big reason to suspect *him*.

I stuffed my curiosity about size of the estate into a narrower question. "Did Miles own property other than the townhouse?"

"I have no idea."

True? I didn't want to be suspicious of Elena. I *wasn't* suspicious of her. And yet . . . I dumped that entire line of thought as if it were a coughed-up hairball. "Well, now if you want to go over and look around the townhouse again, you certainly don't need Stan's permission. You could retrieve your sandals."

"No, I don't need to go over again. I found—" She broke off sharply. "I found that photo I wanted. And the Bible."

The reference to finding the Bible still sounded like an afterthought to me, and I guessed she'd also found something other than the photo, the something she was really after, whatever it was. The identity of that *something* was apparently not information she intended to share with me.

"Okay, then, I'm going on out to the motorhome," I said briskly. "Let us know if you need anything, okay? I'll check on you tomorrow before your appointment. Maybe Felicity and Fancy can get acquainted with Koop later tomorrow."

"Maybe. If they ever come out of hiding. But maybe they don't like it here," she said gloomily. "Maybe they don't like *me.*"

**

By morning, however, when I went over to check on Elena and the cats, the situation had changed from gloom to glee.

"Sometime in the night they both came and got in bed with me," she reported happily. "And now look at them!"

Felicity was stalking a moth fluttering in a patch of sunlight coming through a living room window. Fancy sat on the open rolltop desk and eyed a cup filled with pens and pencils. Then, with delicate precision, she reached out a paw and pushed the cup off the edge of the desk. She looked down as the cup thudded to the carpet, her tail twitching as pencils bounced and scattered. She looked up and saw me watching her, and then, all innocence, started washing the paw that had done the deed.

Elena had chosen older cats because she thought they'd be less rowdy than younger ones, more suitable for an older lady such as herself, but these two didn't seem to have read the memo about sedentary older cats.

"Did you see that? She did that deliberately." Elena sounded indignant, and I thought she was going to be really angry, but she broke into a smile instead. "It makes me think about that old joke about how we know the world isn't flat."

"Cats prove the world is round?" I asked doubtfully.

"Of course. If the earth was flat, cats would have pushed everything off it by now." She giggled and made not a word of complaint as she retrieved everything Fancy had spilled. "They're so curious about everything! I left a drawer open and one or both of them got into it and dragged out the bottom of my bikini and two bras. It looked as if there'd been a . . . a burlesque show in there! One of them crawled in the dryer and pulled out a couple of socks. Oh, I just love them both!"

"Okay, great. We'll see you when you get back from your appointment with the lawyer."

"Would you mind coming over once or twice while I'm gone and checking on them? They have food and water, but I don't have any idea how long I'll be gone. I wouldn't want anything to, you know, happen to them."

I couldn't imagine anything happening to the cats here in the house, although I couldn't say as much for any breakables that might be sitting around on shelves or tables. "I'll check on them," I assured her.

Which I did. I came over about a half hour later. Fancy was in the closet inspecting Elena's shoes. Felicity was exploring under a pillow, only her tail sticking out. Nothing broken yet.

I came back again about an hour later. This time I didn't spot either cat but something lay in the middle of the bedroom floor. Something all wrinkled and ugly. I walked around it cautiously. Ugh. Some unfortunate little creature they'd found and killed?

Perhaps that suggested Elena wouldn't have to worry about a mouse problem from now on. Or anything bigger, either, because this wrinkled, ugly thing was bigger than a mouse.

I got a paper towel from the kitchen and gingerly used my foot to nudge the thing onto the towel. Elena came in through the front door as I was carrying it to the trash can in the kitchen. It didn't look as much like a dead creature now, at least not any dead creature I'd ever seen, but I had no idea what it was.

She looked startled. I thought she'd ask *What is that?* But she didn't. She asked, "Where'd you get that?"

"I think it's something the cats caught—"

She astonished me by dropping her purse and grabbing the thing and stretching it out. I could see now that it wasn't some dead creature after all, that it looked almost like a garish human face, and it was my turn to ask, "What *is* that?"

"Nothing! Nothing at all." She wadded the thing into a ball and dashed to her bedroom.

I followed and found her stuffing the wadded ball on a closet shelf. I had to ask again, "What is that thing?"

She sighed and pulled the thing off the closet shelf. She also went to the jacket she'd been wearing yesterday, which was now lying on the floor. The cats had half dragged something out of a pocket. It looked a lot like the other thing. *Two* ugly, wrinkled things.

She went to a mirror hanging on the bedroom wall and pulled one of the things over her face and head.

The thing didn't fit exactly right, but she'd turned into an old man. A wrinkled, leathery-faced old man! She yanked the thing off and balled it up in her hands again. "It's a mask. A silicone mask. Custom made. They're both masks. I had them in my jacket pocket."

"This is what you got from Miles's townhouse yesterday. What you went there looking for."

"Yes."

"Why?"

"Because I didn't want the police to find them."

Why?

"Because I think . . . Miles was a bank robber."

CHAPTER 12

IVY

I think Miles was a bank robber.

For a moment I couldn't think of any suitable response to that unlikely statement, but finally I said, "What makes you think that?"

"And I may have been an accomplice bank robber," she added. "Or accessory. Or something like that."

"Maybe we'd better go sit down while you tell me about this."

"Are you going to tell the police?"

"Well . . ."

"Because that's why I wanted to get the masks out of the townhouse. So the police wouldn't find them. Because Miles is *dead,* and there's no point in bringing up . . . unnecessary details about his life now."

Robbing banks struck me as a bit more than an *unnecessary detail* about a life, but I confined my comment at the moment to "Umm."

Elena picked up the purse she'd dropped. I saw now that there were some legal-looking papers sticking out of it. "The lawyer gave me a copy of the will." She sounded almost absentminded about it.

She brought the masks along when we went to sit in the living room. She draped them over her knees, and it now looked as if each knee had sprouted some strange malignant growth. With a floppy nose sticking out of it.

"Okay, start at the beginning," I said.

"I'm not sure where the beginning is," Elena muttered.

"Start with the masks, then. Where did Miles get them?"

"In Hong Kong. They're custom made and expensive, and it takes several weeks to get one made. He ordered them when he was there working one cruise trip and picked them up on the next trip."

Not an impulse purchase then. Had we been barking up the wrong crime tree here? Miles hadn't been conning cruise ladies; he was robbing banks? The thought made me feel oddly light-headed, as if I'd stepped into some alternate universe where nice older ladies living in small-town USA have mask-wearing boyfriends who rob banks.

"He was planning way back then to become a bank robber and use them as a disguise?" I asked.

"I think the bank robbing came later. Not long after I first met him, we were at his townhouse looking at some photos taken on the cruises. Sometimes the crew did little skits for the passengers, and there was this wrinkled, bent old man in one of the photos. I asked how in the world had *that* man ever gotten a job on the ship. He looked as if he could barely shuffle around. Then Miles laughed and said that was *him*. He went and got the masks and put one on to show me, and it . . . completely transformed him." She shook her head as if the change still dumbfounded her.

"It wasn't like a cheap little face mask you buy at a store. This mask clung to his skin and actually turned him into a wrinkled old man. He used a different voice when he was wearing it, and walked bent over, and if I hadn't known it was him, I'd have thought it was another person entirely. He said making masks as good as these was considered a real art by people in the business. But he put some acting into it too."

The masks now seemed to stare at me through empty eye holes. Not in a kindly way. I tried not to stare back. But my gaze kept drifting that way.

"So what makes you think he decided to use these masks for robbing banks?"

"I went with him to this little town up north of Sacramento—"

"He invited you to go bank robbing with him?"

"No, no, no. Of course not! Actually, he was quite reluctant for me to go along. He said it was a business trip and I'd just be bored.

But I persisted, and finally he took me along. When we got there we drove around for a while, and then he parked the car on a side street and we walked to a little café with a few chairs and tables outside. It was cool and windy for sitting outside, and we were the only people out there. He went inside to order and came back with a hot mocha latte with whipped cream on top for each of us. He took a couple of sips of his, then looked at his watch and said it was time for his business appointment and he'd be back in a few minutes."

While she was telling me this, one of the cats unexpectedly appeared and jumped up beside her on the sofa. She was so delighted that she momentarily seemed to forget all about masks and bank robbing and started trying to entice the cat into her lap. But Fancy was more interested in a mask on Elena's knee and kept batting at it, with a few hisses thrown in.

I tried to get Elena back on track. "You were saying, you waited for Miles at this outdoor café—?"

"Yes. He wasn't gone long. He came back around the corner really fast, skidding almost. He yanked off his jacket and sat on it and started drinking the latte as if he were dying of thirst. A minute or two later sirens blasted all around us, and then cops were running everywhere. One even stopped and asked if we'd seen an old man run through there. Miles said no, we hadn't seen anyone like that, and the cop said be careful, that the guy was armed and dangerous. And then a young guy came out of the café and looked up the street and said someone had tried to rob the bank on the next street over."

"And you thought then that was what Miles had been doing when he said he had a business appointment? He'd been robbing a bank?"

"Right at that moment, I had no idea what was going on. But then, after the cop ran by, Miles pulled a gun out of his jacket pocket. I think he wanted to get rid of it in case the cop came back."

"So what did he do with it?"

"We ate it."

Now I felt as if I had both feet in that alternate universe. I repeated what she'd said. "Miles robbed a bank, and you ate the gun."

"It wasn't a real robbery because he didn't get any money. And it wasn't a real gun." She sounded impatient. "Miles wouldn't use something that might actually go off and hurt someone. It was a *chocolate* gun. A piece broke off when he sat on the jacket, and then he broke it into more little chunks. I was just eating the last piece when two more cops ran by. They also asked if we'd seen an old man and Miles again said we hadn't. Then we wiped chocolate off our fingers and strolled back to the car and came home."

Fancy made a sudden move, snatched a wrinkled mask off Elena's knee, and raced down the hall with it. I went after her and grabbed the mask away from her. It felt odd in my hands, slithery, almost *alive*. I carried it back to the rocking chair where I'd been sitting and tossed it back to Elena. She spread it over her knee again. It had a rip in it now.

"Did you and Miles discuss this on the drive home?"

She shook her head. "Miles didn't volunteer a word of information or explanation, and I didn't ask any questions. But a few days later he told me about Miranda rights. In case I were ever arrested, he said. Then I went to the library. They have newspapers from all over the state, and I looked at some issues from that town we'd been to. There was a picture in it, on the front page. A surveillance camera had taken a photo of the bank robber."

"Miles?"

"Someone who looked just like that photo of Miles in the mask in the skit on the cruise ship."

"Was the person in the newspaper photo carrying a chocolate gun?"

"It looks like a real gun in the photo. People in the bank no doubt thought it was real. But it *wasn't*. You can buy them on the internet, you know. Chocolate daggers and hand grenades too. Even skulls."

I could probably eat a chocolate gun. I've eaten chocolate Easter bunnies. But a chocolate skull? No way.

"What did the newspaper have to say about the bank robbery?"

"It wasn't really a *robbery* because he didn't actually get any money," she said again, as if she wanted to make sure that point got through to me. "The article said the robber demanded money but the

117

teller asked him what denomination of bills he wanted, and he said whatever you have, and then she asked him did he want the money in a bag or envelope. And the robber must have then realized the teller was stalling because she'd buzzed for help or something, and he ran off without getting anything. So it wasn't really a bank robbery," Elena repeated.

I suspected that not actually getting any money didn't cancel the criminality of holding a gun on a bank teller and demanding money. Even if it was a chocolate gun.

"The newspaper quoted the bank teller as saying the robber was a very polite old man. They were calling him the Geezer Gunslinger and treating the whole thing as if it were mostly a joke."

I doubted the police were amused. I was uncertain about Elena's culpability in all this. Was she an accomplice or accessory? Is there a special penalty in the world of crime and punishment for eating evidence?

"Do you think this was the only time Miles ever did this?"

Elena shook her head. "I think that's what he was doing on those trips he took. He went to far-off places and robbed banks."

"Real bank robberies in which he got real money."

"It was probably just having me along that made everything different that day. I shouldn't have insisted on going with him."

She sounded more sorry about her presence sabotaging that day's bank robbery than sorry about Miles's Geezer Gunslinger career in general.

"You'd said earlier that he owned a real gun. A Glock. Maybe he used that on his out-of-town bank robberies when you weren't along."

She shook her head vigorously. "Miles wasn't that kind of man. He wouldn't want to take a chance on someone getting hurt. Besides, I don't think it's legal to carry a gun on a plane flight."

I couldn't imagine Miles had been too concerned about that illegality if the basic purpose of the trip was bank robbery.

Had the police taken the Glock when they searched his townhouse? There must be a list somewhere of what they'd taken.

That was one of the requirements of a search warrant. Or did they even need a warrant to search a dead victim's home?

"Apparently he was pretty good at robbing banks," she added. "He never got caught."

Which made me wonder about something else. Didn't banks, in preparation for a possible bank robbery, keep a ready stash of cash booby-trapped with a dye pack that would go off and stain money, robber, and anything else nearby? And what about serial numbers; didn't banks keep track of them so the stolen money could be identified if someone tried to use it? Had Miles figured out some way to circumvent these problems? Or was he just lucky?

"Why do you think he started robbing banks?" I asked. "Did he need money?"

"I don't know. He seemed to live comfortably, but he certainly wasn't some big spender. But he said something once about needing to pay off some debts from the past. I think he wanted to get them paid off before we got married. He said that after we were married he wouldn't be making any more business trips, which I see now was the same as saying he wasn't going to do any more bank robbing." She suddenly jumped up and wadded the masks together. "In any case, he's dead now and none of this *matters*."

I had another thought. Had Miles, wearing a mask and tweed cap, made a trial run to the bakery where Nicole worked, figuring if the disguise could fool her it would surely fool anyone? Bank employees and witnesses would never be able to connect silver-fox-looking Miles with the wrinkled old man demanding money and waving a gun at them. Except that with Nicole he'd made the mistake of wearing that identifiable ruby ring, a mistake he probably didn't make again.

In an abrupt change of subject, Elena said, "Let's make some pies."

"What about the masks?"

"I'll burn them in the barbecue later. For now—" She disappeared down the hallway, and I presumed she was temporarily stashing the masks some place where Felicity and Fancy couldn't drag them out again.

So I peeled apples and Elena made pie crusts and chattered about the cats and how nice it was to have them around and how her mother made green tomato pies that tasted like apple pie. "As long as they were warm. When they got cold, they were just green tomatoes." She wrinkled her nose at the memory of cold green tomato pie. I mentioned that fried green tomatoes were quite tasty. We went on to talk about possible health food additions to pies.

Just everyday conversation between two little old ladies making pies. No mention of that alternate universe in which one little old lady helped eat a chocolate gun after an attempted bank robbery.

Mac brought Koop over and we let the three cats get acquainted while the pies baked and gave off tantalizing scents of apples and cinnamon. The two calicos were a bit wary of Koop, but not hostile. Then we ate warm apple pie and ice cream, and Elena gave each of the cats a spoonful of ice cream. Again, all very ordinary.

Except I couldn't stop thinking about what wasn't ordinary at all: a murdered boyfriend who robbed banks. Using a chocolate gun. The thought occurred to me that perhaps that verse in the Bible that said *You shall not steal* did have special significance for Miles, that it covered something he'd done. And there were no footnotes saying that using a chocolate gun altered the commandment in any way.

Now I also had to wonder, did Miles's late-in-life career as a Geezer Gunslinger have something to do with his murder? If Miles was robbing banks, perhaps the matter of who killed him had a much wider scope than we'd been thinking. Our thinking had centered primarily around Stan and possibly cruise ladies. But if Miles had encroached on a territory that some big-time criminals figured belonged to them, would they have retaliated by ordering a hit on him? Were we dealing with a paid killer here, a professional outside our small list of suspects?

Mac was just starting on a second piece of pie when the doorbell rang. Elena glanced out the window and gave a little gasp. I looked out too. Police at the door. Four of them.

Our pie-and-ice-cream party screeched to a halt. This did not look like a friendly group collecting for a policemen's charity.

CHAPTER 13

MAC

The calicos scurried down the hallway when Elena opened the front door. Ivy and I stood at the kitchen doorway as the four officers entered the living room. They came in like a *Star Wars* invading force, rather at odds with the homey scent of apples and cinnamon. Koop wasn't frightened by them, but I picked him up so he wouldn't be in the middle of whatever this was.

I recognized the one handing Elena an official-looking paper as Officer Hutchinson of wet-blotch fame. Behind him the younger officer still eagerly bounced on his toes. If physical exams for officers test for toe strength, I'd guess this officer could lift barbells with his.

The officers spread out through the house. Elena came back to the kitchen, and we all sat down at the breakfast nook. Having four police officers prowling through the premises was a little distracting, but it didn't keep me from going back to my second piece of apple pie. Elena studied the paper in her hand. I suspected what it was. She confirmed my guess.

"It's a search warrant."

"Searching for what?" Ivy asked. "They can't just come in and dig around hoping to find something incriminating. They have to tell you what they're looking for."

"A handgun. And ammunition."

"Nothing else?" Ivy asked, and I wondered what she had in mind. Specifying a handgun allowed them to look anywhere an item of that size might be located or hidden. If they found evidence other than a handgun and ammunition in the search, they could take that also, but they couldn't go poking around in spaces too small to hold the items specified in the search warrant. I figured *ammunition* gave them a fair amount of leeway. They could look for a single bullet in any kind of space larger than a thimble.

"I wonder what makes them think you have a gun. You said you didn't tell them. Is the gun registered to you?" Ivy whispered.

Elena shook her head. "I don't think so. Miles bought it and gave it to me, and I never did anything about registering it. Someone must have told them about the gun." She looked up, her eyes squinting as if she were calculating something. I thought she was thinking about who may have tipped them off about her gun, but her mind was on a different agenda.

"Actually, to be accurate," she said, "I *had* a gun. We all looked for it, remember? And couldn't find it. So, like I told them when I was questioned at the station, I don't really *have* a gun."

I thought, from a legal standpoint, there was probably a hole the size of the Pentagon in that reasoning.

"They may be a while," Ivy said. "Shall we go outside or over to the motorhome while they do the search?"

"The officer said we can't follow them around and watch what they're doing. No interfering. But we aren't required to leave." Elena squirmed against the padded seat under her, as if she were digging in for a long haul. "I'm staying right here."

Ivy patted Elena's hand. "Everything's going to be okay." Although she gave me a glance, and I knew what she was thinking. It would have been better if Elena had told them about the gun to begin with. Now if they found it, an unregistered gun . . .

But they couldn't find a gun, of course. There was no gun here. We'd *looked*. Which still didn't mean she didn't *own* a gun, of course, wherever it was.

We sat and waited. Bouncing Toes came in and searched the kitchen. I don't think it is required, but, after not finding gun or ammunition, he put everything neatly back in place. Elena offered him a piece of pie. He looked rather longingly at the apple pie left on the table but made a comment about being on duty and dutifully declined.

After he left the kitchen to continue the search elsewhere, Elena restlessly got up several times to peer out the kitchen door. We could hear them moving things in the bedrooms. Once the toilet flushed, which reminded me that lawbreakers often think the water tank of a toilet is a fine hiding place. Cops would never look there. Except they always do.

Koop also got restless, and I finally took him back to the motorhome, then took BoBandy out for a short walk. When I went back to the house, an officer at the door wouldn't let me enter. It felt like what my oldest grandson said about events at their high school these days; if you left, that was it. No reentry. I protested, but the officer wouldn't negotiate.

So, like a shut-out teenager, I sat on a chair on the front patio. The windchimes tinkled gently when officers went past carrying plastic baggies, but I couldn't tell what the bags held. The neighbor I'd talked to, the one who'd claimed he had important information about vehicles the night of the murder, walked by with his dog. He craned his neck so hard looking this way that he actually stumbled off the side of the road. After a while, Ivy and Elena came out and sat with me. The yard light came on as dark approached.

Eventually Officer Hutchinson and the other officers also came out. He handed Elena another paper. "This is a list of the items removed from the house."

Elena murmured a polite thanks. We waited until all the officers got in their squad cars and drove away before going back inside. Elena looked at the paper, then handed it to me. It was a printed form, signed by Officer Hutchinson. Handwritten on one of the blank lines was the information that one .38 caliber Smith and Wesson Special, with a long serial number, and one full box (fifty cartridges) of .38 caliber Magtech ammunition, plus another partial box of seventeen cartridges, had been removed from the house.

How had they found a gun when we couldn't find it?

"Does this mean they'll charge me with some crime for not telling them about the gun when I was questioned?" Elena asked.

"I don't know." Actually, I figured not telling about the gun was the least of Elena's worries. The big worry was, what would the gun tell them? Did they have a bullet from Miles's body with which to compare test shots from the gun?

"I wonder where they found the gun and ammunition," Ivy said. "I thought we'd looked everywhere."

The form didn't say. Apparently they don't have to tell you that detail. But I also thought we'd looked everywhere. I know I'd looked in the toilet tank. Had the gun and ammunition actually been in the house when we made our search and we just hadn't found them? Or had someone more recently made them available to be found?

Ivy also looked at the form and, with a glance at Elena, made what struck me as an irrelevant comment. "No masks."

Elena nodded. "No masks." She sounded pleased.

I felt rather like a male customer at a cosmetics counter, where the conversation is all woman-speak, and a man has no idea what is being said. But Ivy, when we got back to the motorhome, gave me the full story about Miles, masks, bank robbing, and a chocolate gun. We were already thunderstruck by the finding of the gun by the police, and now Ivy had given me this new and startling information about Miles to think about.

"The masks surely wouldn't have been hard to find when the officers were searching," Ivy said. "I don't think Elena actually hid them. She's planning to burn them."

"Which means they probably found the masks but didn't think they had any relevance to Miles's murder."

"They could be wrong."

After what Ivy had just told me about Miles and masks and bank robbery, that was my thought too. She also brought up a possibility we hadn't considered before: a paid assassin as the killer because Miles's bank robbing may have encroached on the territory of some professional criminals and they'd managed to track him down.

And where did that put us, if we were rummaging around in murder committed by hit-man professionals?

**

IVY

Next morning Elena let the cats out in the backyard. They wandered around, cautiously exploring, and I suspected that at one time they'd been strictly indoor cats and weren't familiar with the outdoors. Elena brought out some knitting to work on while she kept an eye on the cats. She was making stocking caps to donate to some children's charity, certainly a worthy endeavor. It made me think, as I have before, that perhaps I should take up some similar worthwhile activity. Past experience has not been encouraging, however. My Thumb of Death with plants seems to extend to such activities as knitting and crocheting. I don't believe a knit scarf is supposed to bear a strong resemblance to an oversized toadstool.

So all I was doing at the moment was sitting under the motorhome canopy with Koop in my lap, which, from his point of view, probably qualified as a worthwhile activity. Mac was cleaning out a storage compartment on the underside of the motorhome, BoBandy "helping."

A lovely, quiet morning, murder and bank robbing far away.

Until Stan's unexpected appearance hit the backyard like an avalanche of toadstools.

"I rang the doorbell but no one answered." His hostile stare and tone lifted the statement to accusation level, as if we were deliberately hiding from him. He didn't waste time with small-talk pleasantries about the nice weather.

"I had a call from your lawyer," he snapped at Elena. "He asked me to come in and see him. Which I did. Congratulations. You latched onto everything, didn't you? Very clever."

Elena managed to ignore the snide attack and kept knitting, although I wondered if Stan realized those knitting needles in her hands might qualify as lethal weapons. And Elena was known to be unpredictable. But she merely said, "I don't have a lawyer. You must have heard from Miles's lawyer."

"Whatever. He made it plain enough. Everything in *my uncle's* estate goes to you."

His emphasis proclaimed the righteous power of a blood relationship and that Elena had stolen what was rightfully his.

"Why, yes, I believe that is what the will says," Elena said pleasantly as she switched to a different-colored yarn. The stocking cap she was working on was striped red and white. Some child would love it.

"In spite of how you've managed to manipulate the will, it was to *me*, as next of kin, that the authorities returned his personal possessions yesterday."

"The items that were on his body?"

"Yes. His wallet and a white handkerchief. Some change he had in his pocket. A smooth black stone."

"Miles called it a rubbing stone. He kept it in his pocket and liked to rub it now and then. He said it was supposed to bring good luck."

"No ruby ring?" I asked. I also wondered, was it a clean handkerchief or a used one? Irrelevant, of course, but I guess I liked thinking that Stan was stuck with nothing more than a sneezed-on handkerchief as his inheritance.

Stan looked at me. I don't think he'd even noticed my presence until then. The invisible little old lady thing at work. "Miles apparently wasn't wearing a ring when they brought his body in. But I remember a ring now." His venomous gaze shifted back to Elena. "It's probably in the townhouse. Something else you can latch on to."

I wasn't surprised that Miles wasn't wearing the ring when he was killed. He probably hadn't worn it since Nicole recognized it on the wrinkled old man who'd been in the bakery.

"They also called me, as next of kin, to say the body will be released tomorrow. I'm having it picked up by Anderson Mortuary."

"That sounds like a good choice," Elena said agreeably.

"We'll have the funeral at that church over on Hillside Boulevard."

That was the big church we'd seen when Elena guided us on a tour of the town. Probably the most elegant and elaborate church in the area, the one she'd called "intimidating." I waited for her to object, but she just kept knitting.

None of my business, of course, but I asked a question. "That's the church you and Saundra attend?"

"We've been there," he snapped, and I guessed what that meant. C&E churchgoers. Never miss a Christmas and Easter. "We'll notify the newspaper about the service, of course. And put up a notice in the community center at Sunshine Valley. We'll notify the local senior groups too. Saundra knows a man who has recorded several gospel songs, and she'll contact him about a solo for the service. The church has a social room we can use for a gathering and dinner afterward. I'm thinking a buffet from The Homestead. I'll say a few words."

"Some dancing clowns?" Elena muttered. "Maybe cheerleaders in angel costumes?" I think Stan was too busy with his grandiose plans to hear her snarky comments, and what she said in a more audible tone was something else entirely. "That sounds very nice, but Miles's will is quite specific. He said his body is to be cremated and his ashes scattered wherever I think appropriate. No services."

"No services? You can't be serious!"

"Didn't the lawyer show you the will?" Elena asked.

"Just the portion that . . . applied to me." He ran a finger around his collar, as if it felt a little tight.

"I'll do what Miles wanted." Elena didn't sound so much stubborn as immovable. "I can show you a copy of the complete will, if you'd like."

"I can contest the will, you know. I can tie it up for weeks. Maybe years."

"You'd postpone putting him to rest just to have a fancy *funeral*?"

He hesitated momentarily. "No, of course not. I don't think what you intend is proper, but apparently you're in control." His tone was stiff enough to cut through bricks.

"It's what Miles wanted."

"I can still contest the will about his leaving everything to you."

"I'm sure you know some excellent lawyers who will be happy to do that." Then, surprising me, she added, "Was there something in particular you wanted?"

Stan gritted his teeth, a teeth-gritting that would no doubt bring joy to any dentist scouting for new customers. "Yes, actually there is," he finally said. I was thinking *townhouse, SUV, bank accounts,* but what he said in a controlled tone was, "At one time Miles was working on some family history, a genealogy thing. I'd like to look through the townhouse and see if I could find the information he'd collected. I don't think it would have any value for you, but it's important as my family history."

"That sounds reasonable enough," Elena said, and my feelings toward Stan also warmed by a few degrees. This *was* a reasonable enough request, even a rather heartwarming one. He cared about family. "When would you like to do it?"

He looked startled. She might have said something she had every right to say. *You want in the townhouse? When pigs fly and cats send emails.* But Elena is a good-hearted woman, not given to snark or denying a reasonable request.

"I drove by there," Stan said. "The yellow tape has been removed. So how about this afternoon?"

"That's fine with me. I'll meet you there at, say, one o'clock?"

After Stan left . . . without, I noted, asking Elena when or where she intended to scatter the ashes . . . I asked Elena if she'd like me to go with her to the townhouse to meet Stan, but she said no, that she could handle this alone. I nodded, but by then my warmed attitude toward Stan had cooled considerably, and suspicions returned. My friend Magnolia is fascinated by genealogy; she and husband Geoff will drive halfway across the country to find a third cousin twice removed. But Stan didn't strike me as a man who cared about third cousins or their removal status.

What, exactly, was Stan up to now?

CHAPTER 14

IVY

Elena left for the townhouse immediately after lunch. I asked if she wanted me to check on the cats while she was gone, but she thought they'd settled in comfortably now. Mac, who still writes occasional articles for travel magazines, wanted to visit the local library to check out background material on an old ghost town east of San Isolde. I thought, with a considerable lack of enthusiasm, that it was time to tackle the postponed task of cleaning the stove.

Happily, Mac and I compromised. We cleaned the stove together, using my trusty, old-fashioned mixture of baking soda and vinegar, and then went to the library together. The library, also old-fashioned, had a blocky, tan-brick exterior, with lion statues—one paw missing—guarding the front steps, but the nicely up-to-date computer system made finding the information Mac wanted easy. However, as is usual in a library, we both got sidetracked into other subjects: Mac into information about a local woodworking artist who specialized in carving bears, me into some interesting material about ordinary household materials used as poisons. Nothing I needed at the moment, but you never know when you might run into a poisoner, right? I photocopied some of the pages and, back home, stuck them in my *Poisons* file.

Elena was already home, and I went over to ask her how the meeting with Stan had gone. She was sitting at the dining room table with papers . . . stapled papers, folded papers, paper-clipped papers . . . looking as if she'd been caught in a paperwork pandemic.

"Did Stan find the genealogical material he said he was looking for?" I asked.

"No. It's probably in the file cabinet they removed." She paused. "If it exists. I don't remember Miles ever mentioning any interest in genealogy. We talked once about doing those DNA tests that are supposed to tell you about your ancestors, but we never got around to doing it."

"Do you think Stan may have been hoping to find something other than genealogical information?" I asked cautiously. I didn't want to suggest anything that would raise her hackles about Stan if their relationship was on better footing now. He was, after all, her last connection with Miles. And maybe my suspicions of him were unfair.

"No. Well, maybe . . . oh, I don't know." She threw up her hands in frustration. "I don't trust him. But then, I don't think he trusts me either. I'm pretty sure he still thinks I coaxed . . . or pressured . . . Miles into leaving everything to me. He may even think I killed Miles."

"Did you mention to him that the police had been here to search the house?"

"No. He did ask if Miles had kept papers or anything here. I suppose he was thinking the genealogical information might be here."

"Could what he wants be in these papers you're looking at?"

"These are all financial records I got out of Miles's desk. Paid bills and bank statements and credit card statements. I brought it all home so I could go through everything. He kept them from a long time back."

"Are you looking for anything in particular?"

"I'm wondering about money from the bank robberies. What did he do with it? I don't see any big deposits of cash."

Banks have to report oversized deposits of cash, so I wasn't surprised Miles hadn't put the money in the bank. Had the police located any hidden stashes of cash when they searched the townhouse? Or had he handled it in some more sophisticated, money-laundering way?

"I did find this." She reached into her purse on the floor beside her and brought up a roll of bills encased in a rubber band. "But this is money Miles told me about. Five thousand dollars he kept hidden in an old pair of slippers in case of emergency. His ruby ring was in there too." She placed the ring on the table beside the roll of bills.

Had the searching officers found this money and left it there? Or had they not found it at all? I wasn't sure Elena had a legal right to the money or the ring before the will was probated. But then, I wasn't sure she *didn't* have a right to either item, so I kept my thoughts to myself.

"I'll be glad to help you look through all these papers, if you'd like."

"You're always so helpful, Ivy. I don't know what I'd do if you and Mac weren't here at such an awful time." She shoved a bunch of credit card statements at me, then grabbed my hand and pressed it against her cheek. "Thank you."

I had that small twinge of guilt that comes when someone offers appreciation for my helpfulness. That mutant curiosity gene doesn't necessarily have noble motives; it is sometimes downright sneaky about combining nosiness with helpfulness.

So I sat down at the table and studied statements from credit card companies. Miles had two credit cards, certainly a modest number considering how many cards some people have. He didn't run up exorbitant bills, and he paid off his balances every month. Studying another person's purchases gives the big picture, but details are lacking because credit card statements don't tell you what items were actually purchased. In the older statement I was looking at, Miles had paid $58.73 by credit card at Walmart, but there was no indication of what items he may have bought. Toothpaste? T-bones? Tweed cap for a bank robbery? Same with Amazon and Home Depot purchases. What he bought at gas stations was obvious enough, as were cable and cell phone charges. But there were several companies I'd never heard of, and I made a note to check them out on the internet later.

Then I realized what I *wasn't* seeing: charges for expenses on those trips he took. He could have used cash for food and lodging, but how did he travel? Had he driven his SUV, as he had for the unsuccessful bank robbery when Elena accompanied him? That seemed unlikely, if he was traveling cross-country for his bank activities. Elena had mentioned his bringing back real maple syrup from one of his trips, and it was a long drive to maple-syrup country. I didn't see any charges from gas stations out of this area. But neither did I see airline charges that we could check on and determine his destination. A careful covering of his tracks?

Although this brought up an alternate thought. If Miles wasn't traveling to do bank robberies, as I was assuming, if he was instead visiting cruise ladies on conning missions, maybe they'd provided airline tickets for him. And maple syrup.

At this point, I was fairly certain sweet Miles was into some kind of criminal enterprise; I just wasn't sure what kind.

After a couple hours, Elena threw up her hands in exasperation. She'd run into the same problem I had. "I always write on a check what it's for, but banks don't return cancelled checks anymore. It's impossible to tell from a figure on the bank statement what he actually bought with the check. You know what I'm really worried about anyway? None of this." She swept her hand across the table, sending a small avalanche of papers tumbling to the floor. Felicity, lurking under the table, skittered away. "It's that gun the police found here. That's what I'm worried about. Do they think I killed Miles with it?"

"They're investigating all aspects of the case." A generic comment, of course. And not nearly as pessimistic as my actual thoughts about the gun were.

She jumped up. "I need to see what the cookies say."

"Elena, don't— Look, I hope you won't be angry with my blunt words, but looking to crumbled cookies for anything is just—" I searched for a proper word and came up with one that I remembered my mother long ago using. "Cockamamie."

"Cockamamie!" Elena huffed. "That's what my mother called romance magazines when she found them hidden under my pillow when I was a girl."

"Cookie crumbs are just cookie crumbs, pure cockamamie, not mystical purveyors of wisdom or prophecy. You'd get more out of the cookies by eating them."

"I want to consult the cookies," Elena insisted stubbornly. "I'm going to call Nicole."

Which she did, and then she said she was going over to Nicole's that evening. "You come with me, and you'll see. The cookie crumbs will know what's going on."

**

So here we were at 7:00, Elena perched on the tall chair at Nicole's table, reaching for a cookie. I wasn't here because I wanted to see what the cookies had to say; I was here because I wasn't sure what unpredictable Elena might do with cookie-crumb cockamamie. I was also questioning myself a bit. It did seem a little . . . well . . . *picky* of me to object so strenuously to something that really wasn't much more than a parlor-game sort of thing. *And that's the way the cookie crumbles* wasn't exactly an invitation to a den of iniquity.

Elena was apparently feeling more belligerent than usual this evening; she fist-hammered a peanut butter cookie with enough force to set off earthquake alarms. Cookie crumbs bounced on the table, the floor, and my feet.

She hadn't given Nicole any indication of what she was after with this session, and Nicole studied the crumbs, including a peer at those on the carpet below, without saying anything. I couldn't see any discernable pattern in them, neither on the table or floor or my shoe; I didn't think Nicole could either.

"The crumbs say you're unhappy with what's going on in your life," Nicole finally said cautiously. She gave me a little sideways glance, and we both knew I put that statement in the *duh* category.

I expected Elena to mention being so sad and unhappy about Miles's death, but what she said was, "I'm more than unhappy. I'm scared."

"Scared that what happened to Miles might also happen to you? That you're in danger?"

Elena's head jerked in surprise, as if this were a possibility that hadn't occurred to her before, as it also hadn't to me. But if a hit man had killed Miles, Nicole might be right; whoever had hired him might come after Elena too.

But Elena put a different spin on it. "Yes, danger! The police came and searched the house. They found my gun."

I didn't want to accuse Nicole of being a shyster, but this was how fortune-tellers worked. They elicited a scrap of information and then built on it. Or, as in Elena's case at the moment, let the client herself build on it.

Nicole tilted her head and studied the crumbs from a different angle. "You know, I do see something here. See this pattern?" She waved her forefinger over a scattering of crumbs. "It's the shape of a man—"

"A police officer?"

"No, not the police, but it is the shape of man with authority. Wait, I see it now! It's a lawyer. The crumbs say there's a lawyer in your future. Because you are in danger."

"Maybe it's the lawyer I've already seen. He told me that Miles made out a will and left everything to me."

Nicole looked surprised. "Really? Good. You deserve it more than Stan does."

The comment sounded sincere, but now another thought tumbled into my head. Could Nicole have thought she'd be included in Miles's will? She was a semi-niece, and he was fond of her. Was that motive enough for Nicole to commit murder?

I didn't think so, but *everybody's a suspect.*

"You should see the lawyer again, this time about the police searching for and finding the gun. And see this arrow here?" Nicole pointed to a blob of crumbs that could, with imagination, be identified as arrow shaped. "That means speed, that you should do it *now*. Don't delay."

Elena nodded slowly. "Okay."

The crumbs "said" a few more things. That Elena should be taking care of her health during this stressful time in her life. That her teeth needed attention. That she should relax with some encouraging reading at bedtime.

"I could read Miles's Bible. I brought it home from his place."

"Miles read the Bible?" Nicole again sounded surprised.

"He was working on reading it all the way through. Maybe I'll do that."

"Good, yes, very good." Nicole nodded. "And don't forget a dental appointment."

Nicole finished the session with her signature closing line: "And that's the way the cookie crumbles."

But afterward, while Elena was carrying a handful of crumbs she'd picked out of the carpet to a trash can in the kitchen, Nicole looked at me and said, "You think my cookie readings are just a lot of foolishness, don't you? In fact, you're quite *hostile* toward them." She sounded a bit hostile herself.

"Not hostile enough to suggest tarring and feathering or burning at the stake, but—"

"Whew." Nicole swiped a hand across her face with exaggerated drama. "That's a relief."

"But I can't say that I'm a . . . supporter. In all honesty, I have to say that reading anything into cookie crumbs is what I once mentioned to Elena. Just a lot of cockamamie."

"Reading crumbs may seem a bit, oh, *frivolous*," Nicole conceded, "but it's really no different than reading tea leaves or palms or bumps on your head, and people have been doing that for—what? Centuries?"

Nicole wasn't in her Ms. Cookie Lady costume this evening, though the little apartment did smell deliciously of cinnamon and vanilla. Fake scents, I reminded myself. Like the fake sounds of canned laughter for a TV show. Nothing was actually cooking. And the cookie crumbs, even if Nicole "interpreted" them to say something helpful, were nothing more than cookie crumbs.

"When I decided I could make a business of this," Nicole said, "I went to several palm and tea-leaf readers to study how they did it. I incorporated some of what I learned from them into my cookie reading. I've read some books too." She managed to make it sound like a learned study of a scientific subject.

"I object to palm reading and tea leaves too," I said. "Also astrology, numerology, crystal balls, and fortune-telling of any kind. Including toenail clippings."

"Toenail clippings? I've never heard of anyone doing readings from *toenail clippings*."

"Neither have I," I admitted. "But I figure doing that makes as much sense as any of those other practices."

"Isn't that rather narrow-minded? Just because *you* don't believe in such methods doesn't mean someone else may not find them helpful. I mean, I'm not doing Elena or anyone else any *harm*. The new cats are good for her, aren't they? And with the police searching for and finding her gun, she's going to need a good lawyer, isn't she?"

"I think you're right about both cats and lawyer. And her seeing a dentist is good advice too. I remember her tooth hurting from eating a hard nut the last time we were here." I lifted my eyebrows, and she shrugged, neither admitting nor denying that this bit of advice came from information Elena herself had provided.

"Actually, I think *you* do sometimes give helpful guidance. But cookie crumbs have nothing to do with it." I don't often get up on my soapbox, but the Bible is the core and foundation of my faith and beliefs, so I jumped right up there, more sure of myself than I'd been when the session began. "The Bible is quite definite about rejecting such practices."

"But I'm not some fanatic unbeliever. I'm certainly no Satan worshipper or something like that! I believe God exists."

Still firmly planted on my soapbox, I said, "But you'd rather trust in crumbled cookies than God."

"The crumbs can be quite accurate. The last cookie reading I did for myself showed a figure of a monkey. That's a very bad omen."

"You do readings for yourself?"

"Of course. Didn't I tell you that one time?"

Doing self-readings wasn't the equivalent of a self-appendectomy, but it suggested she took this quite seriously. "Who decides what's a good omen and what's bad?"

She ignored that question. "And the very next day after I saw the monkey in the crumbs, you called to tell me about Miles." She sounded triumphant, as if this were irrefutable proof of the accuracy of the crumbled-cookies system.

"Several books in the Old Testament mention various objectionable occult practices. Cookie-crumbling may be a very mild form of the occult, but it's still in the neighborhood. Right along with sorcery, witchcraft, casting spells, consulting the dead, using divination, looking at entrails—"

"You're lumping me in with witches? Comparing my looking at cookie crumbs with looking at *entrails*?" Nicole asked indignantly.

Elena had returned and was down on her knees again, picking up more crumbs. "Entrails?" she muttered. "I don't want anything to do with *entrails*."

"Actually, I just don't see what the big objection is," Nicole said. "Though I will stick to cookie crumbs rather than entrails."

"They're all systems of belief that take you away from depending on the Lord and trusting him. They keep you from looking to *him* for guidance. One of the Psalms says, 'I will counsel you with my loving eye on you.' The Lord knows the past, present, and future. We're to look to *him* for counsel."

"But he doesn't always let us in on what he knows."

I have to admit that I've sometimes found that frustrating myself, but I also remind myself that God knows what he's doing, even if I don't. "But that doesn't mean we should give up on looking to *him* for guidance. The cookie crumbs don't know what's going on, but *you* are pretty good at picking up on what people need. What did you study back in college, before you married Stan?"

Nicole looked surprised at the unrelated question. "From the time I was in fourth grade, I wanted to be a teacher. I was having trouble in school and that year I had a teacher, Miss MacMillan, who helped me so much. I wanted to be like her. When my friends were playing with glamour Barbie dolls, I had my one Barbie doll standing in front of a class of teddy bears, teaching them." She smiled and shook her head at that long-ago little girl. "It stuck with me, and in college, before I dropped out to marry Stan, that's what I was studying, elementary education."

"But Stan thought being a teacher was a waste of time," I guessed. "That you could work all your life and never have more than a house in the suburbs and a penny-pinching retirement in your old age."

Nicole smiled wryly. "He also mentioned never being able to afford more than a secondhand car and a vacation at the Dead Pines motel and resort. On Lake Scummy, I believe it was. He preferred a showroom-new Mercedes and a five-star hotel in the Bahamas or Tahiti."

"But Stan is out of the picture now. There's nothing wrong with working in a bakery, but why don't you toss Stan's negative thoughts and be what you wanted to be pre-Stan? I think you could become a very good teacher. You must have thought about doing this."

"Sure, I've thought about it." She shrugged. "But I'd have to go back to college. How could I possibly do that? It'd be like jumping off a cliff without a parachute. I wouldn't have enough money to get past the first month of classes. And you'd obviously frown on my crumbling a few cookies for guidance about how to do it."

"You might talk to a college counselor about it," I said.

I thought Nicole was going to make some other sarcastic remark, but she just gave a tired sigh.

"Think about it," I urged.

"There are loans and grants," Nicole finally said slowly. "Going to school part-time and continuing to work part-time. Maybe taking some classes online. I might be able to manage it." After a long pause, she said, "I think I'd like to be able to manage it."

CHAPTER 15

IVY

"I hope Nicole does go back to college," Elena said as we drove home, which sounded like a thoughtful consideration of Nicole's future until she added, "She could probably do Cookie Lady readings at college to help pay for it." Then, in an abrupt change of subject, she asked, "Do *you* think I should have a lawyer?"

"It wouldn't hurt to have someone lined up, just in case."

"Just in case," Elena echoed. "In case *what*?"

"In case ballistics tests show the gun found in your house was the gun used to kill Miles."

"But how could it be?"

I couldn't answer that, but I had a jittery feeling about the disappearing/reappearing gun. I also wondered what had prompted the authorities to search for it in Elena's house. But I answered a question she hadn't asked. "That lawyer you talked with about the will may not handle criminal cases, but he can probably refer you to someone who does."

"But tests should prove that my gun *didn't* kill Miles," she argued. Then she turned her arguments back on herself. "But I suppose, if the cookie crumbs say I need a lawyer, then I should—"

"Elena, don't base important decisions on cookie crumbs!"

"But you're telling me the same thing. Get a lawyer."

True. I felt as if I'd tumbled into a cookie whirlpool, and crumbs were zapping me from all directions.

"Do you think consulting the cookie crumbs is *evil*?" Elena asked.

"On a scale of good and evil, they probably aren't up there with the really evil evils. But the Bible definitely speaks against using divination, like the entrails."

"Okay, I agree. Entrails are out. But it doesn't mention cookie crumbs, does it?"

"No. But that's like setting up rules for children. You can't think of *everything* to tell them not to do. I remember back when I was a librarian, and we had a jar of cookies for the kids at story time. I told them not to get into the cookie jar before the story, that we'd give out the cookies later and everyone would get one. That seems plain enough, doesn't it?"

Elena made a noncommittal grunt/grumble.

"But one little boy saw that as meaning if the cookie jar tipped over and some cookies spilled out, there was nothing wrong with grabbing them. Because we hadn't mentioned anything about cookies from *tipped-over* cookie jars. So he nudges the jar, and over it goes, and he grabs a handful. But, as he pointed out to us, he didn't get *into* the jar to get any cookies."

"And your point is?" Elena muttered. "Outside of the possibility this kid might grow up to be a lawyer charging big bucks for that kind of thinking?"

"God doesn't specifically spell out every possible variation on his words against divination and fortune-telling and the occult. Or various other sins."

"God thinks we're like little kids then," Elena suggested. "Always trying to find a sneaky way around the rules."

"We *are* all God's children, and all too often we do tend to act like . . . sneaky kids."

"So you talk directly to God about everything, and he, in a big voice booming out of heaven, tells you exactly what to do?" she challenged. "'Ivy, that toenail polish looks like rotten tomatoes on your toes. Use a nice peachy-pink instead.' Or, 'Ivy, go to San Isolde and help that weird woman with the dead boyfriend.'"

"God has never spoken to me in a big, booming voice," I had to admit, and I'd never consulted him about toenail polish. But maybe I should. Would that Midnight Blue look as sophisticated on me as it does on that model in the magazine? Or would it just look as if I were beginning to mold, like old bread, starting with my toenails? "Sometimes you have to look for the Lord's message in words in the Bible or a message in a sermon that just 'happens' to apply to your situation. You have to pray about things. God speaks to you in various ways, maybe through circumstances or simply by putting a thought in your head."

"Why not through cookie crumbs, then?" Elena said. Elena, I thought with some frustration, would have been a tipper-over of cookie jars.

"If cookie crumbs, why not toenail clippings?" I countered. "Or the shapes the hairs make when a few stick to the bottom of the sink or shower after you wash your hair? Or the way the taco chips fall in the bowl when you pour them out of the sack? Or the shapes the bubbles form when you take a bubble bath? I grew a tomato once that looked like President Nixon. Do you think that was a significant message?"

Elena gave that a thoughtful tilt of her head. "I tried growing potatoes a long time ago. They didn't do very well, and three of them looked really creepy, like little shrunken heads. I thought that might be a prediction of some coming calamity." She gave a big sigh. "But nothing happened, so maybe the potatoes just grew in creepy shapes because I forgot to water them."

**

The following day we went over to Miles's townhouse and picked up several more boxes, and then Elena called her dentist to make an appointment for her hurting tooth. She also called the lawyer who'd written Miles's will for a referral to a lawyer who handled criminal cases. She made an appointment to see the other lawyer the following week. She wrote his name, Mark Harlowe, phone number, and the appointment time on a scrap of paper and propped it against the salt shaker on the table as a reminder.

Later, taking the copy of the will along for legitimacy, she went to the mortuary and gave them instructions about cremation for Miles. When she returned, she said they said they'd picked up the body that morning, and she could have the ashes on Tuesday.

141

"Have you decided where you're going to scatter them?"

"I'm thinking about it. I guess there's no hurry."

That afternoon we started going through the latest batch of boxes she'd brought home from the townhouse. One held old greeting cards sentimental Miles had saved over the years, everything from Valentine's cards when he was in grade school to a birthday card from Elena showing two penguins kissing on icebergs floating side by side. She'd labeled the penguins Miles and Elena. Now, when we heard a noise at the door, she looked out the window and sighed.

"Can you believe it? The cops are here again." Then she brightened. "Maybe they came to return my gun."

Optimism, thy name is Elena.

She went to the door and I followed. She opened the door and said, "Officers, how nice to see you again!" She lowered her voice to conspiratorial level. "But we really have to stop meeting like this."

The officers, one of whom was Officer Hutchinson, were not into lighthearted banter. He scowled as if she'd just tossed a fresh blotch on his uniform.

"Eleanor Elena Ridgeway, we have a warrant for your arrest on a charge of murder."

And arrest her they did, complete with handcuffs, and took her away in their squad car. It all happened with stunning speed. They didn't give her time to make a phone call or comb her hair or even change her slippers for regular shoes. And her slippers happened to be my garish shark-tooth pair. She'd admired them. . . bless her . . . and Mac had suggested I give them to her, so I did. I doubt murder suspects usually arrive at the station in shark-tooth slippers.

I thought official tests of any kind took days or weeks, but they must have run the test on Elena's gun as fast as dropping coins in a vending machine. But here, instead of a stale Snickers, out had popped an incriminating verdict. It said the gun they'd found here at her house was the gun from which the bullet that killed Miles was fired. I couldn't think of any other reason they'd have to turn their earlier suspicions into an actual arrest.

Mac came in the house as they were putting Elena in the back seat of the squad car, one officer's hand planted on top her head to keep it from hitting the doorframe. We both watched until the car drove away, and I told Mac what had just happened.

"I guess this puts a kink in my theory that Miles's death could have been a contract killing done by a hired professional," I said. "Her gun couldn't have been used by a professional hit man."

"It could have been stolen by the hit man and then returned."

"That would have taken some rather complicated planning. And a lot of sneaking around. Would a hit man do that? How would they even know she had a gun?"

"Hit men don't tend to do complicated," Mac agreed. He picked up one of the cats that was winding around his feet and draped it across his shoulder. "From what I've read, they just pop in, do the hit, and disappear. But that doesn't necessarily mean they didn't do some preliminary investigation about Elena, maybe even surveillance, *this* time. I think a hit man, something to do with the bank robberies, is still a viable possibility."

I contemplated another question that dangled like an invisible hologram between us even as we talked about a theoretical hit man. Mac reluctantly voiced that question.

"But is it possible Elena actually did it?"

"No," I said fiercely. Although I have to admit I hesitated momentarily before saying it. "She didn't do it. Someone took the gun, used it to kill Miles, and then returned it. They did it to frame her for the murder. Which is exactly what is happening."

"Are they framing her simply because she makes a convenient scapegoat or with malicious intent specifically against her?"

Good question. I had another one. "Is it possible that framing her for murder was the goal all along, and murdering Miles was just an unpleasant necessity to accomplish that?"

Mac looked surprised and then shook his head. "Ivy, my dear, you have a devious mind. It's a good thing you're really a sweet Christian lady or you might be a mastermind criminal."

I chose not to comment on that. Although it could be worrisome if authorities ever came knocking on the motorhome and found all my files. *Poisons. Explosives. Autopsies. Fingerprinting. Disappearing.*

Which reminded me— "I wonder if the gun will show fingerprints."

"They'll check, I'm sure, but I'd guess that the gun was wiped clean," Mac said.

"Wouldn't that suggest to the authorities that Elena didn't do it? I mean, why would she wipe fingerprints off her own gun? If the gun was wiped off, it was wiped to get rid of someone *else's* fingerprints."

"Nice theory. You might mention it to Officer Hutchinson."

Right. I might also mention I'd once raised a tomato that looked like Nixon. It would no doubt be just as effective.

But I wasn't through with theories to absolve Elena. "Stan could have done it. He could have come in the house when Elena wasn't home, made off with the gun, killed Miles, and brought the gun back. With fingerprints wiped off."

"When Stan came here after Miles's body was found, he said he wasn't familiar with Eidenburg Street and they had a hard time finding it."

"Perhaps he was deliberately planting misinformation."

Mac nodded.

"And I'm still not sure *why* he'd kill Miles. From what Nicole says, he and Saundra seem fairly well off."

"Maybe they're not as well off as they look," Mac suggested. "Maybe, even if what Stan figured he'd inherit from Miles isn't some large amount, he needs it. Or maybe he knows about Miles's bank robberies and where that money is, and that could definitely be a murder-worthy amount. Perhaps pinning the murder on Elena is not so much malice as convenient. He, or whoever the killer is, figures if the police have Elena as an easy solution to the murder, they'll stop looking right there, and he's home free."

"Convenient for him. Tough on Elena." Another thought hit me. "Maybe Stan knows about the bank robbery money because Miles got rid of it by investing the money through Stan. A money-laundering scheme."

Mac nodded. "Stan said Miles had an investment account with him earlier but he'd sold everything. But maybe he never sold it and now, with Miles dead, Stan can cover up any investment Miles had with him. It just disappears. And Stan knows how to grab whatever is in it for himself. If Miles kept records of that investment—"

"There must be records somewhere." I motioned to the papers littering the dining room table and floor. "Miles seems to have kept records on everything else. But they could be in that file cabinet or on the computer the police took."

I called Nicole at the bakery to let her know that Elena had been arrested, then called the lawyer with whom she had an appointment. We figured she was going to need him.

After making my way through a barrier of receptionists and secretaries, I got to Mark Harlowe and told him what had just happened. He agreed to set up a meeting with Elena at the jail, though he'd need a retainer to actually take the case. I remembered that $5,000 Elena said she'd found in the toe of Miles's slipper at the townhouse. Would that be enough? I have no idea how much lawyers require as a retainer. But even if $5,000 was enough for a retainer, more funds would be needed for bail.

Or maybe not. Because when I asked what bail might be, lawyer Harlowe said that bail might not even be granted in a murder case, and if it were granted, the amount could be extremely high, possibly in the neighborhood of a million dollars.

Not a neighborhood with which we were familiar.

Mac shook his head when I told him. "We'd have to turn to bank robbing ourselves for that kind of money."

Fortunately, or unfortunately, depending on how you looked at it, I suppose, we are not geriatric versions of Bonnie and Clyde. So what now? Would nephew Blake help?

One good thing about Elena being in jail, if the real killer had her targeted next, he wouldn't be able to get to her behind bars.

I wanted to take shoes to Elena to replace those garish shark-tooth slippers, but I knew from past experience that a new arrestee wouldn't immediately be allowed visitors. And what Elena needed more than shoes right now was help from the outside, help in the form of finding the real killer.

**

We went back to the motorhome, and I got on the computer to look up those companies to which Miles had made payments by credit card, the names that were unfamiliar to me. I didn't see how this would help Elena, but I couldn't think of anything else helpful to do at the moment.

One was a men's store; no telling what Miles may have bought there, but probably nothing out of the ordinary. Another company dealt in old coins. Could he have been turning bank robbery cash into collectible coins? It seemed like a good possibility for getting rid of illegitimately acquired money, but so far no old coins had surfaced anywhere. Another company's site merely confirmed what Elena had already mentioned. Chocolate. This company sold chocolate in all forms: ordinary items such as chocolate truffles, chocolate-covered nuts, and chocolate bunnies. Then, less ordinary, at least from my point of view, chocolate guns . . . including one filled with caramel . . . chocolate bullets, angels, mice, lizards, hand grenades, and skulls.

No thanks.

I also spent some time researching *dye packs in bank robbery money* and *serial numbers to identify bank robbery money*. What I learned was that these methods were indeed used by banks, but that they were by no means used by all banks. Miles had, whether by expertise or luck, evaded getting caught by either method. Later that day I remembered something we hadn't yet investigated.

CHAPTER 16

IVY

Miles's little red address and phone book. I retrieved it from where I'd stashed it in the cabinet with my crime files.

There were several names in the little book that looked as if they might be older cruise ladies. I gave two names to Mac and kept Gertrude Livingston, with an address in Wisconsin, and Emily Schaeffer in Illinois for myself. I tapped Gertrude's number into my cell phone. A woman with an older-sounding voice answered on the second ring. Great! Maybe this would be easier than I expected.

"Is this Gertrude? Gertrude Livingston?"

"Who's this?" she snarled.

I was rather taken aback by the rough response. It also didn't give me a clue as to whether this was Gertrude. "I'm a friend of a former acquaintance," I said cautiously. Then I had to pause. That was rather unspecific but avoided falsehoods, didn't it? Miles must be an acquaintance; Gertrude was in his address book. And he was "former" because he was dead. But could I truthfully identify myself as a friend since I hadn't actually known Miles when he was alive? I always try to be truthful, and truth is truth, but sometimes I get bogged down in sticky details.

"You still there?" the woman growled into my bogged-down delay.

"Is this Gertrude?"

"No, it isn't. She passed away six weeks ago. This is her sister, Mona. I'm here at the house trying to get her belongings organized for an estate sale."

This was not in my scheduled scenario, and I was momentarily flustered. "I'm sorry to hear about Gertrude. Had she been ill?"

"No. She had a heart attack. It was very sudden."

"Oh, I *am* sorry to hear that." And I was. In spite of this woman's gruffness, I could hear the undercurrent of grief in her voice.

"Are you another of those shysters who've been calling? Like the one who said Gertie had ordered two Bibles with her name printed in gold on them, and surely I wanted them, didn't I? And all I had to do was pay $179.82 and shipping was included. And that other jerk who claimed she owed him for a financial consultation. But, when it was paid, he'd throw in a free consultation for me . . . oh, happy day! . . . and he had this great group investment in a Hong Kong office building and we all know how Hong Kong is booming, don't we?"

"That's terrible, shysters trying to take advantage after a loved one's death. Maybe you should have her phone shut off."

"I should have done that already, shouldn't I? But I've kept thinking . . . oh, I don't know what I've been thinking. That she was going to call me or something?" She gave a sad, rueful laugh. "But I'll do it. I'll get it shut off right away before some other shyster calls. It's been such a terrible time without Gertie. She always took care of things."

Including sister Mona, I suspected.

"I didn't call because I want money or anything. I just wanted to . . . connect with Gertrude. But to be sure I do have the right Gertrude, I think my friend met her on a cruise ship trip."

"Could be. She took some cruises all right. She always had so much fun that I was thinking I might go with her sometime." Her tone unexpectedly warmed slightly after my comments about getting the phone shut off and not wanting money. She sighed. "Right now, going somewhere warm and sunny sounds wonderful. There's a foot and a half of snow right outside the door. But I don't know, without Gertie . . ."

"I've never been on a cruise, but taking one has always sounded exciting," I said. "But I wouldn't know where to go."

"Gertie went somewhere in Mexico one time. Cancun? Is that on the coast? Another time she went to Thailand, but I don't know . . . That's an awfully long way. I'm not as adventurous as Gertie."

"Australia might be interesting." True. I've always had kind of a yearning to climb that big red rock somewhere in the middle of Australia. "Although that would be a long trip too, and I might get seasick. My friend who knew Gertrude had seasick problems."

"I don't think Gertie ever did. She raved about the food."

"I've heard you can eat practically nonstop, if you want."

"Gertie was so skinny she could eat three desserts and never worry about her weight. I've seen her do it! But me, that's a different story. I can put on pounds just watching a cooking show on TV." She actually laughed, and so did I. I never used to have to worry about weight, but I've put on a few pounds since Mac and I got married.

"Did she ever mention meeting someone interesting on a cruise? A man, I mean. A good dancer, perhaps?" I asked.

"Gertie was more of a bridge player than a dancer," Mona said, and I made a mental note to ask Elena if Miles had been a bridge player. "But I always figured she was hoping to find a man on one of those cruises."

"You mentioned this so-called financial advisor who called. I hope she wasn't having financial difficulties that he somehow found out about?"

"I think he was just some shyster who got a list of old ladies somewhere and was trying his rip-off spiel on all of them." She gave a scornful snort. "I never knew much about her finances, but some time back she was fussing about money she'd put into an investment and lost."

"Do you know what kind of investment it was? I certainly wouldn't want to get tangled up in something and lose money."

"She was pretty closemouthed about her money, so I don't know. But I think she got that money back. Maybe that guy who came to see her helped, because it was right after he was here that she started talking about going on another cruise."

"That's good."

"She left me this house and everything in it—that's why I'm having the estate sale—but everything else goes to Lindsey. Not that I mind, of course! She's Norman's granddaughter, and he's dead too, you know, and she's a nice girl, trying to get a college education and all. Except I don't know why she wants to study *entomology*, whatever that is, and I wish she'd get rid of that awful boyfriend."

In spite of the shyster phone calls, she seemed to have gotten past her suspicions of me and was glad to have someone to talk to. Maybe she was alone now, with Norman and Gertrude gone. "The younger generation has different interests than we do," I said, trying to be encouraging but neutral.

So then I got an earful about the younger generation, including how Lindsey got a tattoo that looked like a barbed-wire bracelet, except it was on her ankle, and the boyfriend was always playing those ear-splitting video games on some machine he had. Plus her blood pressure had shot way up, and she missed Gertie so much, but she didn't know how she was ever going to get rid of all this *stuff* Gertie had. Everything from a collection of old piggy banks to two shelves of old beer cans! She couldn't understand why Gertie had them; she'd never even liked beer.

I didn't break off the conversation. I figured Mona needed this release, even if it took a while. So I told her not to throw out those beer cans until she consulted an expert; people collected them and maybe that's what Gertrude was doing and they might be valuable. Finally, someone rang Mona's doorbell and she said she had to go; it might be an antique dealer coming to look at Gertie's old four-poster bed. I tossed in a quick question about the visiting man before she hung up. Mona, unfortunately, didn't know much about him, except, now that she thought about it, maybe he was someone Gertie had met on a cruise. And, from a distance, at least, he'd looked quite attractive.

"Well, thank you for talking to me. And again, I'm so sorry about Gertrude."

"Thank *you*. I'll check on those beer cans before I throw them out."

Afterward, Mac and I discussed the lengthy conversation. We concluded that Gertrude may indeed have been one of Miles's cruise ladies, although it didn't sound as if he'd conned her. But the part about his having helped her get back a bad investment was puzzling. Although we didn't know for certain, of course, that Gertrude's visitor had actually been Miles.

While I'd talked to Mona, Mac had called the number for the woman in Kansas and found it had been disconnected. Dead end there.

He'd reached Earline Johnson in Missouri. She'd told him she was widowed and had enjoyed several cruises. She was experiencing some "financial complications" at the moment, but she'd like to do some more traveling later on. Did he like to travel? Then she wanted to know how old he was and how tall and what he'd done for a living before he retired.

"I can't imagine why she wanted all that personal information," Mac said.

I could. "She was checking you out as a potential traveling companion. You do have a great voice, you know."

He gave a little snort. "I told her my wife and I were thinking about a cruise—"

"What did she say to that?"

He smiled. "And then she wasn't so friendly. Then I asked her a direct question about Miles, if she'd ever met a man named Miles Willoughby on a cruise, and she got all huffy. She said if that fast-talking Miles was a friend of mine, I could just take a long sail on a leaky boat, and what was I doing calling her if I was *married*. I finally got in a few words and said Miles was dead, but that didn't seem to surprise her. She just said, 'Some people will do anything to get out of their responsibilities, won't they?' Then I added that Miles had been murdered, and she kind of gasped and said Sam hadn't mentioned *that*. Then she asked how he'd been murdered, and I said he'd been shot in the chest. And she made kind of a croaky, choking sound and said, 'Oh dear. Sam was so mad at Miles—' Then she stopped short and hung up. Now I'm wondering who Sam is."

Me too. And how angry was this Sam? Angry enough to commit murder?

"I wonder what she meant by 'responsibilities'?" Mac added.

I wondered that too. Did it mean our suspicions that Miles had conned his cruise lady friends was correct, and this made him responsible for something? Had Earline thought he was going to marry her? Was "sweet, sweet Miles" both a bank robber and a con man? Then another thought.

"I wonder why she didn't seem surprised when you said Miles was dead?"

"I got the impression that this Sam must have told her about Miles's death but not that he was murdered. I think the fact that he'd been murdered came as quite a shock to her."

"Why would Sam tell her one but not the other?"

"Good question. I think Earline wondered that too."

We pondered those questions for several minutes, but all we came up with were more questions. We took a break for dinner . . . a taco casserole recipe I'd seen on a website, which turned out to be quite good . . . and by the time we'd eaten we decided, given the time difference between California and the states back east, that it was too late to call Emily in Illinois today. I glanced through Miles's address book again to see if I'd missed any names and now noticed something I hadn't before. Gertrude in Wisconsin, Emily in Illinois, and the woman in Kansas whose number had been disconnected all had a small *p.* written by their names. So did one other name that I hadn't picked out to call because Terri didn't sound like an older woman. Earline's name had no mark beside it.

I showed the marks to Mac, and we puzzled over them together. They were small, almost insignificant, and I decided they were probably meaningless. Until Mac made a comment.

"It looks like a mark I'd make to tell myself something had been paid. Like if I were collecting for something, I'd make that mark so I'd know that person had paid."

"*P* for *paid.*" I nodded. Made sense. Was this Miles's way of showing a swindle had been successful and the woman had paid what he was hoping to con out of her? Just then Elena's cell phone, which we'd brought back to the motorhome with us after she was arrested, rang and we had to make a hasty decision about whether to answer it. Well, you know me and that curiosity gene. On the third ring, I snatched it up.

"Elena isn't available right now," I said. "May I take a message?"

"Who's this? Elena isn't sick, is she?"

"No, not sick—" Then, oddly, because I hadn't heard the voice all that many times, I recognized it. Deep, rich, distinctive. "Blake? Is that you?"

"Yes. This is Blake Houston. But who—"

"This is Ivy MacPherson. Remember us? Mac and Ivy. We met you down in Cabo San Lucas. You were interested in having us park our motorhome here on Elena's place to keep an eye on her. And you also said you might sell us the property eventually."

"Oh, hey, nice to talk to you again! Aunt Eleanor . . . or Aunt Elena, as she's calling herself now . . . said you'd arrived and you were nice people. Good. I'm glad you're there. But I still haven't persuaded her to go into a retirement home. I'll try to do that when I come up there. Do you like the place?"

"Oh, yes, it's a great place, and Elena is very sweet. But there's a complication. She isn't sick, but I think she told you her fiancé, Miles, had been killed?"

"I didn't know he was a fiancé until she told me he was dead, murdered, in fact, and she mentioned then that they had been planning to get married. Shocking, something like that happening right down the road. All the more reason to get Elena into a safe retirement home. But why isn't she answering her own phone?"

"Well, maybe you'd better brace yourself for this. Elena is in jail. She's been arrested and charged with murdering Miles."

"*What*? I couldn't have heard that right. You said Elena is charged with *murdering Miles*?"

"That's right. They handcuffed her and took her to jail."

"I can't believe it. Aunt Elena *arrested*? There must be some mistake. Look, I just flew in from Dubai. I was planning to stay in my apartment and catch up on a few things before coming up there, but I'll be there tomorrow and we'll get this straightened out."

**

MAC

Blake's confidence was encouraging, though both Ivy and I doubted it was a simple matter of getting this "straightened out."

Next morning, after Ivy had fed Felicity and Fancy and I'd taken BoBandy for a walk around the back side of the property, with Koop tagging along, Ivy tried to call Emily in Illinois and found the number had also been disconnected. She picked two more possibilities out of the address book to call. She tells me I'm great at talking to people, but I think she's better at it than I am. Probably because, although she may be after information, she's always so genuinely interested in people that they wind up *wanting* to talk to her and telling her all kinds of things. But that talent didn't help today, because all she got were canned requests to leave a voice message on both numbers, and we didn't want to do that.

We figured we had several hours before Blake arrived from San Diego, so we decided to use the time to search for Miles's records on an investment with Stan. Ivy went over to the Elena's house, dug the townhouse key out of her purse, and we headed over to Sunshine Valley.

I kept thinking something would keep us from going inside the townhouse because we really didn't have any business being there. Maybe the police would be doing another search, or maybe Stan had managed to get a key and was inside rummaging around. Ivy still suspected he hadn't found what he'd really wanted to find in the townhouse, that it was something other than the family genealogical information he'd claimed to Elena. Perhaps the same records we were looking for?

But there was no police barrier or presence at the townhouse, no Stan, and we marched in as if we belonged there.

Ivy said she and Elena had searched the living area of the townhouse fairly well in the several times they'd been there, but they hadn't gone through the garage, so that's where we started. We found an SUV that was dusty on the outside but looked recently vacuumed and Armor All-ed inside. Had Miles done the cleaning, or had someone else done it to remove traces of their presence? The glove box held only the usual registration and insurance papers, a vehicle manual, and some breath mints. The trunk held a small toolbox, a first aid kit and a blanket, an extra can of motor oil, several bottles of water, and some high-protein bars. Miles was sensibly prepared for emergencies.

Unfortunately for Miles, however, high-protein bars aren't much of a defense against a non-chocolate gun shooting real bullets.

With the SUV here in the garage, he'd apparently gotten home from his evening at Elena's. So how had his body gotten back out to Eidenburg Road? Had he been taken there and killed, or was he killed here or elsewhere and his body moved? There was no sign of blood in or around the car. Did someone other than Miles himself put the car in the garage? Out where we'd found his body, there were no marks to indicate he'd been dragged from a vehicle on the road to the spot back in the trees, and it would have taken someone with a fair amount of strength to carry rather than drag the body that far.

My first thought, of course: Stan was a big, athletic-looking guy, certainly strong enough to carry Miles dead or alive.

We looked in the large cabinets that covered the outside wall of the garage. They were neat and well organized. Car supplies in one section: a case of motor oil, extra air and oil filters, replacement window wipers, a gallon of distilled water. It looked as if Miles had done most of the routine vehicle-maintenance work himself. Another section held tools, well-kept looking, a drill among them. The last section of the bottom cabinets held a set of luggage, not a top-end brand name but not cheapies, but they were well-scuffed, as if they'd had a fair amount of use. Two were wheeled, with long handles, and the other was a smaller, hand-carried type. I started to close the cabinet, but Ivy held the door open.

"Let's look inside. Who knows? Maybe they're stuffed with bank robbery loot."

I pulled the suitcases out and we opened them. No piles of money. The first two were quite empty. The smallest suitcase held two pairs of socks, one pair of red-plaid boxer shorts, and a package of disposable razors. But then we both spotted something else: a stash of papers tucked into a side pocket. Ivy fished them out.

"What are they?" she asked. "They look like schedules of some kind, probably printed off the computer."

"They are schedules." I pointed to the listing of times, some with a D before them, some with an A. "Departure and Arrival times. There are place names too. Denver and Little Rock, and a lot of other places I've never heard of."

"A train schedule?" Ivy suggested. "No, I know what it is, stopping in all those little towns. It's a bus schedule!"

"Miles traveled cross-country by bus to visit cruise ladies?" I said doubtfully.

"And/or rob banks?" She also sounded doubtful, but then she laughed. "Maybe it fits. What friendly senior lady would suspect a nice-looking older man arriving on a bus would be there to sweet-talk her out of her life savings? And wouldn't a bus be a fine form of transportation for a robber armed with a chocolate gun?"

"A bit slow on the getaway."

"But with his mask he didn't necessarily need a quick getaway. Riding a bus to and from a crime might sound unlikely, but if you think about it, it kind of makes sense," Ivy said. She ticked off the reasons. "He pays cash right at the station for a ticket, gets on the bus and goes. All quite anonymous. At his destination, he gets off, puts on his winkled old man disguise, robs a bank, takes off the mask . . . maybe eats the chocolate gun . . . gets back on a bus, and comes home. Maybe takes time to buy some maple syrup for Elena. A time-consuming way to travel, true, but Elena said he was sometimes gone a week or so at a time." She was looking now at the contents of an envelope she'd also pulled out of the pocket of the luggage.

"I don't know if you have to show identification when you ride a bus, but if you do, I think Miles had that covered," she added.

She handed me a driver's license in the name of Robert Anderson, with an address in Santa Barbara. The license showed a birthdate that was probably in the same year as Miles's real birth year. There was also a Medicare card with the same name, and even a card from the Santa Barbara library.

"Phonies?"

"They look real enough to me. But I'm sure it's possible to have documents of any kind made that will pass for the real thing." She paused and looked a little sad. "And it looks as if Miles knew how to do that."

Sweet, sweet Miles was looking more like a crook all the time. The library card was a nice touch. Very convincing. Most crooks don't carry a library card. "Can we figure out from these schedules where he went?"

"I don't know. Maybe." She flipped through the numerous pages that had been folded together. "It may take some time."

I put an arm round her and squeezed. "We may be a geezer and LOL, but I think we can still pull an all-nighter."

CHAPTER 17

IVY

Back at the motorhome, interpreting the schedules was not an all-nighter. It took only minutes to divide the schedules into three separate trips and figure out that one set applied to a trip to Pueblo, Colorado, another to Des Moines, Iowa, and a third set to Gerbyville, Missouri. We compared the towns to addresses in Miles's little red book. No cruise ladies were listed with addresses in Colorado or Iowa, but Gerbyville, Missouri, was where Earline, the woman who wanted a traveling companion, lived.

Did that mean the Colorado and Iowa trips were where Miles had staged bank robberies rather than visits to cruise ladies? Or maybe these weren't trips he'd taken but were instead trips planned for the future? Earline's name didn't have a *p.* by it; had he been planning a trip there to work his con game on her? Although, from her angry outburst on the phone with Mac, it sounded as if she'd already been scammed. We decided that after lunch we'd get on the computer and find out if there had been bank robberies in any of the destination towns on the schedules.

A knock on the motorhome door interrupted our salads and toasted cheese sandwiches. I went to the door.

"Blake!" He must have left San Diego well before the crack of dawn or driven like the proverbial bat out of you-know-where.

He looked even bigger than I remembered him from Cabo San Lucas, his hair longer and darker, his eyes a deeper blue when he yanked off his sunglasses. He was wearing khaki cargo shorts, a *Star Wars* T-shirt, and Reeboks with orange socks. Maybe he and Elena shared an unpredictable gene. He stepped inside, gave me a hug and Mac a hearty handshake.

"Okay, what is all this about Aunt Elena being arrested?"

"We're eating lunch—"

He looked at his watch. It was a big masculine watch, big face, big numbers, band of chunky gold links, but it looked as if all it did was tell time. "Hey, I'm sorry. I didn't mean to interrupt. I'll just go over to the jail now and come back—"

"No, no, I mean, would you like some lunch?"

"Well . . . yeah, I guess I could use some lunch. It's been a long time since breakfast." He smiled. "Thanks."

I had mixed feelings about him as he sat down on the far side of the dinette. He'd seemed nice enough down in Cabo, and I appreciated how he'd rushed up here now with concern over Elena, but there was that totally inconsiderate dumped-date thing he'd pulled on Nicole. He'd apparently never bothered to contact her again to try to make amends.

But he was here to help Elena, and apparently eager to get at it, so I dished up salad, toasted another sandwich, and poured tea for him. We told him the full story, about Miranda finding Miles's body, the lost-and-found gun, and the arrest. He looked a little deflated when we'd finished, as if he hadn't expected there to be any solid evidence against her. Blake was a take-charge, get-'er-done kind of guy—he'd quickly straightened out a problem with our Jeep ride in the backcountry around Cabo San Lucas—and I think he'd planned to storm in and straighten out Elena's problems before dinner. And now he realized that might not be possible.

"How come they're wasting time on Aunt Elena?" he grumbled. "Why aren't they out trying to find the real killer?"

"The fact that it was her gun that killed him, and they found it right here in her house, looks pretty bad," Mac pointed out.

"You don't think she actually did it, do you?" He sounded horrified, although I didn't know if he was horrified that we might think she was guilty or horrified that she might actually be guilty.

"We've been doing a little investigating on our own," I said. I don't think Blake realized that was a detour rather than a definitive answer to his question. I scooted on to something else. "One thing we've been thinking about, when you offered us the opportunity to live here and keep an eye on Elena, you also said something about keeping an eye on her boyfriend. What did you mean by that?"

His brow, big like the rest of him, scrunched. "Well, nothing specific. Miles seemed to care a lot about Aunt Elena, and he treated her like a princess. And I know they had fun together. Attractive too, for a woman her age—"

A woman her age! My foot ached to give him a shin-kicking whack for that one, but I contented myself with setting his refilled tea glass on the table with enough of a slam to tidal-wave the contents. "Yes, Elena is attractive. Very attractive. For any age."

"Oh, yes, that's true," he agreed hastily, and I could tell he recognized that he'd been chastised. With a wary glance at me, he added, "But Miles was several years younger and rather more worldly than Elena, I think. Anyway, I tried to pin him down about a trip he'd taken not long before I was here, and he got really cagey. I never did find out where he'd gone. And later, when we were barbecuing out back, he got two phone calls that he shut off really fast. He said they were robo calls, nothing important, but—" He lifted his shoulders in a gesture that expressed his skepticism. "Or maybe I'm just being overprotective."

Even though we were certainly suspicious of Miles ourselves, on both conning-cruise-ladies and bank robbing issues, I now felt oddly defensive about him. It was difficult to feel too harsh toward a pretzel-making man with a chocolate gun.

"Maybe that's what they were," I said. "Robo calls. Did you ever try to find out anything more about him?"

"I didn't hire a private investigator or snoop around in his garbage, but I did look him up on the internet."

"And found—?"

"Not much." He crumpled his napkin and stood up. "Okay, I'm going to the jail and talk to Aunt Elena now. I really appreciate the lunch."

"You might want to talk to her lawyer too. I'll go back through the house and get his name and address for you."

"Thanks. I'd appreciate that."

I copied the lawyer's information off the scrap of paper on Elena's kitchen table for him. Felicity, curious and much bolder now, came out to see what was going on, and he knelt down beside her. You can tell by the touch whether someone really likes cats or if it's just a polite pretense. Blake liked cats. His long stroke along Felicity's back and tail sent her rear end rising into a happy catosphere.

"I'm glad she got a cat. I know how much she missed grumpy ol' Ricardo."

"Actually, there are two of them. This is Felicity, and Fancy's around here somewhere. If you're staying here tonight, better close your door or they'll probably be in bed with you. *Are* you staying here tonight?"

"I hadn't thought about it, but, yes, I'll stay here. I've stayed in the guest room before. I won't object to the company." Felicity had rolled over, and he knew what that meant. Invitation for a tummy rub. He gave her one that was just right, not too vigorous, not too mild. He laughed. "This seems like an odd coincidence. I used to have a secretary named Felicity. I hope this Felicity is nicer than that secretary."

"You don't have a cat of your own?"

"No. I'd like to, but I'm away from home too much." He let Felicity clamp her front paws around his hand and kick with her hind feet. "Sometimes I think I ought to take the company's offer to work in the home office instead of chasing all over the world."

"Do you need a key to stay here at the house?"

"No. I remember where Aunt Elena keeps it, under that pot by the front door." He grimaced. "I keep telling her that's the first place a burglar would look."

Not that it necessarily mattered. In spite of what she'd said about locking the house, Elena neglected to lock doors much of the time anyway.

By the way," he added after he untangled his hand and we walked toward the front door, "is that friend of Aunt Elena's still around,

Nicole, I think her name was? Or did she marry that guy she was seeing?"

Nicole had been seeing a guy? If she was, she must be hiding him in the woodwork because neither she nor Elena had mentioned a man. "No. She's still working at the bakery."

I didn't mention that if I were him, I wouldn't stop in at the bakery. Nicole might find something more dangerous than a blueberry muffin to throw at him.

**

MAC

After Blake left, we decided, rather than getting on the computer to check out bank robberies, we'd locate the local bus depot and see if anyone remembered Miles.

"We need a photo," I said, so while I used the computer to find the location of the local bus depot, Ivy went over to the house again. She came back and slipped a photo of Miles and Elena out of its gold frame.

A bus was stopped outside the small depot when we arrived, and we waited until a few people boarded and the bus pulled away before approaching the counter. A stocky woman wearing a cap over short gray hair looked up from the papers she was stapling. Ivy said a friendly Hi.

"Can I help you?"

The truth about why we were here . . . *We think this Miles guy was riding the bus to rob banks and/or con older ladies . . .* would probably raise more questions than it answered. I knew Ivy wouldn't make up some phony story about why we were asking questions about him, but I'm always intrigued by how she can make a peculiar request sound reasonable. She kept it simple.

"We're wondering about a friend we think used to take bus trips fairly often. We have a photo of him here and wonder if you recognize him." Ivy pushed the photo across the counter to the woman.

"Are you from—" I think the woman started to say *the police,* but she apparently took a closer look and realized no way were these golden oldies part of any police department. "Are you here in some official capacity?"

I wasn't sure what that meant. That they didn't give information to the authorities on the basis of privacy for their customers? Or that they gave information *only* to authorities, not to just any busybody checking on someone's travels?

Ivy smiled her sweet and disarming LOLsmile. "No. Our friend is deceased and we're just trying to find out about these rather mysterious trips he took."

The woman studied the photo. She shook her head. "I'm pretty good at remembering faces, but I don't recognize him. But we do get a lot of people traveling through here, and I can't remember them all." She smiled. "And maybe my memory isn't as good as it used to be. What's his name?"

"That's part of the mystery. His name is Miles Willoughby, but he may have been using the name Robert Anderson when he traveled."

She didn't question why he had two names, just shook her head again. "Neither name rings any bells with me," she said, apparently also not recognizing Miles's name as that of the man who'd recently been murdered. "But if he was trying to be . . . oh, *discreet*, he may have used a bus depot in some other nearby town. I know one old guy who did that so he could take a bus down to visit a girlfriend in Fresno and not leave his car parked around here where his wife might spot it."

I figured *discreet* was too kind a word for a man sneaking around on his wife to visit a girlfriend in Fresno . . . and also too kind for Miles if he was deliberately hiding his tracks to carry out conning-cruise-ladies or bank robbing schemes.

We went back to the motorhome to pick up BoBandy, then drove over to Lumbaugh, situated between Highway 99 and Interstate 5, both of which run north and south through California. No helpful information at the small depot there. We headed east, back across Highway 99, to Firmont and several other small towns. One clerk thought he may have seen Miles a couple of times, but he wasn't positive. We stopped for lunch at a place called The Fastest Fork, although it should have been The Greasiest Spoon. Maybe not the worst burgers in the world but they needed more than a blessing to make them edible. Even BoBandy was slow at eating the half burger we offered him.

Altogether we made a wide circle with little to show for it, and it was after dark by the time we got home, tired and disgruntled from our unsuccessful day. Even BoBandy seemed glad to be home, and he loves riding in the pickup. Lights shone from the windows in Elena's house, and Blake came over a few minutes after we arrived.

"Can I take you two out to dinner somewhere?"

"Chinese?" Ivy asked.

He pulled out his cell phone and with enviable speed brought up a choice of three local Chinese restaurants. Ivy picked The Dragon Empire, and we said we'd be ready in half an hour.

By the time we went over to the house, Blake had changed clothes, from shorts to jeans, light green polo shirt, denim jacket, and ordinary black socks with his Reeboks. We went in his ride, an SUV. It, like his watch, was big and solid-looking but not fancy.

At the restaurant he suggested a family style dinner that came with everything from won-ton soup to shrimp, barbecued pork, fried rice, chicken chow mein, and broccoli with hoisin sauce. While we were waiting for the food to arrive, Blake told us the results of his day.

"I didn't get in to see Elena. The fact that I'd driven all the way up from San Diego did not impress the jail authorities. She isn't allowed visitors yet."

"Not even the lawyer?" Ivy asked.

"That's what I asked. But a lawyer isn't considered a visitor, and he had been there. So I went to his office. Actually, I didn't expect him to be in on a Saturday, but the secretary said he was there, so I waited to see him.. I read *Lawyers Monthly*. I read *Trial Lawyers Today*. I read an article that someone had tagged with a folded-over corner in some women's magazine about how to get what you have coming when you get a divorce." After the sour recital of his reading material in the office, he did smile. "Fortunately, I've never had to worry about that situation. I've never been married."

"What did you think of the lawyer?" I asked.

"It's hard to tell in one short meeting. He seems knowledgeable and competent, but he wasn't too encouraging. He said Aunt Elena's arraignment is on Monday, and he expects her to be indicted. It came as a surprise to me, never having been involved with criminal activities, but the defense doesn't present arguments at an arraignment. It's all what the prosecution has against him or her. I gave him a retainer to continue with the case."

I was curious about the size of the retainer, but all I said was that it was good of him to do that for Elena. Our food arrived, and I offered our usual blessing. I'm always thankful for what the Lord provides, but I have to admit I was a little more thankful for this meal than I'd been for the greasy-spoon hamburgers.

Ivy waited until we'd filled our plates before asking, "Did you talk to him about bail?"

"Apparently that will be handled at the arraignment."

"He warned us that in a murder case, bail could be quite high."

"I'll come up with whatever it is. Aunt Elena shouldn't be in that place." He lowered the chopsticks of fried rice that were halfway to his mouth. "But what she really needs is someone working to find out who actually killed Miles. I'm afraid the police won't look any further now that they've charged Elena. I'm thinking about hiring a private investigator."

"Could be a good idea," Ivy agreed. She didn't mention our sleuthing efforts.

The food was excellent, and I admired Blake's expertise with the chopsticks. Ivy and I had to use forks. The meal ended with fortune cookies, of course. In some peculiarity, all three fortunes were exactly the same: *Silence is golden, and gold is silent.* There may have been some deep philosophy in that, but I was too tired to try to figure it out.

CHAPTER 18

IVY

We tackled the internet first thing next morning. Even if Blake hired a private investigator, we might be able to give him —or her— a head start with whatever information we could provide.

I'd thought bank robberies must be rare these days, what with surveillance cameras and other high-tech methods available for thwarting them, but I was wrong. A statistics site showed 3,033 bank robberies in the US in a recent year. The perpetrators usually didn't get impressive amounts of money, often less than $5,000, but one robber hit five banks in one day, so his tally added up nicely. Had Miles done that?

Only 112 robberies involved dye packs hidden in the stolen money, so it wasn't unusual that Miles hadn't gotten caught that way. Although it had nothing to do with him, I was startled to read that at least 214 of the robberies involved women. Blessedly, although Miles had drafted Elena to help him eat a chocolate gun, he hadn't pulled her into an actual bank robbery.

Another site showed that some 98% of the robbers were caught, but still, 2% of 3,033 meant some sixty or so bank robbers that year went merrily on their way. A site with surveillance photos taken during robberies showed that for quite a few of the perpetrators, a hoodie sweatshirt was the fashion statement of the day.

Then the shocker: one photo from Georgia didn't show a good angle on the face, but what could be seen bore a startling resemblance to Miles's wrinkled mask.

We were just getting into bank robberies specifically in Colorado when someone knocked on our door. I expected it to be Blake, but when I opened the door, Nicole stormed in. She looked as if she'd had a bad night and had rushed over in whatever she could throw on, which happened to be baggy jeans, a pink sweatshirt with a purple stain shaped like a lopsided version of Texas, purple toenails peeking through purple flip-flops, and hair in a messy topknot.

"Do you know who's over at the house?" She didn't wait for an answer. "Elena's nephew, that's who! Blake is over there."

"He got here yesterday," Mac said. "He came early because of Elena's incarceration."

"And what's he going to do about it? Rush in here and solve the case for them? Fat chance. I tried to see her yesterday, but they wouldn't even let me in."

"Blake went to see her too—"

"I suppose *him* they let in!"

"No. He was just as frustrated as you are to find she wasn't allowed visitors yet."

"I take it you didn't stop to have a chat with Blake at the house?" Mac asked.

She gave him a you-gotta-be-kidding glare. "I spotted him out front with the cats and parked farther down the road. I don't think he saw me."

"He asked about you yesterday," I said.

That did not soften her sour expression. "In what way? 'Is that fat woman whose husband dumped her still hanging around?'"

"Nicole, you aren't anywhere near fat, and he didn't ask a question like that. He mentioned you by name, that's all. He wondered if you'd married the guy you were seeing."

"What guy? I haven't been seeing any guy. He probably has me mixed up with some woman he met in Hong Kong or Buenos Aires or London." She gave a dismissive snort and waved an equally dismissive hand. "I came over because I wanted to talk to you about what we can do to find out who really killed Miles. I'm afraid the police investigation will just stop dead now that they've arrested Elena."

"That's what Blake thinks too," Mac said. "He mentioned the possibility of hiring a private investigator."

She looked momentarily torn, perhaps as if she thought bringing in a private investigator was a good idea but she didn't want to credit Blake with having a good idea. She didn't have a chance to express any thoughts on the subject, however, before another knock came on the side of the motorhome. I opened the door and Blake peered inside. The first thing he saw, of course, was Nicole standing there in her coordinated purple-Texas-stain-and-purple-flip-flops outfit.

"I didn't realize you had company," he said stiffly. "I'll come back later."

"Don't bother," Nicole said. She tried to cover the stain with one hand and stuffed a straggly strand of hair in the topknot with the other. "I was just leaving."

Not at the moment, however; Blake was blocking the doorway, a muscular tank in cargo shorts and purple socks. He didn't show any indication of stepping aside.

"Heading home to your live-in love?" he inquired. "I assume he's moved back in."

Nicole gave him a *what-planet-are-you-from?* look. She glanced around the motorhome as if scanning for an escape hatch. Seeing none, she apparently decided to barrel directly through him. I stepped between them with the idea of running interference, and then realized this was about as smart as getting between two shoppers ready to wrestle over a pair of shoes on sale.

"Don't you have an emergency trip to make?" Nicole snapped at him over my head. "To Shanghai or Tokyo or Mars or somewhere?"

"What was your idea of accepting a dinner invitation from me anyway? Some adolescent scheme to make the poor guy jealous?"

I didn't want to take sides here, but I couldn't see what Blake had to be huffy about. He was the one who'd bailed on the date with Nicole. I started to say something but Nicole interrupted.

"Stan?" she snapped. "You're talking about me trying to make *Stan* jealous?"

"Sorry. I don't believe I ever caught the name."

"Stan is my ex-husband."

"You're living with your ex-husband?"

By now I had the feeling they were blasting each other in two different languages, words shooting like bullets back and forth over my head.

"Look, I have no idea what you're talking about," Nicole said. "I don't live with anyone. I haven't since Stan moved out and we got divorced and he remarried. I have no idea why you think I'd try to make him jealous."

"But Felicity said—"

"Elena's cats are speaking to you now?"

Blake's eyes rolled. "Felicity is my secretary in San Diego. I mean, she *was* my secretary. She was the one who called you before our date to tell you I had to make an emergency trip and wouldn't be—"

"Nobody called me," Nicole interrupted. "I sat there for three hours waiting for you to show up. Three *days* later I got a call from somebody saying you'd gone to Hong Kong."

"That was when you told her that my missing our dinner didn't matter anyway, that you and the guy you'd been living with had decided to get back together, and please don't call you again?"

"I never told her anything of the sort!"

He paused, forehead wrinkling, as he apparently tried to put a timeline together. "No, it couldn't have been three days later when you told her about the live-in guy. Because I called the office the very next morning after I missed our date, and Felicity said then that you'd told her about getting back together with him, and not to call again. But if she hadn't even talked to you yet—" Blake slammed a hand against his forehead. "Sabotage!"

"Sabotage?" Nicole repeated.

"Felicity had . . . kind of a thing for me. I wasn't interested, but I wonder if . . ." He gently picked me up and moved me aside as if I were one of the cats, and he and Nicole were face-to-face. "I wonder if Felicity didn't call you when she was supposed to because she wanted to sabotage a possible relationship between us."

"A possible relationship between *you and me?*" Nicole said the words as if such a relationship was about as likely as a relationship between a paddling swimmer and a passing shark.

"And then she told me that you and this guy had a fight but you'd gotten back together and that you didn't want me to call you." He struck a fist against the palm of his other hand. "Yes, that's what she did. Sabotaged both of us—"

"You didn't go to Hong Kong?"

"Yes, I went to Hong Kong. An emergency to straighten out a deal worth millions with one of our best clients. I told her to call you immediately, because I couldn't make our date, and tell you I'd call you as soon as I could. But then Felicity said you said not to call you— Sabotage, that's what it was," he repeated. "Sabotage!"

"And she really told you I'd said this guy I'd been living with was moving back in?"

"Yes. And not to call you."

They stood there looking at each other, neither exactly convinced the other was totally innocent but neither quite as sure the other was eligible for a Scumbag of the Year award.

"But Felicity isn't your secretary anymore?" I put in. Little ol' helpful me.

Blake answered the question, but his attention was on Nicole, not me. "I had to let Felicity go because on several occasions she totally mishandled client communications. The final straw was when I wound up in Mozambique instead of Munich because of what she'd done. And then she tried to blame one of the other women in the office. I'm thinking now, considering what she did here, and did *deliberately*, that I should have fired her much sooner."

"Look, why don't the two of you go out for coffee or lunch and talk this over?" I suggested.

Stony silence until Blake finally muttered, "I guess I could do that."

Nicole eyed him warily. She made a show of lifting her wrist to look at her watch. "I might have time."

I figured that between the purple socks, purple flip-flops, and purple-Texas stain, they made a nicely-coordinated pair. Although they'd better be sure to pick a place without a dress code for lunch.

They exited the motorhome, and we went back to prowling bank robberies on the internet.

CHAPTER 19

IVY

We spent the rest of the morning investigating bank robberies in various states. Pueblo, Colorado, and Des Moines, Iowa, both had bank robberies that had never been solved. So did every other state we looked at, but we found no more photos that might be Miles in his wrinkled-old-man disguise.

By the end of the morning, we'd established that there were numerous bank robberies Miles *could* have committed and gotten away with. We hadn't established any *probability* that he'd done so. The bus schedules told us he'd looked up timetables for traveling to towns where robberies had taken place but not when or if he'd actually taken those trips. One schedule would have taken him to a town where a cruise lady lived.

Would Elena remember dates he was away on trips so we could compare them with dates of bank robberies?

On Sunday we went to services at that same stucco church with the friendly people, this time with a sermon from Philippians, a verse I've always loved: "Do not be anxious about anything, but in every situation, by prayer and petition, with thanksgiving, present your requests to God." They also sang a wonderful praise song I'd never heard before. Some of the words kept running through my mind afterward. *And his glory came down to earth, all for you and me.* A blessed reassurance!

Later we invited Blake over for dinner, but he said he and Nicole had a date that evening. He seemed quite optimistic about it. I said I hoped he wouldn't be called away for an emergency trip to Hong Kong or elsewhere, and he said he hoped so too. A drizzly rain began

171

about the time I started fixing our dinner. I was trying a new hamburger casserole from a recipe I'd seen on the internet. Hamburger Surprise!! with two exclamation points.

The surprise was that when we tried to eat it, it tasted as if it were made of old shoes simmered in a liniment sauce. Mac, bless him, didn't complain. He takes a philosophical view of cooking disasters, a this-too-shall-pass attitude. My thought was, good thing Blake hadn't accepted our dinner invitation. We made up for the inedible entrée with big dishes of Nuts 'n' Chocolate Fiesta ice cream.

We took BoBandy for a short walk in the rain, watched an old Eddie Murphy movie on DVD, speculated about Nicole and Blake's dinner date, and went to bed before 10:00.

I woke sometime in the night. I thought it must be close to morning, but when I turned the clock on the nightstand around so I could see the face, I found it was only 11:45. I slipped out of bed, intending to get a drink of water. Well, get a drink of water and look out the front windshield to see if Blake was home from his date with Nicole yet. That sneaky curiosity gene can always think of something such as the need for a drink of water as an excuse for snoopy excursions.

I pushed the curtains aside and peered out. Mac padded up beside me.

"What are you doing?" he asked.

"Looking around."

"Trying to see if Blake is home yet?"

Mac knows me so well.

"I was also wondering . . ." This felt so much like that other night, when we'd run into the burglar running out of the house. Had the burglar returned? And if so, was he after something he hadn't gotten that other night? "I think I'll run over and check on the cats. They're as unpredictable as Elena."

"What if you run into Blake wandering around in his pajamas?"

Yes, that could be embarrassing. Especially if Blake isn't the kind of guy who wears pajamas.

"I'll knock first. I'm not going to just barge in," I said righteously. "I'll also look out front and see if his SUV is there. I'm just concerned about what the cats may be doing. The way they bat things around, they might start a fire with a broken lamp. Or something."

Mac was right behind me, of course, when I opened the door. With his baseball bat.

We checked out front, no SUV, and then followed our pathway of that other night. Knock on the back door. Listen. Slip inside the unlocked door.

"Hey, kitty, kitty," I called softly. "Where are you? Felicity? Fancy?"

No cats came out to meet us, but that didn't quell my suspicions about what they might be doing. We moved on down the hallway and then heard the front door opening. No doubt Blake returning. I felt a little foolish, but I didn't want to rush for the back door and then have him catch us like escaping prowlers. We turned and headed back for the kitchen as a light went on.

Blake stood in the kitchen. He was wearing nice slacks and a leather vest, but he looked a bit worse for wear for a man coming in from a dinner date. A couple of greasy streaks marred the tan slacks. Not surprisingly, he looked startled to see us, Mac in his pajamas, me in my nightgown and robe. I was glad I'd worn the robe. The lacy nightgown is one Mac bought for me, short and a bit skimpy in places.

"Is something wrong?" Blake asked.

Mac gave him a condensed version of our concern about the cats and he went down the hallway to check on them. He said, with Elena not at the house, they usually slept in his bed. He returned to say they'd knocked a few things off his nightstand, but otherwise everything was fine. He asked if we'd like midnight tea and we said yes.

With bachelor expertise, he nuked water in the microwave and set out teabags. As we sipped tea at the dinette, I asked Blake how his date with Nicole had gone.

"We had a steak dinner and went to a Sandra Bullock movie."

He sounded unexpectedly gloomy, but I said an encouraging, "Sounds like a schedule for a great date."

"Yeah, well, then I suggested coffee at a place near the theater, and we talked about Aunt Elena and Miles and my hope that I could get into the arraignment tomorrow. Then we got into my thinking about changing to an office job instead of traveling all the time and her thinking about going back to college."

I nodded more encouragement. Thinking about their futures. Exploring whether those futures might mesh. Still sounded like a great date. But Blake was still in gloom-and-doom mode.

"So then I asked if she'd like to have dinner again tomorrow night, maybe an Italian place over near the mall. She said she'd like to, but she had an appointment tomorrow evening. I thought she meant a date, but then she said it was a meeting with this . . . client, I guess you'd call the person."

"A client in her Cookie Lady business."

"Right. Some peculiar thing where people smash cookies—from that 'And that's the way the cookie crumbles' saying, she said—and she analyzes the person's character and tells their fortune from patterns the crumbs make. Kind of like reading tea leaves, I guess. And I made some comment . . . I think something like, 'You've got to be kidding, people pay money for that?' Which I suppose could be considered an insensitive remark. Anyway, she got huffy and said some people found it very helpful, Elena included. Then she said it was time for her to get home, and we went out to the SUV and found a tire was flat. And when I got out the spare, it was flat too."

Which probably explained the greasy streaks on his tan pants and generally disheveled appearance. I murmured something soothing about that being unfortunate, but he did not look soothed.

"I felt like an incompetent jerk, of course. Who doesn't make sure their spare tire is pumped up and ready? Not a way to make a good impression on a woman. So then I said something, just kind of kidding, about maybe if we'd crumbled cookies earlier she could have foretold this, and she accused me of making fun of her. So, while I was trying to find someone to call to get the tires fixed, she called a cab and went home." He took a sip of tea and sloshed liquid out of the cup when he set it down. "I like Nicole. I really do. She's fun and interesting. And my not having a good spare was really stupid. But all this crumbling-cookies business seems kind of . . . flaky."

All I could think to offer was my all-purpose, "Umm."

"Did you get the tires fixed?" Mac asked.

"No. I couldn't find anyone to do anything in the middle of the night, so I also called a cab and came home. The SUV is still outside the coffee shop."

Felicity, doing what she could, came out and jumped in his lap and purred for him.

**

MAC

In the morning, with a return of blue skies after the rain, I took Blake to the coffee shop and waited with him until a guy from a tire repair shop came and fixed both the tire on the SUV and the spare. Afterward, Blake immediately rushed off to the courthouse to see if he could get into Elena's arraignment.

Ivy and I had just returned from taking BoBandy on a longer than usual walk along the road when Blake's SUV pulled into the driveway. We'd never been past the corner before, but this time we'd walked on to what turned into a country road with some actual farms. A dozen black Angus cattle in one pasture, sheep in another. Very pastoral and peaceful and fresh-washed smelling after the rain.

"Did you get in to attend the arraignment?" Ivy asked Blake when we met him in the front yard.

Blake, still in his old jeans and blue T-shirt from the tire-fixing morning, shook his head. "I got there just after it was over, so I don't know if they'd have let me in or not. But I caught the lawyer on the way out. I don't think he had to be there, but he was."

"Good. I'm glad to hear she has a lawyer who's keeping on top of things."

"Anyway, the bad news is that she has been indicted on several charges. From what the lawyer said, that's the way they do it: layer on multiple charges rather than just a single murder charge. Covering all bases, it sounds like."

"Bail?" I asked.

"That's bad too, but not as bad as it could be. Five hundred thousand. But it could easily have been a million in a murder case, so I can be thankful it's not more than it is. I can come up with the five, but it's going to take several days to do it. I don't keep that much in a checking account."

"Who does?" Ivy murmured. She managed to sound sympathetic, as if not keeping five hundred thousand in the checking account was a minor annoyance anyone might encounter.

"The good news," Blake added, "is that Harlowe thinks I can get in to see her tomorrow."

**

IVY

We wanted to visit Elena too, of course, but we decided we should let Blake go first. We were in the kitchen at the house the following morning when he returned from visiting her. I'd brought over a pan of cinnamon rolls I'd baked earlier. He came in and set a box on the kitchen table.

He reported that Elena seemed in good spirits and she'd said the food wasn't as bad as she'd thought it might be. She was concerned about the cats, and he'd told her they were doing fine. She'd asked him to go to the funeral home and pick up Miles's ashes. She'd decide what to do with them when she got home. He'd told her we'd come to see her the following day. He also said he was still thinking about hiring a private investigator to look into Miles's murder.

He'd then stopped by the funeral home and picked up the ashes. He pointed to the box on the kitchen table. I felt an immediate rush of embarrassment. Here we were, carrying on a conversation about cats while the ashes just sat there ignored. The box appeared to be a temporary container rather than something intended as a permanent residence for the ashes, an unremarkable box, vaguely reminiscent of an Amazon delivery.

I hoped Miles had read that Bible and absorbed the truths written there about what comes after life on this earth.

"I think I'll put the box in Elena's room for now," Blake said.

I murmured, "Good idea," but I had a sudden unpleasant thought. How strong was that box? I had an appalling picture of the cats gleefully pushing it off wherever he put it, ashes scattering like confetti. Would they fall into shapes that some morbid fortune-teller might turn into prophecies of the future?

"Put it somewhere the cats can't knock it over," I said.

"Right." Blake disappeared with the box firmly clutched in both hands, as if he too feared droppage or spillage. When he came back, he said he'd put the container in the closet and shut the door. Tight.

But I had a new resolve when we went back to the motorhome. Miles should be right here, marrying Elena, not stuck in that impersonal box. Whoever did this was *not* going to get away with it.

**

We went to the jail the following afternoon. It was not a simple process of opening a door and being greeted with a friendly *Welcome to our jail!* We had to offer identification, fill out forms, wait, get scanned by a metal detector, and leave the sack I'd brought for Elena at the desk. And then we found that only one visitor at a time was allowed.

"You go." Mac gave me a little nudge toward the woman officer, and I followed her. He went back to a bench in the waiting area.

The meeting area was more or less what I expected: a small, bare room and a glass wall with a phone on each side. I sat down and waited. A guard brought Elena to the phone on her side. She didn't look dreary or discouraged. The orange jumpsuit actually looked rather festive on her. She didn't have pins or ribbons, but she'd managed to do her hair in an upswept fluff, and she smiled at me. All of which made me wonder: didn't she realize what serious trouble she was in, that just because *she* knew she wasn't guilty she might still be convicted?

I couldn't see her feet to tell if she was still wearing the shark slippers. I picked up the phone. "I brought some shoes for you, but I couldn't bring them in with me. I guess they'll give them to you later." No doubt after checking to make sure I hadn't stuffed them

177

with drugs or explosives. Being an LOL doesn't mean they aren't suspicious of you.

Elena held up a foot to show me she was still wearing the shark slippers. The movement also showed that her feet weren't shackled, plus an enviable agility to get that foot up there. "These are fine. I get lots of people asking where I got them. They were going to make me wear some of their regular shoes, but I have this big bunion and nothing fit. So they let me keep my own slippers."

"I brought Miles's Bible for you too. But I had to leave it out front with the shoes."

"Oh, great! I met a woman here who has one, but she said there are various versions of the Bible. Isn't that kind of peculiar, there being different versions? Shouldn't they all say the same thing?"

"They aren't exactly different versions. They're different translations. Translation apparently isn't an exact science, especially when dealing with historic languages, and there's some room for interpretation. Actually, it's quite interesting to compare the different translations."

"Miles's Bible is the one I want to read." Being in jail hadn't changed her stubbornness on that subject.

She asked about the cats again and whether Blake had picked up the ashes at the funeral home, and I asked if she could remember any specific dates Miles had taken trips. The closest she could get was maybe a month ago, and maybe six weeks before that. Finally I asked what was really on my mind.

"Elena, while you're in here, you must have time to think—"

"Actually, there isn't much else to do here *but* think." She smiled, but for the first time she sounded a little downbeat about her incarceration. She pulled at the loose jumpsuit as if it felt restrictive. Then she straightened her narrow shoulders and gave an airy wave. "But it's all just an annoying inconvenience. If it were anything more, the cookie crumbs would have warned me that last time Nicole did a reading for me. So I'm fine."

I admired her determinedly optimistic attitude, but attributing it to cookie-crumb fortune-telling made me want to pick up my shoe and hammer the glass wall. But what I managed to say was, "Mac and I are wondering if you've had any more thoughts about who might have killed Miles and why."

"I've thought and thought, but I can't think of anyone who'd want him dead. He was such a sweet guy. But what I've also been thinking is, I want you to burn those masks before the police decide to search the house again. No one needs to know that Miles was . . . that Miles *may have been* a bank robber."

Sweet Elena. Still thinking about protecting Miles's reputation and memory more than of her own danger with a murder charge hanging over her head. I shook my head. "I don't think we can do that. It's possible that whoever killed him is somehow connected to the bank robberies. It may be important to prove he *was* a bank robber and had enemies in that . . . line of work."

She sighed as if I were the one being frustratingly stubborn. "Well, I have been thinking about that young woman who ran out of Miles's townhouse that time, the one who seemed so angry at him about something."

"As I recall you saying, she sounded almost threatening."

"Yes, she did. Very threatening! She said Miles wasn't going to get away with . . . whatever it was she thought he'd done."

"I also remember you saying that Miles said she was a saleslady trying to sell him some timeshare thing and she was angry because he wasn't buying."

"Yes, that's what he said. But now I wonder . . ."

"Wonder if that wasn't exactly the truth?"

"She seemed so *very* angry. As if it were something more personal than just his not buying something. But I don't see how she could have had anything to do with bank robbing. Women don't rob banks."

Well, yes, as a matter of fact, women do rob banks, as we'd learned from our internet exploration. However, another thought occurred to me. Mac had talked with someone else who was also very unhappy with Miles. The angry Earline in Missouri.

CHAPTER 20

IVY

Back out in the pickup, I told Mac about my visit with Elena and my wondering whether some angry woman running out of Miles's townhouse was connected with an angry Earline Johnson in Missouri.

"You said Earline mentioned someone who may have told her Miles was dead. But I can't think of the name. Do you remember it?"

It took Mac a moment, but he came up with it. "Sam. Earline did seem to know Miles was dead, but this Sam hadn't mentioned anything about his death being murder. That, along with the fact that Sam had been so angry with Miles, seemed to trouble Earline. When I told her Miles had been murdered, I think she was afraid Sam may have had something to do with it."

"We need to find out who Sam is. And where he is."

After lunch we got on the internet again and went back to the bank robberies site to compare when Miles took trips with when bank robberies had occurred. There were possible matches, but nothing definite, of course, because Elena couldn't remember specifically when he took the trips.

After that I looked up Earline's number in Miles's little red book. I made the call this time, with the goal of finding out more about Sam. It took five rings before a woman said a rather breathless "Hello," followed by, "Sorry it took me so long to get to the phone. I left it inside while I was trying to catch Tansy before she got out of the backyard."

Tansy might be anything from a pet cockroach to a next-door neighbor, but I took a hasty guess. "Cats are so quick, aren't they? And so independent, always wanting to get out and go places."

"Oh, yes. And I don't know what I'd do if she got lost out there somewhere. Tansy is *family*."

"My Koop is too."

"Koop?"

"He's my cat. Orange, one eye, stubby tail. He can't stand smokers, so I named him after that surgeon general C. Everett Koop, who was so anti-smoking."

"Really? What a strange coincidence! A couple years ago I read what Koop had said when he was in office about smoking. It finally gave me the push to *stop*." She gave a little laugh. "And there's no more ferocious anti-smoker than a former smoker."

"Good for you! Oh, did you catch Tansy?"

"Yes, thank goodness."

"Why I'm calling, is Sam there?"

"Sam?" She sounded surprised. "Oh, my goodness no. Sam has lived out in California for several years now. You're a friend of Sam's?"

I was a little excited. Sam was here in California, within murdering distance! But I dodged the question about my friendship with Sam, and said, "Really, it's been that long, several years in California?"

"Oh yes, ever since college graduation. Is that where you knew Sam, at college?"

Another question to dodge. "I'm out in California myself now. Perhaps I could get a phone number or address for Sam from you? It would be so good to make contact with Sam." To keep it honest, I carefully kept "again" off the end of the sentence.

A moment of silence, as if she suddenly had reservations about giving this information to some unknown person on the phone. Was she thinking I sounded rather old to be a friend of . . . what? Her grandson?

"This is Ivy MacPherson," I said smoothly. "You probably don't remember me." Of course she didn't remember me. There was nothing to remember. "I'm much older than Sam, of course. An LOL. That's little old lady."

"That's what I am too! And you know who get to become LOLs? Survivors!"

I'd never really thought about it that way, but she was right. That's what we LOLs are. Survivors.

Another moment of hesitation, and then she capitulated to answering my question about Sam. Thanks, I guessed, to Tansy and Koop. Who could be suspicious of an LOL with an anti-smoking cat?

"Just let me look at my list of people here. I don't know enough people to have an actual address book, but I do have a list . . . Yes, here it is." She gave me both a phone number and an address: 3672 Y'Bera Drive, Apartment 213, in Bakersfield. I scribbled it down. "Is Bakersfield close to where you are? I'm sure Sam would like to see you again. Sam is one I keep talking to about how bad smoking is. Not exactly nagging, but . . ." She gave another little laugh. "Well, maybe it is nagging. I'm sure Sam thinks it is."

"I'll have to check on how far away Bakersfield is. And thank you so much for the information." I rather liked chatting with Earline about cats and anti-smokers. She seemed like a much nicer person than when Mac had talked to her. I felt a real LOL bond. But I needed to end this quickly before I made some big blunder that didn't fit the facts with grandson Sam. "You take good care of Tansy now, okay? And if I see Sam I'll keep pushing the anti-smoking program."

"Great! And give your Koop a big hug for me. We anti-smokers have to stick together."

So the first thing we did, of course, was get on the internet and see what we could find about Sam Johnson. What we found was a lot of Sam Johnsons, enough to start a Sam Johnson army for some needy third-world country. Everyone from a now-dead Congressman to a football player, plus an assortment of plumbers, lawyers, an army major, and a biologist.

We narrowed it down to Sam Johnsons in California, but even that didn't narrow it down enough. There was still everything from a horse trainer to a psychiatrist. But nothing gave us a specific Sam Johnson on Y'Bera Drive in Bakersfield.

There was also the possibility the grandson's last name wasn't Johnson. He could be the son of a daughter of Earline, whose married name was something other than Johnson.

So we made the decision. We'd drive down to Bakersfield tomorrow. We weren't fully decided on what we'd do there, but Mac said the drive shouldn't take more than three hours.

Which also meant Sam could have driven up to San Isolde in three hours. More than once. An interesting possibility. Had Sam been the person in black who'd flattened me in the hallway? And if so, why? Was he looking for something specific in the house, something that tied him to Miles's murder?

Blake came over that evening. He'd found two private investigators in San Isolde, but one was leaving on vacation day after tomorrow, and the other said she didn't handle murder investigations. Both had given him names of other people to contact in Modesto or Merced or Fresno. He planned to do that tomorrow. He said he should also have Elena's bail money together by then.

Mac and I exchanged glances, as we often do, and silently agreed that we wouldn't tell Blake about our plans for tomorrow. Younger people tend to fuss when older people do something they consider iffy. Was this iffy? Maybe even dangerous? I dodged those questions and asked Blake if he'd talked to Nicole again.

"Yes. She didn't seem quite so mad at me. At least she didn't hang up when I called and told her I'd like to do a Cookie Lady reading. I thought maybe that would soften her up, but she wasn't un-mad enough to crumble cookies with me. I think I'll stop by the bakery tomorrow. Maybe I'll act surprised, as if I didn't know she works there, so she won't think I'm stalking her or something."

I was impressed with Blake's apparent determination to get somewhere with Nicole. "Tell her you heard the bakery has great blueberry muffins," I suggested. "Because they do. And you've just heard it from me."

"Okay, I'll do that. What are you two doing tomorrow?"

"Oh, we thought we'd take a drive," Mac said, very offhand. He made it sound as if we had in mind a peaceful ramble around the countryside looking at scenery and flowers and cud-chewing livestock. Nothing iffy. "We may not get home until late."

"I hope I can have Elena out of jail and a PI working on the case by then. And Nicole willing to do a cookie reading and then have dinner with me again. You two have a nice drive."

**

MAC

Next morning, we debated whether to take BoBandy and Koop along on the drive. BoBandy, yes. He loves riding in the pickup with us. With some doggy sixth sense he already knew we were going somewhere and danced around the motorhome, begging to go along. Koop isn't nearly as enthusiastic about pickup rides as BoBandy, although he's too dignified to throw a catfit when actually required to take a ride. We decided to leave him at home. Ivy opened the curtains so he could watch what was going on outside between naps.

The drive to Bakersfield took a little less than three hours, but finding 3672 Y'Bera Drive took a while longer. At times like this, I start thinking we should get a GPS. But then I also think of the times I've heard about when GPS does something strange, such as send a traveler to a mountain road blocked by snow. Anyway, we don't have GPS but we finally managed to bring up a map on the phone and find the street.

The address was a fair-sized apartment complex. Not luxury-living but well-kept looking, maybe a motel in a previous life. Lemon-colored stucco with big bushes putting out beautiful red blooms even at this time of year. We had to get out and walk to find apartment 213. It was on the second floor, down a balcony walkway.

We walked on by while we considered, *what now?* Midday on a weekday, we decided that Sam was probably working and not at home. Which was okay. We'd ring the doorbell, then when we got no answer, start ringing other doorbells and asking questions about Sam. Where did he work? When did he usually get home? What did he drive? Was he a friendly neighbor? What do you know about him? We might even ask what he looked like, with the quick explanation that we were hoping to meet him but hadn't yet.

Step #1: ring the doorbell. Ivy did it. I stood right beside her, one hand on her waist.

Surprise. The door opened on the first push of the doorbell. But no cigarette-puffing grandson stood there. Instead, although she was smoking, it was a young woman who held the door open. She was barefoot, wearing scruffy green shorts and a white tank top, her dark hair short and spiky. A necklace with a scorpion embedded in what was supposed to look like amber, but was probably yellow plastic, hung around her neck. A snake tattoo spiraled her lower leg. She reached over to squash the cigarette in an ashtray with an all-too-realistic-looking rattlesnake coiled around it.

Ivy stiffened, I thought from the peculiar snake motif of the woman and apartment, and then I realized it was because she recognized the woman. It took me another moment, but then I recognized her too.

What did this mean? Sam had a wife or live-in girlfriend? A wife/girlfriend we'd seen coming around the backside of Miles's townhouse?

"We're looking for Sam," Ivy said.

"Congratulations! You've found her." The greeting wasn't totally sarcastic, but neither was it overly welcoming. "Are you selling something?"

"No, no . . ." Ivy stumbled verbally, as startled as I was to realize "Sam" was not the grandson we were expecting.

I was at a loss as to what to say next, but Ivy came up with, "Your grandmother says you should stop smoking."

"Grandma sent you all the way from Missouri to harp at me about *that*?"

"Is Sam your real name?" I asked.

Her attention shifted to me. "It's Samantha. But I switched to Sam when I flattened Andy Devier with a pineapple I'd brought for show-and-tell in fifth grade. I got in big trouble, of course. I thought maybe I'd be sent to prison. But then I decided it was worth it. Andy never tried bullying me again after that."

Samantha was either a tough young lady or making a good pretense at being a tough lady. Tough enough to murder Miles in a flash of temper? I leaned over to get a better look inside the apartment. What I could see was not reassuring. A corkboard with a variety of pictures pinned to it. An alligator. A mountain lion. A wolf. Samantha was apparently into predators. A mirror had another snake draped around it as a frame. Hopefully a phony snake, although I wasn't too sure. A water-filled aquarium stood on the far side of the room. Given Sam's taste in home and body decoration, I had to wonder what was in it. Piranhas?

Ivy took off in a new verbal direction. "You aren't working today?"

"No. I've been working from home since—" She touched her midsection, winced, and eyed us with sudden suspicion. "Who are you anyway? Why are you here?"

Ivy had noticed Sam's sudden touch to her midsection too. "Did you hurt yourself?"

"I leaned over and bumped into a cabinet door. I'm kind of . . . sore."

I suspected she bumped into something, all right. My baseball bat in a dark hallway. Although, at the moment, I was relieved that I hadn't hit harder. Even if she had no business being in Elena's house, I was uncomfortable realizing I'd clobbered this young woman. But I decided to go for a direct attack now and catch her while she was still a little off-balance with her manufactured story about an injury from a cabinet door. "We understand you knew Miles Willoughby."

She hesitated momentarily, then said warily, "Who's Miles Willoughby?"

"You told your grandmother Miles was dead," Ivy said.

"Did I?"

"But you didn't tell her Miles was murdered," I said. "Why not?"

I thought she was simply going to deny knowing him, but instead she crossed her arms and eyed me defiantly. "I thought it would make her feel bad. In spite of what he did to her, creep that he was, she was still hoping he'd show up again. Now, because of that old goat, she's lonely and also doesn't have enough money for those cruises she saved up to go on. She loved those stupid cruises."

Sam might be a little odd, at least from our older point of view, but it was obvious she cared about her grandmother. Admirable . . . but did it also mean she was willing to commit murder for Grandma?

"So you did know Miles," Ivy said.

Sam jutted her jaw out and planted her feet a few inches farther apart. Her arms fell to her sides, fists clenched. "No, I didn't know him." She looked Ivy, and then me, right in the eye again when she said it. The message was plain: *That's my story and I'm sticking to it.*

She looked capable of flattening us just as she'd done to that kid back in the fifth grade: steel in her gray eyes, earrings shaped like exotic curved knives, black toenails filed to sharp points. I had an irrelevant, Ivy-type thought: how many pairs of socks did she rip through in a week with those toenails? Then I decided she probably wasn't a sock-wearing type of person anyway. I pulled Ivy several inches back from the doorway.

"We saw you at his townhouse," Ivy said. "Before he was killed, someone else also saw you there. You ran out his door yelling that he wasn't going to get away with it."

"Someone should get their vision and hearing checked," Sam snapped. "Now, if you'll excuse me, I need to get back to work."

Not a noisy door slam, but a moment later we were looking at a closed door.

**

IVY

Samantha "Sam" Johnson knew something, and she had some kind of midsection injury, but she obviously didn't intend to share anything with us. Would giving her name to Officer Hutchinson accomplish anything? Doubtful. We had no evidence against Sam other than a peculiar taste in home and body decoration and the fact that we'd seen her at the townhouse. Officer Hutchinson might even chalk that up as a mistaken sighting by seniors watching too many crime shows on TV. He was obviously convinced they had their killer in Elena.

But if Blake hired a private investigator, he might be more open-minded about what we'd seen. Although I had to admit that, while seeing Sam at the townhouse several days after Miles was dead was suspicious, it was hardly handcuff-level evidence. If we just knew why both Earline and granddaughter Sam were so angry at Miles...

Well, you find out things by watching and asking.

We went back to the pickup, took BoBandy for a short walk, and then settled down to wait until she left so we could talk to her neighbors. We could see Sam's doorway from the pickup. It took a good two hours, interrupted by another short walk for BoBandy and the comings and goings of various residents, but it finally happened. Sam came out the apartment door, now wearing jeans and a slouchy hat, trotted to the closest stairway down from the second floor, took the stairs in a few quick bounces, and jogged to a white car parked with a line-up of other vehicles at the curb. The same car we'd seen at Miles's townhouse? Maybe.

Oh, to have all the youthful energy and agility Sam had! I know. Irrelevant. *Thank you, Lord, that I can still get around as well as I can. Even if I can't wear high heels anymore.* We waited a few minutes, then went back up to the second-floor balcony walkway.

We rang the doorbell at the apartment next to Sam's. No response. Two doors down, a woman about Sam's age opened the door. She looked a little groggy. Maybe stoned on the drug du jour? She was still in a bathrobe, hair a semi-blond tangle, flip-flops on her feet.

"We're sorry to bother you, but Samantha Johnson—" I broke off as I remembered Sam hadn't given us a last name.

"Isn't home," Mac filled in helpfully. "We wondered if you know her?

"Sam? Sure, I know her. She works out of her apartment on her website business, so if she's gone it's probably just to the grocery store or Starbucks for a few minutes."

"We don't actually know Sam, but we've talked to her grandmother," I said hurriedly. We needed to get this done. I doubted Sam would be pleased to come home and find us questioning neighbors. If she'd bought a pineapple, we might be in for a rough time. "I think Earline is worried about her."

"Earline? That's her grandmother's name?" The way the woman spoke suggested she'd never realized grandmas had names; they were just Grandma. "I don't know anything about her grandmother, but I do remember Sam saying once that she and her grandmother might take a cruise together."

"Does Sam ever go up north to see other family?" I asked.

"I have no idea. I mean, I know her, but since I've been working nights and sleeping days, I hardly ever see her." She yawned, and I guiltily revised my drug-du-jour assessment. Just a hardworking, sleep deprived young woman.

"Does she have other friends here whom we might talk to?"

"There's a guy in an apartment down on the first floor. I see him up here occasionally."

"Do you know his name or which apartment he lives in?" I asked.

"Jake, I think. He works at home too. I think he draws a comic strip or something. But I don't know what apartment he's in."

"Sam seemed to have some injury to her stomach area. Something about hitting a cabinet," I said. "She said it was sore."

This woman might be sleep-deprived, but she caught that slipup. "I thought you said she wasn't home."

I stumbled into my fallback comment. "Umm."

Mac said, "This was earlier."

The woman let it go. She yawned again, then laughed. "If she's like me, she bent over that cabinet in the bedroom and whacked her belly. These apartments are all alike, you know. Someone should have their head examined for the way they built those cabinets. A real design mess-up. The tangle of pipes under the sink is weird in these places too."

"Oh." I gave Mac a glance. Did this cancel our suspicion that Sam's midsection injury came from a baseball bat in Elena's dark hallway? *No.* "Well, okay. Thanks."

We went down to the first floor and tried the apartment directly below Sam's. No answer to the doorbell. No answer at the apartments on either side. But three doors down, a bookish-looking guy with dark-rimmed glasses answered. He had neatly cut brown hair, faded jeans, and a plaid shirt with sleeves rolled up. Behind him, the apartment looked neat too, more office than apartment actually. Desk, easel, filing cabinet, framed collection of comic strips. No snakes, real or manufactured, no aquarium with questionable residents. Maybe opposites attract? Although I then noticed that he was also barefoot and had a tattoo on the top of his foot. His tattoo, however, was a cartoonish figure of a kangaroo holding a flower. Rather sweet, actually.

Mac's thinking didn't wander the way mine did. "We're looking for Jake," he said.

"I'm Jake." He appraised us with mild interest.

"Sam in the apartment upstairs isn't home, but someone told us you're a friend of hers?"

He didn't comment on the *friends* aspect. "Who are you?"

"We're from up north," I said. "San Isolde. We're wondering if Sam has been up there looking for us."

He shrugged. "If she isn't home, wait around."

"Did you go up to San Isolde with her?" Did he fit into that shadow in black that crashed into me in Elena's hallway?

"Why would I do that?"

"Why not?"

He scowled as if that was not a proper response from an unfamiliar elderly couple at his door. "Well, for one thing, we aren't going anywhere together. Sam and I were seeing each other for a while, but we broke up not long ago."

"Why?"

He gave me back my own inscrutable question. "Why not?"

"This is really quite important. It's possible Sam was involved in—" I broke off. Did I want to mention murder yet?

Mac filled in for me. "Or she knows something about—"

I finished our two-person, one sentence dialogue. "Something that happened up at San Isolde."

"I don't know anything about San Isolde. I don't even know where San Isolde is," Jake said. "We broke up because Sam has a temper that goes off like a Molotov cocktail once in a while. Sometimes it's a good anger. She's a strong conservationist, you know. A preservationist. She cares about—" He hesitated momentarily, as if thinking about Sam's interest in predatory creatures. "All life forms."

"She has an aquarium, doesn't she?"

"Yeah, but it may be empty now. She was pretty upset when her oscar fish ate her angelfish. But throwing something in my face was what broke us up. I'm not into all that drama."

"Why did she throw something?"

He shrugged. "I may have said something . . . disparaging when she mentioned getting a leopard tattooed on her back."

"What did she throw?" I know. Irrelevant question. But my curiosity gene has little tendrils that squiggle out in all directions.

"A kale smoothie." He scowled, but then he must have realized that a kale smoothie sounded somewhat less than life threatening, and in spite of a determination to stay angry with her, a smile tugged at his mouth. But could the kind of temper that resulted in a throwing of kale smoothies escalate into a gun-shooting murder? "She's kind of a health-food nut." he added.

"Health foods . . . and smoking?"

"Yeah, well, I keep nagging her about that."

"Does Sam own a gun?" I asked.

"A gun? What's that about?"

"It's related to something that happened in San Isolde."

He considered the possibility, then scoffed at it. "Sam's into health food stuff, not weapons. That's why she had a kale smoothie, not a flame thrower, in her hand."

"Do you think Sam is capable of doing something more dangerous than throwing a health-food smoothie?" I asked.

"Like what?"

"Like, well, maybe murder."

His head jerked back as if a puppet string had yanked it. "*Murder*? Sam? Whose murder?"

"A man named Miles Willoughby up in San Isolde," Mac said. "Has she ever mentioned him?"

"What are you, a couple of busybody *Murder, She Wrote* wanna-be's?"

"They arrested a friend of ours and charged her with Miles's murder—"

"And now you're trying to do . . . what? Pin it on Sam?" In spite of his breakup with Sam, he sounded both protective and hostile.

I opened my mouth to say something, but he didn't give me a chance. "I think I've said enough. I have to go now. Don't bother to have a nice day."

Another closed door.

I figured that two minutes after Sam got home, Jake would be up there telling Sam about our visit. Two minutes after that, they'd be laughing about the tempestuous smoothie-tossing incident and the weirdos who came asking about her.

Well, if nothing else came of this day, I figured we'd revived an interrupted romance.

CHAPTER 21

IVY

We didn't see Blake when we got home that evening. We were hopeful that meant he was out with Nicole. When he came over the following morning, however, he said he hadn't gotten home until late last night. He'd talked with a couple of private investigators and finally hired one who worked out of Fresno. Today he planned to meet with Elena's lawyer and get her released on bail, and then the PI would be here tomorrow morning to interview all of us.

Blake said the PI he'd hired, Rod Steele, had just nailed a woman who burned down the house where her ex-husband and his new wife were living. His success with the arson woman sounded like a great recommendation for his investigative abilities. Although there was that name. Rod Steele sounded like something out of some lurid old pulp-detective magazine, someone who called women "dames" and always had a cigarette dangling from the corner of his mouth.

I determinedly quashed that thought. Stereotyping someone on the basis of a name was both unfair and foolish.

With a professional private investigator on the job, Mac and I, I told myself firmly, could just step back from any further investigating and let him do his job.

Blake didn't get Elena home until mid-afternoon, and the salad in the special lunch I'd fixed for her homecoming was a little limp by then, but she rushed in with big hugs for both the cats and us. Over lunch, she talked about jail and the people she'd met there, including a rather nice male guard. She'd given her shark-tooth slippers to a young woman in jail for domestic abuse; the woman had clobbered her wayward husband with a frozen fish. Elena said the next step in her own legal process was a preliminary hearing in about ten days.

Elena talked vivaciously for a couple of hours, like someone relating details of a memorable vacation, but then, like a light going out, she collapsed into a nap with Felicity and Fancy snuggled up beside her.

Blake took off for the bakery to buy more blueberry muffins, although there were still a half dozen in the fridge. He was still hopeful about perking up his disaster-prone relationship with Nicole.

**

Next morning the private investigator hadn't yet arrived by the time we'd finished breakfast, taken BoBandy for a walk, and talked to Mac's family up in Montana.

I'd just gone over to the house to ask if they'd heard anything from Rod Steele and was looking out the kitchen window when a big SUV skidded to a stop in front of the house. I couldn't identify the make of vehicle, of course; I never can. But I can tell an SUV when I see one, and this one was black and enormous, conspicuous as a tank dressed up for a fancy soiree. Several antennas bristled from the top.

Blake looked out the window too. "Oh, good. He's here."

My first thought was that Rod Steele was never going to do any discreet investigating in that vehicle. Then I chastised myself for again prejudging the man. Sometimes looking big and bad was no doubt effective for a PI.

He strode from vehicle to house with an impressive swagger. Blake jumped up from the dinette table to let him in. Mac came in the back way.

"Sorry I'm late," Rod said when Blake brought him to the kitchen. "Had a call from a former colleague back East. He needed advice on a serial-killer case. I brought down a serial killer a few years ago for a client whose sister was murdered. Bad stuff." He shook his head.

He wasn't tall, but he was solidly muscular in black jeans and a black turtleneck. Black hair, mustache, good looking, in a Burt-Reynolds-in-his-prime kind of way. A silver eagle with wings spread dangled from a heavy chain around his neck.

Impressive. Masculine but stylish. But I couldn't help wondering, wasn't that chain a little risky? It would make a handy choke-hold weapon if some guy with less than friendly intentions grabbed it.

Then I once more chastised myself. Was I just looking for some way to criticize the guy? Was I actually just a little envious of him? Although we had solved a few mysteries and murders, we weren't authentic private investigators. And he was.

Blake made introductions, and Rod shook hands all around. I could tell his handshake with Mac was forceful enough to qualify as a wrestling move, but he apparently didn't feel the need to impress Elena and me, and our handshakes were little-old-lady limp. I tried to feel pleased with his consideration, but I had to groan when he said what a pleasure it was to meet "you young ladies."

I gave him a beady-eyed glare. *That's shin-kicking territory, mister hotshot private eye.* But I don't believe he noticed me or the glare.

"Coffee?" Elena offered.

"Yes, please. Black." Rod accepted the cup she handed him and then said briskly, "So, let's get right down to business." He spotted a chair in the corner and in a take-charge move pulled it up to the dinette table.

"I'm sure you're all interested in my qualifications for this case, so I'll give you a little rundown on what I've done." He then proceeded to elaborate on the arson-lady and serial-killer cases, another case involving a man who had multiple wives and families, a couple who made off with the life savings of an elderly woman they were supposed to be caring for, and a woman who'd murdered four husbands.

Rod didn't quite proclaim himself to be a masked and/or caped superhero, but he was definitely the star of each of these cases. I felt a snarky urge to ask him where superheroes changed clothes these days since phone booths were no longer available.

"Blake here has told me something about your fiancé's death—" He nodded gravely to Elena. "And how you've been unfairly charged. We'll get the goods on the real killer."

That sounded good. He really believed in Elena's innocence.

He then shot questions at each of us, often interspersing our answers with comments about how that was similar to some other case he'd handled. He took notes on an electronic gadget with which I was not familiar.

Mac and I had earlier talked about whether we should reveal what we suspected about Miles's bank robbing activities and had decided we probably should. I was afraid this would upset Elena, so I was relieved when she told him herself and even brought out the wrinkly masks to show him. I was further surprised when she mentioned that Miles may have had an ongoing relationship with several women he'd met on cruises, possibly conning them out of money. This did enable us to mention our phone calls to the cruise ladies and our meeting with Sam/Samantha in Bakersfield.

"So you've been investigating on your own into who killed Miles?" Rod's eyebrows scrunched in disapproval.

"We thought whatever we could find out might be helpful," Mac said.

"That's a worthy goal, but I must caution you against blundering around in any of this. Amateurs can endanger themselves or others or contaminate or destroy important evidence. And people of your age . . ." He shook his head, apparently appalled at the damage we creaky old folks might do. "You should leave this kind of thing to professionals who have the tools and experience to know what they're doing."

I felt properly chastised even though his displeasure with our old-age "blundering" made it sound as if we'd been poking around in brain surgery with a potato peeler. He made some kind of note on the electronic gadget.

He might be right, of course. I had to admit that our investigations in the past have occasionally tangled us in dangerous situations. But we'd also turned up a killer or two.

Rod then said he'd be talking to Stan as well as neighbors here on Eidenburg Road and then taking a trip down to Bakersfield in the near future to talk to this Sam/Samantha Johnson. Elena emphasized that we did not want to incriminate Miles in any illegal activities, that we were telling Rod these details only to aid in finding the killer. Rod nodded and assured us everything we told him was strictly confidential.

I felt doubtful about that. Confidential until he was bragging to another client about how he solved the killing of a notorious bank robber?

"I'm curious about your name," I said when he stood up to leave. "It seems so . . . private investigator-ish."

He chuckled. "Actually, Rod Steele is a pseudonym I use to keep my professional life separate from my private life." He did not offer his real name, which I suspected was considerably less PI sounding. "I'll probably publish memoirs of my experiences as a PI one of these days, and I'll use the Rod Steele name then, of course. This guy I know who's had a book published says it'll be a super-size best seller and will probably make it into a movie production as well."

Blake eventually walked with Rod out to the SUV, and Elena, Mac, and I looked at each other as we followed as far as the living room.

"Seems like a nice young man," Elena said. She sounded rather morose.

"He's apparently solved quite a number of cases," I said.

"He took a lot of notes," Mac added helpfully.

Silence, then, until Elena, in a rather small voice, asked, "Does this state have a capital punishment penalty for murder?"

"I don't know."

Another silence, until Elena finally said, "I appreciate that Blake is trying to help by hiring a private investigator, but I'm not sure I want to bet my life on Rod Steele's investigative skills. I don't think I have quite as high an opinion of him as he does of himself."

I figured there was no ladder tall enough to reach up to the height of Rod Steele's opinion of himself, although I didn't say anything. I looked at Mac, and we exchanged thoughts without words as we often do. This thought said that even if there was now a professional PI on the job, it wouldn't hurt to do a little more investigating on our own. Just in case Rod Steele ran into his very first case where his superhero abilities came up short and some crook's fist yanked the silver chain tight around his neck.

Blake returned from his walk to the SUV with what I thought was an over-hearty smile on his face. "He seems to know what he's doing, don't you think? Very successful." Then the smile disappeared, and he plopped down on the sofa. "Quite dazzled by his own success, in fact."

I used my handy-dandy, fits-all comment. "Umm."

"I've never hired a private investigator before," he muttered. "Maybe I should have looked around a little longer. But I figured we needed to get going on this right away."

Elena jumped up from the burgundy recliner. "I'm sure he's very capable," she said, "but what I need is a cookie-crumb reading from Nicole."

I groaned inwardly. I had my doubts about Rod Steele, but my thoughts about cookie crumbs weren't just doubtful; they were as negative as Koop is about having a bath. I made an attempt at dissuading Elena.

"Don't you think it would be better to leave these things to the experts, the police and all?" I didn't mention Rod.

"The *experts*? All the 'experts' have done so far is put an innocent person, *me*, in jail," she scoffed. "Along with that nice young woman who gave her philandering husband exactly what he deserved. Except she should have used a bigger fish and hit harder. And they should have given her a big trophy commemorating the occasion instead of sticking her in jail."

Elena's fervent comment gave me an uneasy squirm. We'd pretty much eliminated her from any suspicion in Miles's death, but her comments about her jail companion were pointed proof about how she regarded philandering males. And if Miles had been philandering with those various cruise ladies, and it was her gun that had killed him . . .

Elena immediately called Nicole at the bakery. Nicole was happy to hear from her and delighted she was out of jail, but she said she had clients already booked for the next several evenings. I had the unexpected feeling Nicole was trying to wiggle out of doing a cookie-crumb reading for Elena right now. But Elena persisted, and Nicole finally agreed to cancel her Sunday evening appointments and do a reading for Elena then.

**

We went to church on Sunday morning, of course, a communion Sunday, which felt good. It's always a joy to share that special time with the Lord. But now here we were in Nicole's apartment on Sunday evening, quite a crowd of us, actually. I came because I was concerned about Elena and how easily she seemed to be influenced by what the cookie crumbs "said." Mac came because I did. Blake was here because he wanted to use a cookie reading to get into Nicole's good graces.

Nicole greeted both Mac and me with hugs. Blake didn't get a hug, but he didn't get anything thrown at him, à la the fish-hurling woman in jail. Nicole simply asked him right at the door why he was there.

"As I told you before, I want a cookie reading. I'm here as a client. A cash-paying client." Blake was looking quite handsome and not at all oddball tonight. Sports coat, jeans, loafers. No orange or purple socks. No socks at all, in fact. I thought that was normal for the generations younger than ours, and certainly saved on sock expenses, but I've never been able to embrace socklessness as a way of life for myself.

"I'm not sure I want to take on any new clients," Nicole said. "I may decide to discontinue the Cookie Lady business."

"Oh no, you can't do that!" Elena wailed. "Why would you quit?"

"I won't have time if my evenings are spent studying. I'm talking with a college counselor about going back to get my degree, and I think it's going to happen." She smiled at Elena. "But I'll still be here for special clients. Like you."

Elena clapped her hands. "Good! Thank you."

"How about me?" Blake said. "I'm a special client's special nephew."

Nicole gave him another look. The compressed line of her lips looked tight as a zippered purse, but she finally said, "Okay, I'll do a reading for you. *One time.* I do appreciate your putting up the bail money to get Elena out of jail."

Which was the real reason she agreed, I suspected; she felt she owed Blake for helping her friend.

"Blake can go first," Elena said. I figured she was afraid that, given a little time, either Blake or Nicole might back out.

We all trooped inside. The scent of cinnamon and vanilla was absent tonight; in fact, the scent in the apartment was distinctly onion-ish. Nicole motioned Blake into her cookie-reading room and then to one of the tall, padded chairs at the table. The chair looked flimsy under Blake's masculine physique, as if it might do a chair-crumble before the cookie crumbling even got started. Elena and I crowded the door to watch. A tray of cookies and accompanying tools were already on the table. Nicole went through her usual routine.

"First, you pick a cookie."

Blake used his fingers to pick the top cookie on the pile, a peanut butter cookie with little lines drawn across the top. He slapped it down on the table.

"Is there anything in particular you want to learn from the cookies this evening?" Nicole inquired.

"*Learn* from the cookies?" Blake repeated.

"Yes. Learn from the cookies."

"Well, uh, just the usual, I guess. Am I going to get rich or fall in love or have some big disaster. Maybe something about whether I should take the position where I wouldn't be traveling so much."

"Okay. Crumble."

"How?" He eyed the tools.

"However you want."

Blake shifted uncomfortably on the chair, but he picked up the cookie and crumbled. He did it in what I considered an unusual way, by putting the cookie between his palms and briskly rubbing his hands together. When the cookie was reduced to crumbles, Blake dusted his hands against his jeans.

I leaned over to get a better look at the crumbs. They'd fallen into a neat pile with some ridges but practically no scattering. Oh, my. It looked much like a pile scooped up by Koop when he had nice, soft dirt in which to do his business. I looked at Nicole. Surely she couldn't "see" anything in that.

"This is a rather unusual pattern." Nicole kept her hands in her lap. It seemed to me she was stalling while she tried to figure out something.

Finally she said, "There's not enough scattering for a comprehensive reading, but these ridges are a good indicator of character and personality traits. I see generosity in this long ridge here." Her finger traced the ridge from above. "Loyalty over here. Kindness. A sense of humor. Intelligence. Self-confidence. Determination. A dedication to work."

It was the kind of flattering character reading that would surely delight most clients.

Blake grinned and made an exaggerated show of puffing out his chest. "That's me all right. All the qualities of a great man. Surely it also says something about how humble I am?"

Nicole almost smiled too, but she managed a deep forehead wrinkle instead. "It is, however, as shown by the shape of this concavity in the crumbs,"—her finger hovered over a faint dip in the crumb pile that with some exaggeration might be called a concavity—"a dedication to work that might more correctly be considered workaholic. With a definite tendency toward stubbornness."

Blake nodded, not arguing with the crumbs. "Stubborn can be good," he said. "What about my thinking about moving to a job with the company where I wouldn't have to travel so much, maybe have more family time?"

Nicole moved her finger to a minuscule bump on the pile of crumbs. "I see an impressive future for you whatever you decide to do. Although I don't see you settling into family-man status any time soon."

I couldn't see any of that in the pile of cookie crumbs, of course. There weren't even that many ridges. In fact, the flattering traits Nicole had listed were fairly obvious to anyone who knew Blake. He was loyal and generous to his aunt Elena. Intelligent and hardworking or he wouldn't be as successful in his high-paying job as he obviously was. He seemed determined in his pursuit of Nicole. Nicole had carefully made no specific predictions for the future.

She began her customary wrap-up to a reading. "And that's the way the cookie—"

Blake didn't give her a chance to finish. He groaned, like a man in the midst of a bellyache. He tucked his hands into his armpits as if he were trying to control them, but he couldn't do it. The hands jerked out, smashed the pile of crumbs, and then tossed them like confetti.

"Nicole," he said, "I like you. I admire your plan to go back to school and become a teacher. I intended to sit here and try to believe all this cookie-crumbling mumbo-jumbo. Or at least pretend I believed it." He shook his head. "But I just can't. I appreciate your thinking I have all these good qualities, and I hope I do have them. But a ridge or a dip in a pile of cookie crumbs doesn't give some magic insight into my character or future. It's just . . . nonsense."

Nicole drew back from the table, her neck stiff. "A reading isn't intended to be a professional psychoanalysis. Most of my clients see it as fun and perhaps a little helpful."

"But some of your 'clients' take it seriously, just like some people take astrology and reading tea leaves and looking into crystal balls seriously. And they're *all* just nonsense."

"Don't be shy, Blake," Nicole snapped. "Say what you really mean." The sarcasm erupted like an explosion of metal cookie crumbs.

Blake stood up. "Okay, I will. It's more than nonsense. It's baloney. Gibberish. Hocus-pocus. Hogwash. I think you're sharp and smart, so I don't see how you can take any of this even semi-seriously. I also think it could be really dangerous if someone hearing this stuff did take it seriously."

"You didn't mention cockamamie, which was a word Ivy used earlier. Perhaps you and she should get together and discuss more insulting comments." Nicole shot me a frosty glance.

Elena broke into the hostile moment. "Okay, my turn!" She nudged her way past Blake to the chair.

"I'll wait outside," Blake muttered.

"You forgot my fee," Nicole said tartly.

They hadn't discussed fees, but Blake yanked out his wallet and threw a hundred-dollar bill on the table.

"Oh, I don't charge that—"

"Keep the change."

CHAPTER 22

IVY

Blake didn't exactly stomp to the door, but neither did he do a gentle tippy-toe.

"He's really quite a nice guy," Mac offered.

"Very nice," I echoed.

Elena just frowned. I knew she loved her nephew and thought highly of him, but she was also fond of Nicole. Now she just wiggled onto the tall chair. "I'm ready."

Nicole's glance at the doorway suggested she'd like to follow Blake with a blast of something more formidable than cookies . . . maybe a frozen fish or two . . . but she managed to confine her anger to scouring the wooden cutting board with enough force to rid it of any particles down to microbial level.

She finally slid into the chair opposite Elena. "Okay, pick a cookie."

Elena used tongs to extract a sugar cookie from the middle of the pile. She used the tips of her fingers to crumble the cookie rather daintily. The crumbs scattered nicely.

"What I want to know is what I should do about this awful accusation that I killed Miles. I think I know who really did it, and I think I know how to prove it. But first I need to know what the cookies say."

My first thought was that she'd be better off trusting even Rod and his over-inflated ego than some "opinion" from the cookie crumbs. My second thought, of course, was, who did she think killed Miles? Another thought was a distinct worry. What did she have in mind doing to "prove" this person was guilty?

Then I saw that Nicole was looking at the crumbs as if she were seeing a cockroach among them. Elena suddenly slammed both palms on the table as she apparently also saw what Nicole was seeing. "I am right. The crumbs say yes. I do know the killer!"

I'd have expected her to jump and squeal with delight; but she sounded more dismayed than pleased with this "confirmation" from the crumbs. Did this mean she'd rather the killer *wasn't* who she thought it was, and she'd hoped the crumbs would produce a different name?

Nicole frowned and shifted on the chair. "It looks that way." She sounded as if she wanted to add a "but," but couldn't think of one.

I moved around to Elena's other side. "I don't see—"

"It's right there!" Elena's finger followed the wavy tail of the *y* all the way to the edge of the board. "It's a *yes. Yes* to who I think killed Miles. *Yes* on how to prove he did it!"

And then I saw it. It wasn't as plain as skywriting, definitely not as readable as a computer printout. The *y* had a long, rather sinister-looking tail, like part of an eerie title on some horror novel. The *e* was some distance away, a little distorted and set at a catty-corner angle. The *s* had an extra curve in it.

But it was, with only a small stretch of imagination, a *yes.*

"Are you going to tell us who you think it is?" Mac asked.

"Or go to the authorities?" I added.

Elena hesitated. "Not yet. I still need proof."

"Don't do anything foolish!" Nicole sounded alarmed.

"Me, do anything *foolish?*" Elena threw up her hands to scoff at that possibility. "When have I ever done anything foolish?" She broke off with an unexpected laugh. "Don't answer that!"

Elena stood and gave Nicole a hug. "I knew I could count on you and the cookies. Thank you so much." She turned to me. "Ivy, don't you want a reading tonight? The cookies are *hot.* Or Mac, how about you?"

Mac said a polite, "No, thank you."

I said, "No, I don't think so," at the same time that Nicole said, "Not tonight."

We were agreed on one thing anyway. No cookie crumbling for the MacPhersons. We said rather awkward goodbyes. Nicole offered another warning about taking the cookie crumbs too seriously, but Elena just gushed more thanks.

Blake got out of his SUV when we went out to the pickup. "You okay?" he asked Elena as if she'd just undergone some unpleasant treatment in a doctor's office.

"I'm fine," she said, her tone cool.

Fond as she was of him, Elena was obviously annoyed with his outburst at Nicole. I supposed he could have been more diplomatic with his wording, but he was right. Cookie crumbling, even if done in fun, was like other devices of fortune-telling: baloney, gibberish, and hocus-pocus. Hogwash too. I mentally applauded him for telling it like it is, for being honest about his feelings even when he knew it wouldn't endear him to Nicole.

"I think I'll stop somewhere for a cup of coffee," Blake muttered. "I'll be back at the house later."

"We have coffee at home," Elena said. "Cookies too—" But then she caught the drift of what Blake was saying, that he didn't want to come right home and get into more cookie-crumbling arguments.

In the pickup, Elena also avoided the subject of cookie crumbling. She chattered gaily about the one time they had cookies in jail and someone had stolen hers, but she'd subdued into silence by the time we got home. Mac and I headed around back to our motorhome. I was frustrated with Elena for her stubborn faith in something as preposterous as a crumbled cookie. So a "yes" had showed up in the crumbs; so what? Nixon had showed up in my homegrown tomatoes one time too.

But Elena called after us, "Hey, how about some coffee? I'll make decaf."

I hesitated but then made an about-face to the front door. If Elena had some foolish scheme planned to gather proof, we needed to know what it was.

We gathered at the dinette to wait for the water to drip through the coffee filter. Elena set a plate of oatmeal raisin cookies on the table.

"Elena, you said you knew who killed Miles before you went for the cookie reading, that you wanted the crumbs to tell you if you were right." I detoured asking directly who it was, figuring she'd just clam up, and instead asked, "What made you focus on this person?"

"Just before I went to jail, I found something. It was in with some other financial records, so I just hadn't noticed it before. But now I know what Miles was doing with his bank robbing money."

"What?" Mac asked.

"He was giving it to those women. The cruise ladies."

"Why would he do that?"

"He was paying them back what he figured he owed them." Elena swallowed. "I guess he must have . . . conned them out of it earlier. But now he was paying them back. I think he wanted to get them all paid back before we were married."

That was conscientious of him, nice that he wanted to start the marriage with a clean slate. But paying them back with stolen money wasn't exactly the most ethical or legal way to handle it, even if it was kind of a Robin Hood-ish thing to do. I recall that Robin came to a rather dismal end at the hands of an evil aunt, at least in some versions of the legend.

"You found something that proves this?" I asked.

"I'll show you."

She disappeared down the hallway and into her bedroom. She returned with a sheet of folded notebook paper. It was an inconspicuous piece of paper; I could see why she'd missed noticing it earlier. Mac and I studied the page together. Several of the names written there were familiar. Gertrude Livingston. Emily Schaeffer. Earline Johnson. There were other names that I recognized as coming from Miles's little red book, but they were women we hadn't been able to reach on the phone. There were dollar figures after each name. Earline Johnson's dollar amount was in the midrange of the figures, $17,500.

"Why do you think this means he was paying them back these amounts?"

"Well, I just kind of put two and two together," she admitted. "The money from his bank robberies is missing, so it just seems logical that this is where it went. I think some of his trips were when he took cash to pay the women in person. He couldn't send a check if it was bank robbery money, but he wanted everything made right before we got married."

I thought about that little *p.* after names in Miles's red address book. Mac nodded.

"I'll be back in a minute," he said.

He disappeared down the hallway and out the back. Elena got out coffee mugs and filled them from the pot. When Mac came back with the little red book, I showed Elena the same names that were written on the folded paper, with the little *p.* beside each one.

"So you could be right. He was repaying a debt he thought he owed each of them, and he marked it down here," I said. "Except he hadn't yet repaid Earline—there's no *p.* by her name—and that was why both she and her granddaughter were so angry with him. Perhaps murderously angry."

"You think Earline's granddaughter drove up from Bakersfield and killed him?" Elena sounded surprised.

"Isn't that what you think?"

"No! I mean the notebook pages and Miles's little red book together show he thought he owed each of these women money and that he repaid it. I'm sure he intended to repay Earline too. But that doesn't mean a cruise lady, or someone connected with one of the cruise ladies, killed him."

"I guess I'm confused, then." I looked at Mac. He nodded agreement. He was confused too. "You said something you found before you went to jail was what helped you figure out who did it. This is the paper you found." Mac helpfully tapped the sheet of notebook paper. "So—?"

"I mean it helped me *think,* not that something I found pinpointed the killer for me. And in jail, I had plenty of time for thinking. I thought about the falling-out Miles had with Stan a while back, and I figured it out. And the cookie crumbs say I'm right."

By now I was feeling more than a little exasperated. Elena and the Cookie Crumbs. It sounded like a children's fairy tale. And fairy tale was what it was.

"So who do you and the crumbs think did it?" Mac asked.

If Elena noticed that the question was a little on the snarky side, she ignored it. "Stan," she said. "Stan did it. Which is why I felt kind of . . . downhearted when the crumbs confirmed it. I mean, he's Miles's *nephew*."

"Nephews have been known to kill uncles." From somewhere back in my librarian days, when I also spent spare time doing crossword puzzles, came a word I probably thought I'd never have use for, and yet it popped up now. "Avunculicide. That's the word for a nephew killing an uncle. Avunculicide."

Elena gave me a strange look, as if I'd just come up with something in cat-speak, but then she waved a hand to dismiss this peculiar bit of knowledge. "In any case, I think he did it."

"Why?"

"I'm pretty sure he and Saundra are having marriage troubles, and he wants out, but he figures in a divorce she'll get most of what he sees as his. But if Miles was dead, Stan thought he could manage it. He could let Saundra have the house . . . they're head over heels in debt on it anyway, Miles once told me . . . and he'd be fine because he'd inherit the townhouse. All paid for. Plus whatever other assets Miles had."

This seemed a little complicated, but we'd certainly had our suspicions of Stan so I couldn't dismiss Elena's conclusions. "How are you planning to come up with proof of this?"

"I'm not going to tell you." She tossed her head of blond curls and gave me a sly look. "Because if I tell you, you'll try to stop me. And the crumbs said yes, it would work, but you never believe the cookies."

Mac and I exchanged glances. She had that right.

And this was definitely a time to, as Blake had once requested, keep an eye on Elena.

Elena with an unpredictable plan was as big a worry as a stick of dynamite in my coffee cup.

CHAPTER 23

IVY

We kept a careful eye on Elena, watching her, as the old saying goes, like a hawk. Two hawks, actually. Senior version. But in the next few days she didn't do anything unusual. At least nothing unusual we could catch her doing.

She spent her time on ordinary activities. Baking. Making more knit caps for the children's charity. Meeting with her two lawyers, the one handling Miles's estate and the other handling her criminal case. Accustoming Felicity and Fancy to walking with a harness and leash. With better results than I'd ever had with Koop, I must admit. She even spent some time reading Miles's Bible.

The only activity we weren't sure about was the time she spent on the computer. We could see her, of course, and know she wasn't off on some dangerous mission, but we didn't know what she was *doing* and her actions were suspicious. She'd hastily shut the computer down whenever one of us came near, and if we asked what she was doing, she'd say vaguely, "Oh, looking at recipes and stuff."

We kept hoping that Rod Steele would show up with news that he'd gotten "the goods" on the killer, but Blake said he hadn't had more than a couple of brief texts from Rod. We did know Rod talked to some neighbors on Eidenburg Road because a man with a dog came over to tell Elena if that arrogant investigator came snooping around again, he was going to get out his shotgun.

Even though we were impatient with the lack of results from Rod Steele's investigation, and had some doubts about his investigative techniques, we hesitated to barge in with more investigation of our own. *He* was the experienced, professional PI; we were the "blundering amateurs." But we were concerned about Elena's safety, apprehensive that if we let her out of our sight she'd instantly put some dangerous plan into action.

Once we went into frantic search mode when she said she was going to take a nap and then just disappeared. She meandered in an hour later remarking with all innocence that she'd just felt like inspecting the fence on the back side of the property. Another time, when she was on the computer, I got an unexpected chance to actually peek at what she was doing. Which was watching videos of cute kittens.

She gave me a sly grin, and I realized what was going on. She'd just been having fun messing with our heads. I was a little annoyed . . . and a little admiring. Unpredictable Elena.

When she finally decided to go somewhere, which was over to Miles's townhouse late one afternoon to see if everything was okay there, she asked me to go along. Mac took the opportunity to go to the hardware store to pick up some weather stripping to fix one of the storage compartments under the motorhome.

The townhouse was beginning to smell a little stale when we stepped inside, but we inspected all the rooms, including the garage, and everything looked the same as the last time we'd been there. On the way out, something occurred to me.

"What about Miles's mail?"

"His mail? Oh my, I've never even thought about his *mail*. How could I forget that? There are several mailbox clusters for the townhouse occupants. Each townhouse has an individual locked box in a cluster." She pointed down the street. "Miles kept the key in the medicine cabinet."

I didn't ask the *why* of that.

She went back inside and returned with a key and a plastic bag in which to put the mail. We drove down the street to the cluster of metal boxes. Clouds had almost darkened the sky by then, but a streetlight illuminated the bulky collection of boxes. Miles's box bulged with mail when Elena opened it. She pulled out a few envelopes at a time.

"Junk . . . junk . . . electric bill . . . junk . . . car insurance bill . . . junk . . . junk . . ." She dropped the junk in the plastic bag and put the few important items in her purse. "Hey, what's this?"

It was a 9 x 11 brown envelope, heavy with contents and carefully sealed with tape. There was no return address. We both peered at the postmark. It was dated two days before Miles's murder and showed the envelope had been sent from right here in San Isolde.

"How peculiar," Elena said. "Should I open it?"

I started to say, *Of course.* It was probably just junk mail from some outfit sending calendars or address labels to encourage contributions. But then I stopped. More dangerous things than a calendar from the Protect Our Blue Lizards organization have been sent through the mail.

Miles had been killed by gunshot, but maybe someone had a backup system in place in case the gunshot plan didn't work out?

"Opening it could be dangerous—"

"What's the worst that could happen?" Elena scoffed. "I get a paper cut and an infection inflates my finger into a permanent obscene gesture?"

I blanked out the image that thought brought. "You need to take this more seriously. Remember the anthrax and ricin scares from some years back? Several people died from opening those envelopes that came in the mail. Anthrax and ricin aren't something the recipient has to *eat*; they work by inhalation."

She shook the hefty envelope. "It feels like a bunch of papers."

"You could take it to one of the lawyers and let him open it."

"I'll think about it. But if it's just junk mail, either one of those stuffed shirts will think I'm a senile old lady with a paranoid imagination."

"Better to be paranoid than dead," I said, which came out sounding more prim and prissy than the wise statement I intended. "Let's at least wait and see what Mac thinks."

Elena tossed the bag of junk mail behind the seat in her car, and back at home, I found Mac had finished the weather-stripping repair and was inside the motorhome watching TV. I told him about the big envelope that had come to Miles in the mail, and we discussed what the envelope might contain and what should be done about it.

Which turned out to be moot questions because Elena came over a few minutes later with the big envelope. Ripped open.

"My curiosity got the better of me," she admitted.

"So, what's in it?" I asked.

"Nothing powdery and poisonous. Just pages and pages of computer printout stuff. There are all kinds of dates and figures, but I can't tell what they mean. Maybe some kind of investments."

"Can you tell who sent it?"

"Actually, it's kind of odd. I think Miles may have sent it to himself. I looked at the address label again, and the writing looks like his." She frowned and thrust the envelope at Mac. "Here. You figure it out. Maybe it's a man thing."

I was mildly indignant at the "man thing" designation, as if it were beyond our female comprehension, but I didn't say anything. Elena went back to the house, and we spread the pages across the table.

**

A couple hours later, after a dinner of sandwiches eaten while perusing the printed pages, we were still puzzling over what they said. Intriguing was the fact that we'd run across the same cruise ladies' names with which we were already familiar, plus the name Secure Your Future Investment Club.

"That sounds familiar too. I think I've heard it somewhere . . . But why would Miles send this stuff to himself? It must be on his computer."

"Maybe he wanted to get the printed copies out of the townhouse so they couldn't be found. Or in case someone got into his computer and deleted everything."

"Who would do that?"

"Stan was anxious to find something in the townhouse after Miles died. Maybe this was it."

Stan! "Now I remember where I heard that Secure Your Future Investment Club name. It was when I first called Stan to tell him Miles was dead, and he thought I was a member of the investment club with that name. But I don't understand. Are you making any sense out of it yet?"

"I think so. This part looks like a record of Miles's dealings with the club. These figures show what he invested,"—Mac pointed to several early pages—"and these are dividend payments he received. Rather large payments."

"Didn't Stan say something once about Miles having some investment with him, but he sold it?"

"From the looks of this, he didn't sell. The payments were still coming in, although smaller than early on. The cruise ladies' investments started out paying good dividends too, but then they lost everything. Except Earline, as a later investor, never received any of those large initial payments. She just lost everything."

"That doesn't sound like a very well-run investment club."

"It sounds to me like what's called a Ponzi scheme, deliberately set up to swindle investors. Early investors earn big 'dividends' to encourage them to invest more and to get them to spread the word to their friends so they'll invest too."

"A 'you gotta get in on this' kind of thing?"

"Right. But the payments they receive early on aren't monies the club has earned. The payments come from money later investors are putting into the club. If the shysters can keep enough new investors bringing in new money, the scheme can go on for quite some time. With the shysters skimming off most of the investment money for themselves along the way, of course. Some of the well-known Ponzi schemes have swindled millions out of investors."

"So Stan let Miles make good profits all along, but he was scamming all the other investors."

"Looks that way to me."

"But why was Miles paying back what the cruise ladies lost investing in the scheme?"

"I'm guessing he promoted Secure Your Future as a good investment to them. Because the women took his advice and invested in it, Miles felt responsible for their loss."

"Aren't there rules and regulations about investments?"

"Lots of them. But there are laws about murder and robbery and all the other crimes too, and they still happen. I'd guess Miles planned at least one more bank heist so he could pay Earline too, but he didn't live long enough to pull it off. Although he doesn't mention anything in these papers about repaying the ladies' lost investments. Or robbing banks to do it."

"So why would Stan kill him?"

"I think what we have here is Miles's analysis of how the scheme worked with specific examples using what the cruise ladies lost. I think he intended to go to the authorities with this to get an official investigation started, which could ruin Stan professionally and probably put him in prison as well. Maybe Stan got suspicious Miles was going to do that. Or maybe Miles actually warned Stan he was going to do it, with the idea Stan might clean up his act and repay the investments himself."

"But Stan killed Miles instead. Should we go to the authorities with this information?" I asked.

"They may find it on his computer that they already have in their possession, but not necessarily. I think the most effective action would be to take it to the lawyer handling the murder charge against Elena."

"Let's go over to the house and talk to Elena about doing that."

But when we got outside, we could see that all the lights in the house were off. That should have made us suspicious, but at the moment we just presumed she'd gone to bed early and decided not to disturb her. Blake was apparently out somewhere. His SUV wasn't parked out front. We decided we'd have some ice cream and then go to bed early ourselves.

Then . . . disaster!

Okay, I suppose discovering you're out of ice cream isn't really a *disaster*, but it was a disappointment. My taste buds were all set for the Nuts 'n' Chocolate Fiesta we'd had a few days ago.

"We can have cookies and tea," I said. But cookies and tea fall short when you're anticipating a taste fiesta of chocolate and nuts.

Mac read my mind. "I'll run in to that convenience store next to the gas station and pick up a carton."

215

"Oh, you don't need to go to all that trouble—"

"I'll get a jar of caramel sauce too."

Who can resist an offer like that?

He went out to the pickup, BoBandy running to accompany him, and I changed into my nightgown, a flannel one because it was much cooler tonight. I was just looking for my slippers when a tap sounded on the door. I looked out, saw Elena standing there, and opened the door. A sprinkle of rain was falling behind her.

"I thought maybe you were gone," she said. "I heard the pickup leave."

So she came over to visit when she thought we were gone? Hmm.

"Mac went to get some ice cream. Would you like to come in and have a dish with us when he gets back? He promised caramel sauce too."

"Oh, thanks, sweetie. That sounds good. But I'm going right to bed. I just wanted to pick up that envelope of Miles's papers I left with you. Maybe I'll put myself to sleep trying to read through them. Did Mac figure out what it's all about?"

"He says it looks to him like proof Miles had worked out that Stan was running some kind of shady investment scheme. A Ponzi scheme, he called it. We think these papers are what Miles was planning to take to the authorities to get an investigation started."

"Which is why Stan killed him. The cookie crumbs and I were right!"

"We'll get together in the morning and discuss what to do, okay?"

I scooped up the papers, stuffed them back in the envelope and handed it to her. She gave me a wave with the big envelope as she headed back to the house.

A few minutes later I opened the motorhome door to see if I'd somehow left my slippers outside, and that was when I heard a car engine running out in front of the house. Blake coming home? Or was sly Elena trying to put something over on us?

I tiptoed barefoot over to where I could see around to the front of the house. The sprinkle of rain had stopped, but my nightgown dragged on the wet grass. And there she was, sitting in her little Ford

Fiesta, engine running. She must have decided that with Mac and the pickup gone, this was the time to carry out her plan, whatever it was. She'd even come over to the motorhome to check on us and make sure no one could follow her.

Then the car door opened. Elena slipped out and dashed for the front door. She must have forgotten something—

I hadn't time to make a sensible plan. I just scurried around the house and across the yard. I yanked the door to the back seat of the Fiesta open and stumbled in, wet nightgown tangling around my legs, bare feet slippery from the rain-wet grass.

I flung myself flat on the floor just as the door opened. At least as flat as I could get in the crowded space between the front and rear seats of the small car. The plastic bag of junk mail fell open, and a sea of advertisements flooded around me. Elena tossed something on the passenger's seat and scooted behind the wheel.

She eased the car away from the house, apparently cautious even though she knew, with the pickup gone, I couldn't follow her. Sneaky Elena; she'd been watching for a chance such as this! I could tell when the car made turns, but after a couple of turns I had no idea what direction we were going.

Now what?

I took stock of my status and was not impressed. I doubted slick professional Rod Steele ever found himself in the undignified position of doing his detecting while hunkered down in the back of a car headed to some unknown destination.

Surrounded by a flotsam of junk mail.

In a wet nightgown.

Barefoot.

CHAPTER 24

IVY

I lay there with every muscle rigid. I was relieved Elena hadn't looked in the backseat area and found me, but I was also a little disturbed with her. Didn't she know a woman alone should always check the back seat for lurking boogeymen (or boogeywomen) before getting in?

Maybe she should also check the peculiar scents in the car carpet. I hadn't noticed the scent earlier when just riding in the car, but with my face pressed against the carpet I couldn't miss it.

I mulled over the wisdom of sitting up and making my presence known. I had no idea what Elena's plan was, but I figured it had to be something iffy or weird. Even worse, probably dangerous. She had to figure we'd disapprove or she'd have told us what she had in mind. But maybe I could talk her out of it—

Or maybe she'd agree with me now, and later, when she was actually alone, go ahead with the plan.

While I was still mulling, she pulled over to the side of the street. With my only view the dark underside of the front seats, I couldn't tell what she was doing, but a moment later a faint glow told me she'd turned on her cell phone. Still without doing a back-seat check for lurking boogeypeople.

"Hi. This is Elena."

A response from someone I couldn't hear.

"I know you must be surprised to hear from me, but I have something important I need to discuss with you."

Who was she talking to? Her next words gave me a clue.

"It's concerning the Secure Your Future Investment Club. I think you may be in danger."

Stan! She wanted to discuss those papers in Miles's mailbox with *Stan*? Why would she think he could be in danger? Because we might tell the authorities about his scam? Then an even more disturbing thought: had she and Stan conspired in murder and that was why she was contacting him now?

"I can come to the house and bring the papers with me," Elena said. "Though it might be better if we met somewhere."

Frustrating that I couldn't hear the responses to anything she said. But not exactly an appropriate time to pop up and ask her to put the phone on speaker.

"How about if I meet you at the end of the driveway? I'll show you what Miles put together."

Another moment of silence from Elena, then, "Okay, see you there in a few minutes."

Those papers that had been in Miles's mail were what she'd tossed into the passenger's seat. Rather than prudently taking the incriminating evidence about the investment club to the authorities or her lawyer, she was going to show the papers to Stan.

The glow from the cell phone went off, and we started moving again. Several more minutes of turns and then the car stopped. I couldn't see anything, of course, with the side of my face jammed against the rough carpet, but I presumed we were in Stan's driveway now.

Again I debated with myself about sitting up, but if Elena and Stan were in cahoots, letting her know I was in the car would be dumber than the time I bought a fasten-in-front bra and mistakenly put it on backward. Hello, strange anatomical protuberances. If they were willing to murder Miles, they certainly weren't going to have any inhibitions about doing the same thing to me.

I heard a click as Elena unlocked the car doors. The dome light came on when Stan opened the door. I caught a whiff of the smoke scent that always clung to him. I scrunched harder against the rough and smelly carpet.

Elena said, "Hi."

The voice that answered sent a shock wave through me. A recognizable voice, yes, but not Stan's.

"I'm surprised you called me," Saundra said.

Me too.

This is what the crumbled cookies and Elena agreed on? That Stan was the killer, and Elena should contact *Saundra*?

"You've never called me before," Saundra said. "I've always had the impression you disliked me and resented my marrying Stan. Because of Nicole."

"Our relationship hasn't been close," Elena agreed. "I've had some . . . misgivings . . . about you, and I've been friends with Nicole for a long time. But I have become concerned about your safety recently. You probably don't know it, but Stan has had some kind of shady investment scheme going. He's defrauded thousands of dollars out of various clients. I was hoping you could provide some inside information to the authorities about the scheme."

"You think I'd be willing to help prove Stan is a crook?"

"I think you're in danger."

"From Stan?"

"Yes.

I expected some shocked response from Saundra, but what she said was, "Let's get out of here before he spots your car and comes storming out."

Elena backed onto the street and drove to where lights from above filtered into the interior of the car. A parking lot of some kind. She turned off the engine.

"I work with Stan in the office and know about the investment club, of course, but he's always been very secretive about it. So tell me what this is all about."

"Miles figured it out, and I think Stan killed him to keep him from reporting it to the authorities. I got to thinking that if Stan was willing to kill Miles, you might well be his next target. I've had the impression you and Stan have been having some, uh, marital problems. And he might decide to go with murder instead of divorce. Even if we haven't been friends, I didn't want that to happen to you."

"You think Stan might decide to murder *me*?"

"That way he doesn't have to split anything with you. The grieving widower keeps it all. It also keeps you from turning him in if you do know incriminating details about his scheme."

"You're right about marital problems," Saundra said. "And you're also right that I don't know anything about Secure Your Future being a shady scheme. I thought it was just another of Stan's not-so-brilliant business dealings. You say Miles had proof of what Stan was doing with the investment club?"

"The envelope is there in the seat. You must be sitting on it."

Elena turned on the dome light, which made me feel uncomfortably visible. I reminded myself of all the times when I've been invisible. Times I've overheard conversations because the people talking just didn't notice me. Times I've passed through a crowded room, invisible as a bug underfoot.

But what I've learned from those experiences it that invisibility can be a rather handy asset at times. I hoped it wouldn't fizzle now.

The papers rustled as Saundra shuffled through them. One thing I felt, in spite of my precarious position here, was relief. What Elena was doing meant she hadn't been in cahoots with Stan in murdering Miles after all.

"I have no idea why he did it, but I think Miles sent these papers to himself a couple of days before he was killed," Elena said. "I didn't think to look in his mailbox until today."

"Stan and Miles had a meeting there at the townhouse a night or two before Miles was murdered—"

"An appointment that Miles wanted? Or did Stan set it up?" Elena asked.

"I hadn't really thought about that, but now that you mention it, I think Miles asked for the meeting. Maybe it was because he wanted to talk to Stan about the phony scheme. They'd had a falling-out a while back, which Stan never explained to me, of course, but I'm guessing now that this scheme was what the split was about."

"More of Stan's secretiveness."

"Right," Saundra said. "But I'm sure Miles still cared about Stan as his nephew and may have wanted to give him a chance to make things right. But he sent himself a copy first in case Stan had a meltdown at their meeting and tried to destroy the proof Miles had."

"Stan kept wanting to get into the townhouse to look for something after Miles died. He told me a story about wanting to find some family ancestry information Miles had, but I think it was these papers about Secure Your Future he wanted to find."

"Has anyone else seen these papers?" Saundra asked.

"Just my friends Mac and Ivy. You've met them. They're the older couple who have their motorhome parked out back of my house. Mac pointed out to me what the information in the papers meant. He called it a Ponzi scheme."

My ears felt oddly tingly, hearing Mac's and my names mentioned by someone who didn't know I was listening. I also felt uncomfortable, although I couldn't say just why, with Saundra knowing we'd seen the papers.

A piece of junk mail shifted fractionally and touched my face, bringing a sudden urge to scratch where the touch made my nose twitch and itch. *No, no, no. Do not move. Do not scratch.* I scrunched my mouth around, trying to make that substitute for a scratch. Didn't work. All the mouth-scrunch did was pick up some stray carpet fibers, and now I needed to cough. I think I made a gurgling sound.

"Did you hear something?" Saundra asked.

I didn't hear any response. Without looking in the back seat, Elena must have shaken her head *no*

And I was again reminded of how PI Rod Steele would undoubtedly manage his sleuthing better than hiding in a back seat with junk mail, an unknown scent, and an itchy nose.

Silence, then, except for more rustling as Saundra apparently took a closer look at the papers.

"What Miles has here certainly makes a strong case that Secure Your Future is some kind of phony scheme," Saundra agreed. "I appreciate your letting me see this."

"I did a cookie-crumble reading with Nicole. The crumbs agreed with me that Stan killed Miles and also with my plan to contact you."

"Then Nicole also knows you were planning to contact me?" I thought Saundra sounded rather alarmed about that.

"Oh, no. I didn't tell anyone my plans," Elena said. "Mac and Ivy thought I should take the papers to the lawyer representing me on the murder charge, but I wanted to ask the crumbs if my idea about contacting you first was the right thing to do, and the crumbs said *yes*."

"Do Mac and Ivy know you came to see me tonight?"

"No. They've been watching me, but I managed to sneak away tonight." Another sound that I was pretty sure was a giggle from Elena. She was still enjoying how she'd outsmarted us.

A few more rustling noises I couldn't identify until Elena said, "What are you looking for in your purse?"

"I need a smoke. I'm looking for my lighter."

"I'd rather you didn't smoke in my car—"

Then a flare of light. Saundra was smoking anyway?

No. The flare of light was too big for that—

"What are you *doing*?" Elena yelped. "Don't burn those papers!"

Slapping and grunting noises as Elena apparently tried to put out the paper blaze, then the sound of Saundra opening the car door. I caught a flicker of flame through the open door as she tossed the burning papers outside. "Now you can just forget you ever saw them."

"I don't understand! Those papers were the proof that Stan was pulling some awful scam on innocent investors, and now you've burned them up!"

Unexpectedly, at least unexpected to me, Saundra laughed. "Actually, it was a very *good* scam. But Stan was so wimpy about promoting and marketing that it never brought in the kind of money it could have. We should have had it on a fast track with promotion. Late-night infomercials on TV. Seminars, with a free dinner at a good restaurant to bring people in. An email blast. Maybe a contest, with winners getting shares in the club."

A few moments of silence as Elena apparently processed what Saundra was saying. I did too.

"You lied to me," Elena said finally. "You knew about the scam."

"Knew about it?" Saundra laughed again, all pretense now as vanished as the cruise ladies' money. "It was *my* idea. We bought up a ton of worthless mortgages and stocks that we got for pennies on the dollar and put them all in that investment club. We could have made a killing if Stan hadn't been so wimpy about it." Another laugh. "Sorry. *Killing* probably wasn't the most . . . ah . . . sensitive choice of words there."

"Why are you telling me all this?"

That was my question too: why *was* Saundra telling Elena all this incriminating stuff?

Saundra's response was flippant. "Why not?"

"You were even scamming Miles?"

"Miles didn't get scammed." Saundra suddenly sounded resentful. Had she wanted to scam Miles too, but Stan had objected? "We kept paying him the 'dividends,' but he got his shorts all in a twist when he realized those little old ladies were losing a few bucks."

"He was paying them back. He seemed to think he was responsible for their losing the money."

Saundra laughed again. "He was responsible."

"He didn't cheat them out of their money. It was *your* phony scheme!"

"Stan was paying him a commission on sales in addition to the dividends, and I have to say, Miles was some salesman." Her tone turned reluctantly admiring. "Good ol' Miles could sell ice cubes to a tourist stranded on a glacier. But then he went all softhearted about those little old ladies, and we had to do something when he threatened to expose the investment club as a fraud. Except Stan was also too spineless to do anything, of course."

"Too spineless to kill Miles, is that what you're saying?"

Saundra didn't answer that question, but she didn't have to. The truth sat out there like a rotten tomato. But Elena spelled it out, as if she still couldn't believe it.

"Stan didn't kill Miles. *You* did!"

Saundra also ignored that. "You said Miles was paying back what the old ladies lost. How was he doing that? The commissions and dividends we paid him were pretty good, but not *that* good."

Elena hesitated a moment before saying, "I think he was . . . getting it from banks."

"You mean he had accounts tucked away that we didn't know about?"

"No. I think he was . . . robbing banks."

"Robbing banks! Miles a *bank robber*?" After a moment of apparent astonishment, Saundra laughed again. "Oh, that's awesome. I always thought he was such an honest, straitlaced old guy, but if he was a bank robber there was definitely more to good ol' Uncle Miles than I ever realized."

"He *was* an honest old guy," Elena said hotly. "That's why he was paying the ladies back. He felt responsible for what they lost in your scheme. And you killed him," she repeated.

"And you know what wimpy Stan was going to do when Miles told him he knew the investment club was a big swindle? He was just going to fold up and sneak off into the night."

Silence then. But suddenly everything felt different, as if the very air in the car had drained away.

Then Elena spoke again, this time with a catch in her voice, and I realized what had changed. "Why did you bring a gun?"

"My philosophy is that it's always better to have a gun and not need it than to not have a gun when you do need it."

No doubt a shrewd philosophy. Sometimes Mac and I have needed a gun and not had one. But a little worrisome coming from Saundra. Why did she need a gun now?

"Is that the gun you killed Miles with?" Elena asked.

"Of course not. *Your* gun killed Miles. This is Stan's gun."

Another, "I don't understand."

"Brains never were your strong point, Elena dear. Now start the car. We're going to take a drive."

That sounded like something out of an old grade-B gangster movie but ominous just the same. Elena apparently had her suspicions too.

"Why?" she asked.

"Because you're not going to go running off to the authorities to accuse Stan and me of something."

"Mac and Ivy read Miles's papers about how the scheme worked. Even if you . . . do something to me—" Elena stumbled over the words as she apparently realized this drive involved her own demise. "They'll still turn you in."

I groaned silently. *Thanks, Elena. Just what we needed. A handy addition to Saundra's to-do list: get rid of those old folks in the motorhome too.*

"The papers are gone now," Elena said. "They won't have any way to prove some wild accusation. But I'll take care of them if I have to."

I doubted that meant she'd put us on the Secure Your Future payroll.

"Now *drive.*"

Elena apparently couldn't think of anything else to do, and she turned off the dome light and drove. Saundra gave instructions for several turns along the way. I had no idea where we were going, but Elena suddenly figured it out.

"This is the back way to my place, where the far end of Eidenburg Road runs into Eastern! Why are we going there?"

"Because that's where I want to go."

"It's the long way around to get to my place."

"It's the way I'm familiar with. Aren't you wondering why?" Saundra sounded gleeful. "Because it's the route I always took when I wanted to watch your place, so I'd be on the far side of the house without actually going past it. I could park down the road in our beat-up old pickup no one ever notices. Then I'd walk back to where I could watch your house from back in the trees without anyone seeing me."

Saundra laughed again, a laugh that made me want to reach over the seat and pound her head with something large and heavy.

"You wouldn't believe how many evenings I spent out there in the dark watching your house, waiting for you to go somewhere. Bor-ing." She stretched out the word.

"Didn't Stan wonder where you were all those evenings you were out there watching me?"

"He goes to his gym several evenings a week. At least he says that's where he's going. I think he has a girlfriend on the side. And, having been the girlfriend-on-the-side with him myself, I know he's an expert at it."

"I thought you and Stan didn't even know where I live."

"Stan didn't. We wandered around that day we came to your house. I wasn't about to let on that I knew exactly where your place was. But the internet knows all. A few clicks of the computer keys, and there you are. Name, address, phone number. Police record too, if you want to pay for it."

"But I don't understand why you were watching—" Elena slammed the steering wheel with her fist. "Yes, I do understand. You were watching the house so you could sneak in and steal my gun to kill Miles with!"

"Bravo! Give the lady a gold star. You leave that back door unlocked most of the time, you know. I checked it out one time before I actually went inside. And the gun was easy to find, right there in your nightstand."

"Why did you want the gun? You didn't know yet that Miles was aware of the investment scheme and might turn you in."

"He started asking a lot of questions. Being really nosy. I knew we'd have to do something about him sooner or later. I figure it's always good to have a plan ready ahead of time." She managed to sound virtuous. A good person prudently making a sensible plan.

I just wished Elena had figured *this* plan better ahead of time, because what it felt like was a one-way trip to a dead end. With emphasis on the *dead*. Yet I had to say one thing for her: she was driving as slowly as if she were trying to lose a race with an arthritic snail. She was also keeping Saundra talking. Was that deliberate too?

"And then later on, I went in again to return the gun so the police would find it there. Although that was more difficult, with your busybody friends hanging around. I saw you leave the house in your car, but then I had to wait for them to go to bed. Then, wouldn't you know, nosy old snoops that they are, they came sneaking into the house right while I was there."

Hey, we weren't sneaking! Then I clamped down on that indignant thought. Irrelevant.

"I didn't have time to put the gun back where I'd found it. I just tossed it under the bed and ran. And then the old geezer hit me out there in the hall. *Hit me!* I don't know what he used, but I was sore for three days afterward."

Busybody friends. Nosy old snoops. Mac and me! Now my ears really tingled.

And now I knew who'd crashed into me in the hallway that night: Saundra, returning the gun. And it was Saundra that "old geezer" Mac had hit with the baseball bat. He was right when he said later that he should have hit harder. He should have hit her like he was clobbering a killer. Which he was.

"You told the police I had a gun," Elena said. "That was why they came looking for it."

"I believe that was an anonymous call."

"From Saundra 'Anonymous' Moore."

Saundra just laughed. "It's so easy to make your voice sound different on a phone. There are all kinds of gadgets you can get on the internet to do it. I didn't even sound like a woman on the call. I sounded like a young boy and I told them I'd done some yard work for you and saw you cleaning the gun. And I was afraid of you."

"How'd you even know I had a gun?" Elena asked.

"Miles once mentioned that he'd bought a gun for you for protection, so it seemed logical the gun must be there in the house somewhere. I was just lucky you hadn't hidden it in some weird place, like strapped inside the toilet or stuck inside a box of cake mix."

"I never use a cake mix," Elena said indignantly. "I make everything from scratch."

"Yes, of course you do! The perfect little housewife for Miles. Too bad he messed up. You two could have had a great happily-ever-after together."

Okay, now, right now, before this reached some no-turning-back point, I had to do something. Frantically . . . but slowly, hoping my old bones wouldn't creak . . . I turned my head, searching for some kind of weapon.

And what did I see? Junk mail. It was all around me, maybe even multiplying as I lay there.

"I guess I shouldn't have trusted the cookie crumbs when they agreed I was right about Stan killing Miles and thinking you'd want to help," Elena muttered. "Ivy told me fortune-telling is not a good thing to do."

"Really? I've been intrigued by those cookie readings. Stan mentioned them. I'd have given them a try, but not with *Nicole* playing Cookie Lady. But if the cookie-crumbling system was any good, the cookies would have warned that you were wrong about Stan killing Miles, wouldn't they? And just as wrong about coming to me."

Elena muttered again, something I couldn't catch this time.

"So I think I'll just stick with my marvelous little lady who reads tea leaves for me. She tells me something good is about to happen in my life."

"Something good as in getting me out of the way?"

"Whatever."

"How did you manage to get Miles's body over the embankment and down there in the woods?"

"I was waiting down the road from your house that night in the old pickup our gardener uses around the place. I knew I had to do something before Miles squealed to the authorities about the investment club. I followed the SUV when Miles left your place. I let him get to the townhouse and put it in the garage. Then I ran up and pounded on the garage door."

Again I wondered why Saundra was telling Elena all this. It certainly wasn't some conscience-stricken confession. Ego, I decided. She was just bursting to let someone see how smart and clever she was at managing this whole deadly scheme. Even if her audience was just short-on-brains Elena.

I should have a recorder strapped to my ankle and then I'd have all this incriminating information down solid. Or my phone. A phone will record, won't it? If you know what you're doing. Which

I obviously didn't, or I'd have my phone or a recorder of some kind with me.

Hotshot detective PI Steele would surely have the latest in electronic gadgets with him at all times.

"And then you got him out there in the woods where you could shoot him," Elena said. "How'd you do that?"

"I told him I'd gone to your house because I wanted to talk to you about doing a reception after your wedding." Again she sounded pleased with herself.

"And he believed that?"

"I also told him you weren't at the house but I'd spotted you walking down the road. That I went after you and you were acting all strange and disoriented and ran off into the woods. I said I'd looked for you and couldn't find you and I was so worried. I was afraid you'd get lost or injured. And he was all concerned, of course."

Yes, Miles would have been concerned if he thought Elena was wandering around in the woods in some sort of daze.

"So I told him to jump in the pickup and we'd go search for you."

"And then you got him down there in the woods looking for me and you shot him. With my gun."

"Which worked out rather well, don't you think? Although I suppose that depends on your point of view." She laughed, that superior, self-satisfied laugh that made me want to choke her. Would stuffing a handful of junk mail down her throat do it?

No, not an acceptable course of action. *Sorry, Lord.* Also, probably not possible. Saundra was years younger, pounds heavier, and no doubt a lot stronger than I am. I'd be the one who wound up choking on a mouthful of junk mail.

"And now you're planning to do the same thing to me as you did to Miles. Kill me down there in the woods."

Exactly. After Saundra had fed her ego by letting Elena see how cleverly she'd handled everything, she surely wouldn't let Elena free to run off and share the information.

"It'll work out great," Saundra said, her tone confident. "This is Stan's gun. It will look as if he did it. I'm wearing gloves, in case you hadn't noticed. My fingerprints won't be on the gun, only his."

"You'll frame your own husband?"

"I'd never have bothered stealing him from Nicole if I'd realized what a wimp he is. Good looking and charming, sometimes even fun. But wimpy as a mashed potato. And I don't exactly appreciate his having a new girlfriend."

"But I'm not going to walk down there in the woods with you," Elena said, stubbornness rising in her voice for the first time. "I just won't do it."

"So they find your body right there by the edge of the road." The shrug in Saundra's voice dismissed Elena's refusal as irrelevant.

Silence then, as Elena apparently digested the unpleasant possibilities looming ahead. Mac would be home with the ice cream by now, and he'd be worried about where I'd gone. If he looked and saw that Elena's car was also gone, he'd no doubt realize I was with her and be even more worried.

But I couldn't do anything more than send him frantic across-the-cosmos messages. *Hey, Mac, you out there? I need help!* Even though our thoughts often seem linked, and we're pretty good at knowing what each other is thinking, I'd never given our old-married-folks telepathy a long-distance test. Maybe there was a space limit to our dual thinking. Like across the room.

I did wonder one thing about Saundra's plans. She obviously intended to shoot Elena . . . as she would also do to me as soon as she discovered I was a back-seat lurker . . . and leave our bodies by the side of the road or down in the woods, but what would she do next? She couldn't just drive off in Elena's car. But if she left the car, she'd be on foot in the middle of nowhere. Had she thought about this problem?

I had a solution. I didn't intend to share it with her, of course, but she'd probably come up with it on her own. She could call Stan to come get her. Without telling him, of course, about her little plan to frame him for Elena's murder. She was probably even now practicing her later dialogue with the police to frame him and absolve herself of any guilt.

We eased into another turn in the road and Elena, in a very small voice, said, "I can see my house up ahead now. The lights are on. Blake must be home."

"Yes. Very cozy looking, isn't it? Stop right here. It's wide enough to park on the shoulder. I've parked here before."

It must be the corner Miranda had led us to, the corner where we'd found Miles's body.

Elena braked and pulled over to the side of the road. The interior of the car momentarily lit up as the headlights of a passing car swept through the windshield. The first of a swarm of traffic we could reach out to for help? Doubtful. Night traffic on Eidenburg Road was barely a trickle, never a swarm.

Elena thought of something. She slammed a hand on the horn and the honk blasted through the night. Great idea! In the silence of the night it sounded like an oncoming monster.

Well, maybe a little tinny for a real monster. It was a small car. But at least a semi-monster. Surely someone would hear. Maybe even Mac—

But the tinny blast ended abruptly, and Elena cried out in pain. I couldn't see what had happened, but Saundra must have hit her hand or arm, probably with a slash of the gun. Elena hadn't turned the engine off, and the car jerked forward a few feet before she hit the brakes again.

Think, Ivy, think!

I had only a few minutes before Saundra forced Elena out of the car and killed her. Or killed her right here in the car.

A careful lifting of my head confirmed what I already knew: in the faint light from the dashboard I could see there was nothing on the back seat to use as a weapon.

Oh, Elena, why aren't you a woman with a messy back seat loaded with stuff? An umbrella for boogeypeople whacking. A sweater to throw over boogeyperson's head. A bottle of water to toss in a boogeyperson's face.

Nothing. Other than an oversupply of junk mail and that smell in the carpet, the back seat was as pristine as a new vehicle on a car sales lot. And you can't pick up a smell and overpower someone with it.

Carefully I edged to a sitting position on the back seat. The headlights of the car now angled into the tops of the trees beyond the embankment. The way Saundra was holding the gun, muzzle aimed at Elena, I could actually see its shadowy outline in the space between the two front seats. In another moment or two, Elena . . . or worse, Saundra . . . would realize they were not alone in the car.

I could grab a handful of junk mail and throw it on Saundra and hope for the best.

I could reach for the gun and try to wrestle it out of Saundra's hands . . . and get Elena or myself shot.

Or . . .

Carefully, noiselessly as possible, I untangled my feet and legs from the clinging wet nightgown and drew my feet back.

"I heard something," Saundra said. "Don't try anything."

I've never thought of myself as a lethal-footed LOL—

But here goes!

CHAPTER 25

MAC

Where was she?

I'd come back from the store with the carton of Nuts 'n' Chocolate Fiesta and a jar of caramel sauce . . . but no Ivy. The lights were on, the jeans and sweatshirt she'd worn earlier draped across the bed, Koop curled up on top them. It wasn't likely she'd gone outside for a walk in the dark . . . and what was she wearing if she did go out? . . . but I stuffed the ice cream in the freezer and stepped outside to call her.

BoBandy jumped past me through the open door and headed for the corner of the house, tail snapping back and forth, but I couldn't tell if he was trailing a recent or older scent of her. Or maybe trailing a bug in the grass. BoBandy is a great dog and an enthusiastic sniffer, but he's rather easily distracted. He's better at tail-wagging than bloodhounding.

She must have left in a hurry or she'd have written a note. I looked back and saw her cell phone lying on the dinette table. Although that wasn't unusual. She isn't welded to her phone and often doesn't have it with her.

I went to the corner of the house and peered around. In the glow of the yard light I could see Blake's SUV parked out front. I crossed the yard and knocked on the door. Blake yelled at me to come on in. I found him slouched on the sofa in the living room, TV tuned to an ancient episode of *Gunsmoke*, can of Pepsi in his hand.

"I was just wondering if Ivy was over here?"

"I haven't seen her. I just got home a few minutes ago. I needed to fax some papers to the company, and it took me a while to find someplace to do it after hours. She isn't home?"

"I went to the store, and she was gone when I got back. Elena isn't here?"

"I haven't seen her either." He straightened on the sofa and set the can of Pepsi on the coffee table.

"Mind if I check the garage to see if her car's there?"

We both went out to the garage. Empty.

"Looks as if they may have gone somewhere together," Blake said.

That was what worried me.

"Would they go over to Nicole's?" Blake asked. "I'll call and find out."

Blake tapped Nicole's number into his cell phone as we went back inside. She apparently wasn't in his speed-dialing system, but he did know her number. I wondered if I should have done the calling. Nicole might just hang up on Blake.

She didn't, but perhaps only because he skipped small talk and immediately asked about Elena and Ivy. I could tell from his end of the brief conversation that Nicole hadn't seen either of them.

"There's probably nothing to be worried about. They most likely just decided to go to the store or somewhere . . ." His voice trailed off. He sounded worried anyway.

I don't tend to go into panic mode easily, but where Ivy is concerned, panic mode is definitely possible. I explained my worries to Blake.

"Elena thinks Stan killed Miles. Maybe you already know that. But it wasn't until earlier today that we learned Miles figured out that Stan was running some kind of phony investment club and possibly intended to turn him in to the authorities."

"A good motive for murder, I suppose. If you're the murdering kind."

"Exactly. And Elena had some plan—I don't want to, uh, jump to conclusions—but I'm afraid it could be a plan not necessarily well thought out."

Blake didn't argue the point. He nodded and phrased it more succinctly. "Knowing Aunt Elena, she might come up with a harebrained scheme."

"Anyway, she had some idea about getting more proof against Stan or something like that. She wouldn't tell us what she intended to do, but that strange cookie-crumbling thing of Nicole's told her *yes*, it was a good idea."

Blake groaned. "Oh, no. Not the cookie crumbling again."

"I'm afraid Elena and Ivy might be together . . . somewhere."

"I love Aunt Elena dearly, but we all know she's . . . unpredictable. But would *Ivy* go along with some harebrained scheme?"

"Ivy might be trying to stop her from carrying it out. I'm going to find Stan's place and see if that's where they went. I think that's where the danger is."

"I'm coming with you."

"He lives somewhere on the Hill, but I don't know where—"

"I'll find out. We can go in my SUV."

I ran back to the motorhome door and grabbed my baseball bat. I intended to put BoBandy in the motorhome, but he scooted around me. By the time I got out to the SUV, he was waiting by the door for me. By then, Blake not only had Stan's address, he also had a map on his phone showing how to get there. BoBandy, determined not to be left behind, clambered over me to get in the SUV. We'd just started down the road when I heard something.

"What was that?"

Blake braked the SUV, and BoBandy bounced frantically from window to window, yelping to get out. "Sounded like a horn blasting somewhere."

Blake looked in the rearview mirror, and I turned in the seat to look at the road behind us. No streetlights on Eidenburg Road, but there were lights back there at the sharp curve where Miranda had crashed over the embankment and found Miles's body. Not actual headlights aiming down the road; more as if a vehicle was parked there at an angle, with the beam of headlights shooting off into the trees.

We both listened and watched for a minute. No more horn blowing, and the angled lights didn't move. BoBandy jumped over the seats and hit my lap like a leggy sack of potatoes.

"Maybe some kids out goofing around," Blake said. Bo Bandy bumped into Blake's shoulder, then bounded back across me to stick his nose against the window.

"I don't know what's got into him." I tried to boost BoBandy into the back seat, but he suddenly seemed to have more than the usual four doggy legs and every leg resisted my boost. "He isn't usually like this."

We started down the road again.

Another sound. BoBandy barked. Blake braked again.

"That wasn't a horn. It sounded more like a gunshot." Blake peered in the rearview mirror again. BoBandy had his paws up on the dashboard now. His whapping tail caught me on the cheek.

Gunshot? Ivy and Elena? A worry. But I couldn't think how they could be out here in the dark with someone shooting at them. The danger was surely at Stan's place.

"It was probably a backfire," Blake said.

A backfire. Yes. I'd talked to that neighbor the morning after Miles was killed and the noisy old pickup went by. The backfires from it had sounded like a Wild West gun battle. But this was just one sharp *bang*—

BoBandy jumped into the back seat on his own, then reversed directions and roller-coasted over me again.

Another gunshot/backfire noise cut through the night. Was the old guy out driving his noisy pickup in the dark? The neighbor with the dog had said he sometimes did that. Didn't the cops ever pick him up for those backfires? But the lights back at the corner still didn't seem to be moving.

The guy was probably having trouble getting the old pickup going. Or maybe kids were having fun deliberately making some vehicle backfire. I remember doing that when I was a kid. You couldn't do it with today's cars, but they probably had some old heap they were playing with.

But still . . .

"Maybe we should check it out anyway," I said.

BoBandy's claws dug into my leg. I thought about those weird tales about werewolves and a full moon. There was no full moon tonight, no moon at all. But BoBandy was certainly behaving as if he were a little moon-crazy. Once more he bounded over me into the back seat, leaving more doggy-foot imprints in my leg.

Now he stood on his hind feet to look out the back window.

"I think we should get over to Stan's place as fast as we can," Blake said. "No telling what Stan may do if Aunt Elena and Ivy show up there alone and he realizes they know he's a crook."

Right. I also realized that in my thinking a minute earlier I'd given the robot vacuum cleaner credit for finding Miles's body. As if it were some kind of super-PI in disguise.

I gave myself a mental thump. Sheesh. *Get a grip. That's geezer territory.*

"You've got me really worried about them." Blake took his foot off the brake and hit the accelerator.

I felt another moment of uneasiness about the backfire noises, but when the SUV leaped forward I just grabbed the handhold above the door and held on.

**

IVY

I braced myself against the seat and put everything I had into the kick. Wham!

My bare feet slammed into the gun and Saundra's hand. Both moved and then separated under the blow—

The gun thundered. The flash from the muzzle momentarily lit up the car, and for a moment I saw everything like an old photo negative. The car seats, Elena's hands stopped in mid-motion, my own foot poised in midair. My ears rang and echoed with the thunder. Stars ricocheted from my eyes to my brain. The rear window exploded behind me—

I shook my head and covered my ears trying to erase the thunder of gunshot and blaze of stars. And a flash of panic too. The bullet must have missed my head by mere inches. Had Saundra managed to fire the gun before I kicked it out of her hand? No, it must have slammed into the dashboard or floorboard and gone off when it hit.

I offered the Lord a quick thanks for protecting me.

Now, no longer trying to conceal myself, I leaned forward and saw shadowy blobs rising and falling in the front seat as Saundra and Elena fought to retrieve the gun. Grunts. A booted foot rising out of the moving mounds. A curse.

Another blast from the gun.

I felt my head and chest. Was I shot? No, just deafened again. Was Elena shot? Or had Elena shot Saundra?

In the darkness I couldn't tell what was going on, who was shooting or who had been shot, and then my feet tangled in the wet nightgown again. It ripped as I kicked my feet free.

Hotshot sleuthing expert Rod Steele surely never got his feet tangled in a wet flannel nightgown in the middle of a bullet storm.

Then the car moved, rocketed forward, following the headlights arcing into the trees—

Hey, no, we can't do that! We'll go over the embankment—

"Elena, stop! Don't—"

The car tilted and careened downward. The motion threw me over the front seats, and then there were three of us tangled like wildcats in a gunny sack. Arms and legs and heads and feet everywhere. Also a steering wheel, a gearshift, a rearview mirror, and a wet nightgown. Something hit me in the ribs. I *oofed* and kicked and someone else *oofed*.

It was a multi-person wrestling match, no holds barred, and I knew that somewhere in the tangle was a gun—

The car hit something and whammed to a stop. A hot scent bloomed around the tangle of arms and legs. Would the car explode and go up in flames? No, that only happened in movies . . . or did it?

"Get out!" I yelled. "Before the car explodes!"

Doors opened on both sides. I tumbled out the passenger's side. Saundra was there too. Under me . . . no, on top me! Fingers pulling my ears, fingernails scratching my face. I struggled and pounded my fists and kicked my feet. More ripping nightgown. My hand hit something and I grabbed hold. Hair! I yanked and got a screech in return. Fingernails raked my hand and I let go and rolled.

Old leaves under me. Scent of mold and dampness. Something digging into my back. I rolled over again and grabbed it—

The gun! I wrapped my fingers around it and staggered to my feet. The headlights had gone dark in the crash, but the car had not exploded. Maybe car explosions were a movie myth—or maybe it could still happen. I should get farther away. Find Elena—

I staggered a few steps but the ringing in my ears disoriented me. A light flashed on the car . . . or was it inside the car? Maybe it was inside my head? Where was everyone?

I had no idea, but then I realized the gun was still in my hand. Hey, great! Better me than Saundra. Not so great was the realization that I had no idea what to do with a gun. Mac and I had talked about taking shooting lessons, but we'd never done it. But I knew there was a trigger here somewhere—

Yeah, and if I messed up with that trigger, I'd shoot myself in the foot. Or belly. Or accidentally blast Elena—

Something rustled in the darkness. No, more than rustled. Bigger than rustles. Something rushing toward me. Saundra? Or maybe Stan. Had he followed us?

I tried to steady the wobble of the gun in my hands.

A blinding blaze of light hit me in the eyes. I flung my hands up to ward it off. And hit myself in the face with the gun.

Great going, Ivy.

Piece of advice: never try to shade your eyes with a gun in your hand.

My head reeled again. I heard a voice, but I couldn't make out who it was or where it came from.

A cannonball slammed my midsection and the gun flew out of my hand—

**

MAC

The beam of Blake's flashlight swept over the car with the front end wrapped around a stump at the bottom of the embankment. Both doors stood wide open. Hey, that car looked familiar—

The roving light caught a ghostly figure beside the car. A ghost with a gun? No, that was—

"That's Ivy!" Blake yelled.

Ivy with a gun?

The gun wobbled back and forth in her hand and a tattered something wound around her body and legs. I recognized those tatters. Ivy's *nightgown*. With bare feet beneath it.

A barefooted, nightgown-clad Ivy with a gun?

Something sprawled on the ground a few feet away from her. A dead body?

BoBandy barreled through the weeds covering the embankment where I stood, body angled as I tried to keep my balance. How'd he get out? I thought I left him in the SUV but I must not have shut the door tight—

He headed straight down the embankment, so eager to reach Ivy that he went airborne, a flying doggy missile, and momentum crashed him headlong into her midsection. She went down, gun flying out of her hand. BoBandy stood over her, tail wagging wildly, tongue slobbering her with doggy kisses.

I floundered down the embankment, but I hadn't yet reached Ivy when the dead body rose out of the matted leaves beyond her.

Saundra!

Saundra with dead leaves in her disheveled hair, legs spread like a gunfighter, the gun now in her hand. I felt as if I'd stumbled into a zombie horror movie on TV.

"Stop right there," she yelled. The blaze of the flashlight was now in her eyes and she couldn't see either of us, but she waved the gun wildly in the direction of the embankment. "Back off or I'll shoot!"

She didn't wait for us to back off. She just shot.

I heard a crash behind me, and the flashlight Blake had been holding rolled and bounced down the embankment. A wild tangle of beams from the flashlight arced across trees and sky. I lunged for the flashlight as it hurtled past me, but all I managed to do was crash headlong into weeds and gravel.

The flashlight went out.

I lay there a moment trying to stop the dark universe from spinning around me. "Blake?"

He groaned, only a few feet away from me. "I'm hit. My leg—"

The gun blasted again.

Then silence. And darkness.

Deadly silence. Deadly darkness.

Had she shot Blake again? Or *Ivy*?

I didn't wait to call her name and find out. I floundered to my feet, fell again, rolled, stumbled upright. I knew I must be making a lot of noise, noise that would give that crazy woman with a gun a target to aim for. But I didn't stop.

Because I had to get to Ivy.

CHAPTER 26

MAC

Another gunshot.

How many times had she shot? How many bullets did she have left? If she had a full magazine of fifteen, she could still—

Blake yelling. More noises from down below. Crashes. Crunches. Barks. Thunks. Dying wheezes from the car. Something running through the brush. The darkness enlarged each sound. A woman screamed.

"Ivy?" I yelled in full panic mode.

I lunged down the embankment trying to get to her. Fell again. My body hit something when I went down. The flashlight! I untangled myself from weeds and grabbed it. Another frantic moment until I floundered to my feet and found the switch.

Light from the flashlight turned the trees into a ghostly jungle. I struggled to turn the flashlight and aim it where I thought the car was, desperately trying to find Ivy . . . afraid of what I'd see—

Then I saw her.

Elena too.

And Saundra.

What—?

I dropped back to the ground, uncertain whether to be astonished or relieved. Or maybe just smile at what I saw.

Never underestimate an LOL. Two of them actually.

Ivy sat square in the middle of a facedown Saundra lying flat on the ground. Elena weighed down Saundra's ankles. BoBandy ran enthusiastic circles around them.

"You okay?" I yelled.

"BoBandy knocked Saundra down," Elena yelled back. "I think he knocked her out!"

No, Saundra wasn't knocked out. She shrieked again and then bucked and twisted like a rodeo bronc. But Ivy and Elena rode her back and ankles like a couple of bronc busters.

Saundra finally gave up, or wore out, and lay there motionless, arms spread on the ground. Ivy squirmed to adjust her position, but she didn't stand up. Good for her. Sneaky Saundra might be faking it.

"You know, you really should do something about that smell in the carpet of your car," Ivy said.

Elena answered, "I spilled some of the *natto* I bought at the health food store a few days ago. It's hard to get rid of the smell."

"I don't think I've ever heard of natto."

"It's a Japanese food made from fermented soybeans. A natural probiotic. It's supposed to be really good for you, but I'm not sure I like it. It does have a rather strong scent."

"I'll have to try it. I like kimchi. It's a good probiotic too."

Leave it to Ivy and Elena to have a health food discussion at a time such as this.

Above me on the embankment, Blake whistled and clapped.

Sounded good to me. I whistled and clapped too.

In the distance, I heard sirens.

CHAPTER 27

IVY

Two weeks have passed since that night Elena crashed her car down the embankment and the bullets flew. A deliberate crash, I now know. She said she remembered reading if you were ever hijacked in a car, crash it into something. So that's what she'd done.

Mac and Blake had found us there because they were on the road, headed to Stan's, when they turned around instead. Because Mac heard a frantic mental call from me for help, two people joined by a telepathic bond of love transcending time and space? A sweetly romantic notion, but nope, that wasn't it. Mac had asked Blake to turn around because, when BoBandy scrambled over him to get in the SUV, he'd dropped his baseball bat. He figured he might need it in a confrontation with Stan, so they'd turned back to get it. And then, just as they'd reached the house, they'd seen the headlights go over the embankment.

Blake had immediately called 911. Response from police and ambulance had been blessedly quick.

Various things have happened since then.

A tow truck winched Elena's twisted and battered car up the embankment. She decided against getting it repaired and is using Miles's SUV for transportation now. The murder charges against her have been dropped. Saundra is now in jail and won't be getting out on bail. She's awaiting trial on various charges, including murder (Miles), attempted murder (Elena and me), and shooting Blake. Stan has also been charged with various crimes relating to his fraudulent investment club, but he is out on bail. The information about the shady investment club was all on Miles's computer, and Stan and the investment club are now the center of a complete investigation.

Elena, once the probate is taken care of, will be moving into Miles's townhouse. She took his ashes to a cliff on the coast, a place they had enjoyed together, and let the ashes fly free in the wind. I'd gone with her, but I watched from a distance when she released the ashes. Her last goodbye to Miles was something she needed to do alone.

Was Miles actually a bank robber? That trip Elena took with him, when they ate the chocolate gun, certainly suggested he was. But maybe that unsuccessful attempt was the only time he ever tried bank robbing and he was paying the cruise ladies off with other money that it was taking him time to gather up. I guess we'll never know. Some other assets have turned up in scattered accounts. Elena plans to use some of that money to pay back what Earline lost in the investment club.

Or maybe Miles was a successful bank robber and just never got caught. Elena burned those expensive masks a few days ago. Mac and I haven't felt inclined to bring speculations about him to the authorities.

The guard Elena met in jail has called a couple of times to check on her. Although she acts fairly cheerful, she's a long way from healing after losing Miles, but I figure when the time is right, the guard will be there. I doubt he calls all his jail acquaintances to inquire about their health and safety; he has something more in mind. She's been reading Miles's Bible daily and went to the little church with us last week.

Nicole is working on getting her return to school covered by various grants and loans, although she'll continue to work in the bakery on weekends even after she's in school. Mac and I have filled in for her a couple of times at the bakery when she went for interviews. She's brought Blake goodies from the bakery several times, since he's not getting around much. Will they ever get together for more than blueberry muffins or cookies? Good question.

Right now, we're all gathered in Elena's living room.

Blake is stretched out on the sofa, broken lower leg not in a solid cast but stabilized to protect it while the surgery that had been done that night heals. He, with a metal rod and screws in his leg. . . gunshots are pretty hard on bones . . . is getting around, cautiously, with crutches. Eventually, he'll be working in San Diego most of the time, no more jaunting to far-off places with, as he puts it, barely time to change underwear between trips.

Nicole is sitting beside him on the sofa, Fancy and Felicity draped between them. BoBandy is lying on the floor beside Mac, and Koop is standing at the opening to the hallway. He's quite fascinated with Miranda and is watching as she comes out for her daily cleaning duties. I think he's planning to jump on for a free ride. Elena is in the kitchen getting coffee and cookies to bring to the living room.

Actually, this is a little goodbye gathering for Mac and me. The canopy is rolled up on the motorhome, the slide-out pushed into storage mode, jacks raised, small items inside tucked away for safekeeping. We're ready to roll as soon as the goodbyes are over.

"You're sure you don't want to stay a while longer?" Blake says. "Take a little more time to decide if you want to buy the place and live here permanently?"

Mac and I have already talked this over. We like the house and the town and the little church. But that standard we'd already set for a place where we'd settle down permanently—no murders—has held firm. Now, without mentioning that point in our decision, Mac says, "Thanks, but we'll be moving on. But you never know when we might come around this way again."

Elena set a plate of cookies on the coffee table. "Anytime," she says.

"Actually, I may decide to keep the place," Blake says, his tone offhand, although he gives Nicole a little sideways glance. "I may be able to do most of my work online, so I could decide to live up here in San Isolde."

Nicole makes no comment.

"I don't think I told you that private investigator, Rod Steele, called a few days ago, did I?" Blake added.

"Did you tell him the culprits have been apprehended and his services are no longer needed?" I asked.

"Actually, I didn't have to. He called to resign. It seems he ran into a few problems with the investigation."

"What kind of problems?"

"He went to question a woman in Bakersfield, a Samantha Johnson. She's the granddaughter of one of the women Miles had persuaded to invest in Stan's scheme. I believe Rod got her name from you, so you may remember her." He lifted his eyebrows in question.

Mac and I exchanged a glance. Remember Samantha "Sam" Johnson in Bakersfield? Oh, yes. Sam of the spiky hair and snake tattoo. And quick temper, according to the boyfriend.

"We remember her," Mac said in a noncommittal tone.

"It seems Ms. Johnson didn't appreciate Rod's nosiness when he came to her apartment. She clobbered him with a full-sized crab she'd just bought at a seafood market. A crab claw got stuck in his ear. In his effort to get rid of it, he crashed into her aquarium, which broke and deluged both her apartment and the one below. In hastily exiting the apartment—"

"Still with crab attached?" Mac asked.

"Oh yes. And out on the balcony walkway, he collided with an elderly neighbor lady who whopped him with her rather large purse. Then they both crashed through the railing on the second-floor walkway and landed on top of a vehicle parked down below. The elderly neighbor fortunately was not injured because she landed on top Mr. Steele, but he suffered a finger injury. His trigger finger, actually, and he feels a permanently rigid finger will dangerously inhibit his safety as a private eye. He has, therefore, decided to give up PI work and write his memoirs." Blake told all of this with a straight face, but I could see he had to keep making an effort not to laugh at Rod Steele's problems. "The apartment owners have threatened to sue him for damage to the apartment, but I told him I'd cover the cost of repairs."

"That's a rather impressive . . . chain of events," Nicole commented.

I felt sorry for Mr. Steele and his loss of a nimble trigger finger, but at the same time I felt a certain guilty satisfaction with this outcome. We might be "blundering amateurs" where crime investigation is concerned, but neither of us has ever gotten a crab claw stuck in an ear, and our trigger fingers are still intact. In case we should ever need them in further amateur blundering. And we did wind up with a killer and a fraudster for the police.

Perhaps Mr. Steele's memoirs will prove to be a bestselling book and movie. We'll do what we can to help out by buying the book and seeing the movie.

Blake eyed the plate of cookies. "From the bakery?" he inquired.

"No. Nicole made these herself and brought them over."

"You were thinking about doing a cookie-crumbling session?" Blake asked Nicole.

"No, after the results of Elena following what looked like the crumbs' approval of her plan to contact Saundra to get more evidence against Stan, I've had some second thoughts about cookie crumbling. Ivy and Elena could both have been killed."

"I'm having second thoughts about advice from crumbled cookies too," Elena muttered.

Blake didn't comment.

"I've also done some thinking about what Ivy said to me about fortune-telling in general." Nicole picked up a sugar cookie and examined it critically. "I've come to believe it is, as Ivy once mentioned, cockamamie. I have, therefore, made a decision."

"This sounds serious," I said.

"It is. I've decided to abandon my career as the Cookie Lady. This is what I'll be doing with cookies now." She popped the cookie into her mouth and chewed.

Blake grabbed a chocolate chip cookie and held it high so that the crumbled pieces fell directly in his mouth. Elena did the same thing. Mac and I looked at each other and then did the same thing with our cookies.

"And that," Nicole said, "is the way the cookies crumble now."

We finished off the plate of cookies, and then it was time to gather up our animals and head for the motorhome. We shared hugs and goodbyes.

Finally, Elena said, "You haven't told us where you're going."

"That's because we aren't certain ourselves," Mac said. "Our friends Magnolia and Geoff are down in Texas, at Padre Island. We may go spend some time with them.

"Or we may go up to Montana and visit Mac's son and grandchildren," I offered.

"Or there's a ghost town in the mountains that sounds interesting," Mac said.

"But you can't just drive off without *knowing* where you're headed," Nicole protested.

Mac and I just looked at each other and smiled.

Oh, yes, we can.

The End

If you enjoyed *That's the Way the Cookie Crumbles,* I'd very much appreciate a review on the site where you purchased the book.

Watch for the next Mac 'n' Ivy mystery! A list of other Lorena McCourtney books is on the following page.

Books by Lorena McCourtney

THE MAC 'N' IVY MYSTERIES:
Something Buried, Something Blue
Detour
Desert Dead
That's the Way the Cookie Crumbles

THE IVY MALONE MYSTERIES:
Invisible
In Plain Sight
On the Run
Stranded
Go, Ivy, Go!

THE JULESBURG MYSTERIES:
Whirlpool
Riptide
Undertow

THE ANDI McCONNELL MYSTERIES:
Your Chariot Awaits
Here Comes the Ride
For Whom the Limo Rolls

THE CATE KINKAID FILES MYSTERIES (also available in print):
Dying to Read
Dolled Up to Die
Death Takes a Ride

CHRISTIAN ROMANCES
Midnight Escape
Three Secrets (Novella)
Searching for Stardust

Yesterday Lost (Mystery/Romance)
Canyon
Betrayed
Dear Silver

Connect with her on Facebook at:
http://www.facebook.com/lorenamccourtney
    Visit the website at https://www.lorenamccourtney.info If you'd like to be on the list to receive an announcement when a new book is available, contact the author through the website.

Happy Reading!

www.ingramcontent.com/pod-product-compliance
Lightning Source LLC
Chambersburg PA
CBHW070816180626
46818CB00001B/288